GUILTY DEEDS

SCOTT D. SMITH

PROMONTORY
P R E S S

Promontory Press
www.promontorypress.com

ISBN: 978-1-987857-67-2

Cover Design and Typeset by Edge of Water Designs, edgeofwater.com

Printed in Canada
987654321

"I would forget it fain,

But oh, it presses to my memory,

Like damnèd guilty deeds to a sinner's mind."

William Shakespeare, *Romeo and Juliet, Act III, sc. 2*

GUILTY DEEDS

CHAPTER ONE

Detective Stephanie Monroe pretended to examine the papers and files on her cluttered, gun-metal gray desk, transferring a few sheets from one pile to another before remembering she had twice performed that ritual already. She then checked her phone for the third time in the last twenty minutes, silently chastising herself and throwing it as far back into an open desk drawer as she could manage before slamming it shut a little louder than she had intended. She cast a quick look around the station, but if anyone heard anything they were long past repeating the mistake of acknowledging it.

Feeling herself rebuked by her own thoughts, she slowly slid open the drawer and cast a sideways glance at the innocent device. It wasn't truly the source of her frustration, and she knew it. It was guilty only of possessing the one quality she normally admired most simply because it was one of the few good qualities she saw in herself. It was always honest. Today, however, that honesty was taking the form of two pieces of information that separately were hardly worth noting, but together were almost unbearable: it was 9:00 a.m. and it was ninety-two degrees.

Welcome to Houston, she thought. *Where it's hot enough to boil your brain inside your skull, but at least the mosquitoes are the size of seagulls and every major freeway has been under construction since the Reagan era.*

Stephanie allowed herself another half-moment of slouching self-pity, eyeing the one item that was, she knew, actually the source of her frustration. She sighed. Ignoring the problem for another hour wasn't any more likely to solve her current situation than obsessing over the weather report was to produce a cool front.

"At approximately 4:00 a.m. on the morning of June 21ˢᵗ, 2014," the shift sergeant's report that had lain partially crumpled on Stephanie's desk from repeated re-readings stated, *"a large Caucasian male calling himself Robert Grayson (no identification) entered the station. Individual was visibly agitated. Asked to speak to someone in homicide. Would not remain in lobby and became increasingly upset when asked to wait.*

"Individual then claimed to have murdered multiple women and demanded to see someone immediately. Saw individual's hands at this point, which appeared to be covered in dried blood. Detained and referred to Detective S. Monroe. End report."

Stephanie let the paper float back to the pile and rubbed her temples, cursing herself again for her habit of coming in to work so early.

"Find out who this guy is and if his story is even remotely a possibility," her captain had barked at her when she had tossed the file on Stephanie's desk that morning.

"Sounds like a nut job," she said, barely looking up from the report. "Serial killers don't walk in and confess, Captain. You know that. Can't you give this to one of the new guys? I've got actual cases that need solving."

"What do you want from me, Stephanie? I just handed you a confessed killer who literally has blood on his hands, and you're what? Too busy? Talk to him. Find out who he is and if his story checks out. If it does, arrest his ass and you can get back to your other cases."

"And if it doesn't?"

"Just get it dealt with, Detective. And when this is over, come see me. It's time for us to have your favorite conversation again," she announced, turning on her heel and spinning away before Stephanie could rebut her.

"I don't need another partner," she called after her boss, but her objection fell on selectively deafened ears.

"Just get his permission, then get a unit to his place and get him interviewed. I want this wrapped up before lunch," her boss answered without bothering to turn around.

Stephanie let the matter drop, and then, after an appropriate amount of time had gone by to pass for some semblance of pride-restoring defiance, she had begun. Now, as she punched up the video file and pushed her ear buds in place, wincing slightly at the strange sound of her own voice and vowing again to work on dropping her southern accent, she wondered why she had bothered.

"Mr. Grayson," her video-self began, "my name is Detective Monroe. I understand you have something you want to talk about."

Robert's large frame was crushed down by some invisible weight, his shoulders drawn and his back hunched.

Too bad he's a nut. He'd be good looking under other circumstances, she thought. *But for such a large man, he seems so frail.*

The effect was magnified by the fact that his hands were bound to the metal table at which he sat by a pair of handcuffs that were themselves chained down, and the skin on his face was taut the way it sometimes is on people who've not eaten enough for several days or more. He didn't speak at first. Instead, Robert turned over his hands, exposing the palms and the dried blood crusted onto them by way of an answer.

Stephanie only nodded her acknowledgement. Pushing him, she knew, would be as futile as trying to part the ocean with her hands.

"I've done a terrible thing," he finally said, his normally deep, gravelly voice just barely a whisper. "Terrible *things*. I … I killed women. A lot of them, I think." His eyes were cast down at the table, focused on something only he could see.

She saw the metal of the cuffs biting into his large wrists as he twisted his hands, the chain holding them in place pulling taut and scraping against the snow-cold metal of the table. If he felt any pain, he gave no indication of it.

"Mr. Grayson, I should interrupt. Those cuffs you're wearing are only a precaution. You aren't technically under arrest, and you aren't being formally questioned or even detained, so you don't have the right to an attorney yet, but we could probably arrange one for you. Do you want me to do that?"

Robert's head swiveled slightly from side to side, but he otherwise gave no indication he had heard her. Mutely, he squeezed the fingers of both hands closed into tight fists until the digits were swollen and purple. Then, he released them and watched the color fade back to normal.

Stephanie watched him, her brows knitting together, as he repeated the process several more times. Dr. Burns would have to confirm it later, but her money was on this guy being completely disconnected from reality. A fascinating case study for the doc, but she had real work and real cases to get back to. She'd need a different approach.

"Mr. Grayson, it's clear you want my help with a very serious problem. I think I can do that, but there are things I need from you in order to get you that help, to get you in the right place. We'll have to work together. Okay?"

Robert's reaction was immediate. His head whipped up and

his body was at once tense and hopeful. Stephanie saw a scared stray that sensed a handout.

"The other officers treated you like some kind of lunatic, didn't they?" she asked gently. "As if someone could possibly lie about the kinds of things you've done. But it's okay. I'm here to help. You can trust me." She risked reaching her hand across the table to cement the connection.

Robert cocked his head, studying her closely as her hand settled onto his.

Stephanie jerked her arm back with a start as Robert bolted up and back in his chair. He had nowhere he could go, but his eyes searched every corner of the room for escape. The chains strained against their moorings so much that Stephanie thought they might snap any second. She had seen huge men out of their minds on PCP and God knows what else pull those same chains with no effect at all. However frail and gaunt he might appear, Robert was as powerful a man as she'd ever seen.

"Mr. Grayson?" she asked. "Can you hear me?"

At the sound of her voice, Robert's panicked eyes found hers and focused there. His face was scarlet, and at the rate at which his chest was rising and falling, Stephanie thought his heart might explode, but he appeared at least to hear her.

"Mr. Grayson, are you alright? Do you need anything?"

Robert jolted slightly as Stephanie's question snapped him out of the awful, blissful recollection that had seized him at the touch of her hand. He squeezed his eyes shut now against the image of the detective and leaned back as far as the cuffs would allow. The cold metal cut deeper into his skin, but where he should have felt pain there was only relief, relief that the bonds had held. When he was sure he could not run, he risked opening his eyes.

"Mr. Grayson, what's happening? Can you look at me?" Stephanie asked in her calmest voice.

It took Robert a moment to answer, and when he did he still would not meet her eyes.

"I'm sorry," he managed. "It was a woman. You touched me and it reminded me of one of them. Maybe … maybe I could talk to a man?"

She nodded a little, trying to give the appearance she was thinking over his request. "Maybe we should just try to finish what we've started," she countered. "For instance, what woman do I remind you of? Can you tell me her name?"

He scanned the spaces in his mind around the other details of the girl. What was her name? He had taken everything else from her. Had he taken that too? After a time, he gave up and shook his head.

"How did you know her? Do you remember that?"

Another shake, but he added, "I don't think I did. I only talked to her for a minute. At a zoo somewhere, I think. And then I followed her home and …" He was having trouble finding the right words to describe everything that had happened after that. Words categorized things, described them, and made them tidier somehow in our minds. There was nothing tidy about what he had done.

"You killed her?" Stephanie offered. "You can tell me. It's part of my job to hear these things. What happened when you followed her home, Mr. Grayson?"

He shrugged his shoulders and answered, "I choked her." He looked down and began flexing his hands as before. "Other things too, afterward. That's why you have to lock me up. It's your job to keep me from doing this again, right? Please just keep me here. If you let me out, more people are going to die, and you will be sorry. I promise you that." He finally looked up, this time holding her gaze as his eyes repeated the promise he had just made.

Stephanie could recall dozens, maybe hundreds, of times she

had been threatened by people since joining the force. Most of the time it was simple bluster, not even worth acknowledging. Other times called for an immediate response to neutralize the threat. She was equally comfortable with both scenarios, but in this case, she had no idea what to do. He was obviously serious about what he said, but Stephanie had never encountered anyone about whom she was more sure that violence was the last thing he intended. The department shrink was going to be earning his year's pay with this guy.

"I will, sir. I promise that I will help you, okay? Just a few more questions. Do you remember when this was?"

"No."

"Okay. Well, what did you do with her body? Can you tell me that?"

Yet another shake. "Sorry."

Stephanie let out an exasperated sigh and leaned back in her own chair, letting her hand fall to rest on her leg.

"You have to give me something here, Mr. Grayson. You said I reminded you of one of the women. Can you describe her to me?"

Robert was so accustomed to the holes in his memory that he found his head shaking again even as he realized he was able to describe her. Every detail of her was vivid and alive in his mind—the color of her hair, the shape of her eyes, a tattoo of a clover in a place he shouldn't know about. All of the details he could recall came rushing out to Stephanie.

With this retelling, Stephanie was able to get enough information for a sketch artist and for a search in the missing persons database. She had seldom had a suspect able to recall with the kind of clarity Robert Grayson was now demonstrating, especially given that he could remember absolutely nothing else about the woman apart from her physical description.

Easy part over, she thought.

Now, all that was left was to have the lab run an analysis on the blood from Robert's hands, verify that there was a missing woman who matched the description, find out if Robert even was who he said he was, have the psychiatrist determine whether he was fit to make any claims that could stand up in court, and then find the body of the missing girl, which, assuming she existed, could be literally anywhere, and, finally, see if she had been choked to death. All of that work for a case on which she already had a confession.

Well, she told herself in an attempt to look on the bright side, *if it turns out he's wasting my time and lying, maybe I can find an excuse to shoot him later.*

CHAPTER TWO

"If you don't mind my saying so, you seem disappointed, Detective. Figured you'd be happy his story checked out."

Stephanie looked up at the patrolman who had handed her the evidence bags. Laminated cards and various documents attesting to his identity stared out at her through the clear plastic. Stephanie hadn't even needed to open them before tossing them on the small landfill of office debris on her desk. "I'm not sure what I am, Dave. This guy is clearly unhinged. I guess maybe I was hoping he was making up who he was so I could pawn him off on Burns for good."

"That where he is now?" the officer asked.

Stephanie nodded. "For hours. This guy is right up Burns' alley, too." She made a pantomime of running her index finger in circles around her temple.

The officer tapped his fingers on his gun belt and fixed his gaze down at Stephanie.

"What?" she asked.

"It's not my business, but take it easy on him if you can. The guy's a vet. And you should have seen his place. I could wallpaper my kitchen with the citations he was awarded. I was in for eight years, and I never met anybody with half that many. Whatever he is now, this guy used to be something special. Maybe he still is."

An hour's worth of digging into the life of Robert Grayson later, she was forced to agree.

He was single, had no children, and had joined the Army immediately after graduating from Hastings High School in southwest Houston. His school records showed him to have been an above average student and a well above average athlete. His military record was even better. He had served for almost fourteen years, most of it in the Middle East, and all of it right on the front lines. He had earned a Purple Heart, the Army Commendation Medal, a handful of other medals Stephanie had never heard of, and had twice been recommended for citations for valor, including the Silver Star. Even as pressed as the Army was for soldiers, he could have rotated back to the states five years earlier than he did, but he had chosen to remain deployed in Iraq and, later, in the Islamic Republic of Afghanistan. In his down time, he had helped the villagers build wells and housing. This guy was the Army's wet dream, but he had gotten out with only six years to go until retirement and a virtual certainty of doing it all at any post he desired. It made no sense to her, but then, neither did anything else about this guy.

His current employer had told pretty much the same story over the phone. Great guy. Always on time. Always worked hard. Mostly kept to himself on the job but not in a strange way. He was just kind of quiet. His ex-girlfriend was the next track on the same broken record. Terrific guy. Strong, silent type. Just kept his feelings bundled up too much. Wouldn't ever really open up. Typical guy stuff. More importantly to Stephanie, no history of violence or criminal behavior, and no trouble of any kind, especially not with women. If this guy had somehow turned the corner to serial killer as he claimed, he was hands down the friendliest goddamned sociopath on the planet.

Stephanie checked her phone again. Almost lunchtime. She deliberated for a half-second getting up and walking the thirty feet to her boss's office before sliding out her keyboard and firing off a quick email. An update to her captain might buy her an hour or so, but not much more. In the unlikely event Dr. Burns didn't stamp him *non compos mentis*, she needed to make the next sixty minutes count.

Thankfully, several women had already come up as potential matches for the woman Robert claimed to have killed. Not enough to verify Grayson's story for sure, but close enough to pass for progress on the search in her boss's eyes. Stephanie ignored the older ones and was reading through the files of the ones in the last two years, going from newest to oldest, when, at last, the department psychiatrist and, she hoped, her savior, Dr. Benjamin Burns, approached her. He was not a man prone to guile, but he seemed now to Stephanie to be taking great care to keep his face inscrutable. She frowned but made a clear space on the chair next to her desk for him. She also made what she knew to be a wasted mental note to herself to get her desk cleaned off this week. Again.

"Tell me you got something good, Bullet," she said, removing a pencil from between her clenched teeth. Since she'd read somewhere chewing a pencil was a good way to relieve the buildup of a stress headache, she'd developed a pack of No. 2 Colombia Pencil Company's finest per week habit. "I don't actually want to have to follow up on this one, but as hot and cranky as I'm getting, I might beat that guy to death if he's been yanking my chain."

Taking a seat on the just-cleared chair, the older man simply smiled and ran his hands through his thinning gray hair, his only real sign of age. "I'm afraid I am unable to say exactly what I have for you, Detective," he began in his honey smooth voice. Years of higher education and lecturing at schools all over the country had removed all traces of his original southern twang, but he retained the easy, slow speech patterns of all true southern gentleman of his era. "I've been plumbing the darkest depths of the human psyche for nearly thirty years, and, for the first time in my professional career, I am utterly flummoxed."

Stephanie gawked. She was accustomed to his erudite vocabulary, but she was completely unaccustomed to him failing to deliver a diagnosis on a subject. Dr. Burns, she knew, viewed his profession the same way a safe cracker did—every lock can be opened; it was only a question of having the right tools and enough time. He'd certainly had plenty of the latter, and she'd never known him to have a shortage of the former.

"Jesus Christ on a cracker, Bullet," she finally managed. "You mean nothing? That is a first." She was unsure whether to be more disappointed in the shrink or impressed with the subject.

"I didn't say I had nothing," he corrected, wagging a finger at her. "I said that I didn't know what I had. I have copious amounts of data, and all of it is contradictory. And would you please cease using that nickname? You know how I detest it."

She ignored his protest. "Contradictory? So you think he is making it up?"

"Not exactly," he replied, removing his small wire-framed glasses and laying them on a pile of papers. "Let me put it this way—I am as reasonably certain as I can be that he believes he has committed horrible atrocities against women, and I am as reasonably certain as I can be that he didn't actually do those things. Normally," he held up a hand to stop Stephanie before she could interrupt with the obvious question, "this would mean that he is suffering from some kind of delusion, guilt about some other issue perhaps manifesting itself in this way or unresolved feelings that stayed buried so long that they came out as this paranoid and psychotic scenario his brain developed as a coping mechanism. But in this case, I don't believe those diagnoses apply."

Stephanie's teeth began to grind. "Would you care to share with the rest of the class?"

"My dear, the medical explanation is both lengthy and tedious, but basically it is because if his mistaken belief were part of a mental breakdown of some kind, there would be other symptoms. There are none. That man is, to use the vernacular, sane. Though I will grant you he's under more stress than any person ought to have to endure. I had to give him something to calm him down for fear his heart might give out."

"Doc, you know I love how you care about all living things or whatever that bullshit is you're always spouting, but his heart isn't the organ you were supposed to be checking out. All I need you to tell me is if the guy is playing with a full deck."

"Your saint-like humanitarianism aside, let me make it as plain as I can for you, Detective. I can assure you that his playing deck is quite full."

Dr. Burns leaned back into the heavily worn, vinyl-covered chair and stretched his feet in front of him, crossing one wrinkled, chino-covered leg over the other and looking back at Stephanie as a tenured professor would a first-day undergraduate student, daring her to form her next questions with anything other than the greatest of care.

Stephanie briefly wondered how good her defense team would need to be in order for her to claim she had shot the doctor on accident while showing him her gun. Better than anything she could pay for, she decided. "Forgive me, Doc, but you said he didn't make up his story because he actually believes he killed a bunch of women, a fact with which you disagree, but you also don't think he's crazy. You mind telling me what I'm supposed to do with that information?"

He spread his hands in a gesture of surrender and shrugged, offering only, "You? I've no idea, my dear. I, on the other hand, intend to publish one hell of a paper. I can probably retire on the fees from the speaking engagements alone."

"A paper? That's great. I'll put that in my report. Very helpful, really," she huffed. "Burns is going to write a paper about having his head up his ass."

"What can I say? Mine is not always an exact science. What about you? Were you able to ascertain anything on your end?" Dr. Burns had, for some years, been granted the exclusive privilege of ignoring her insults and, on occasion, even her threats of bodily harm.

"I was just going over the records when you came over here to tell me you managed to do nothing with the last three hours and yet somehow still seem glib about it," she said, calling up the files and scanning the ones within the correct timeframe.

Dr. Burns rose and walked around her desk to peer over her shoulder at her monitor.

"Dammit," she hissed. "There's nothing in any of these that's a sure match."

"What are these other ones?" Dr. Burns asked, tapping the on-screen folders Stephanie had not opened.

"Those are older files from when he was in the military and out of the country. He couldn't have done those, so they won't help prove he's the killer. But maybe," she added as an afterthought, "they could help prove he's not."

"You think he's just matching details to old killings he read about?"

"I don't know, but if I do end up arresting him, it's not like he's going to put up any kind of defense for himself in court. After your half-baked diagnosis, I need to be sure about this one."

Dr. Burns began to say something, but immediately fell silent.

"What?" she challenged.

"Well, aren't you usually more the 'arrest them all and let the courts sort them out' sort of detective?"

"I'm not sure, Bullet. Aren't you usually more the 'keeps his opinions to himself and his teeth intact' sort of psychiatrist?"

"My, my. Even by your standards, you're in rare form today, Stephanie," he admonished.

She managed to hold the look Bullet gave her for nearly two whole seconds before yielding and returning to her screen. After several minutes and a scan of each of the files, she hit on one that looked like a good candidate. Three years ago. Physical description was a match, as was the cause of death. She pulled up the photo from the file and was startled at how close the sketch was to the woman. Allowing some distortion for the fact that she had been dead several days when found, it was nearly exact. She felt her heartbeat begin to accelerate the way it always did when she knew she was onto a good lead.

"If there's a zoo ticket stub listed among her possessions, Doc, you can officially take this innocent crackpot off of my hands."

Stephanie read through the file carefully for several minutes. She had no luck on the ticket, but as she kept reading, she did come across one photograph that stood out. It was an autopsy photo, and on it she could just make out a small green blur high on the woman's inner thigh. As she zoomed in on the object, she was unable to deny the obvious and troubling truth staring her in the face—the four-leaf clover tattoo that Grayson had described.

"What is it?" Dr. Burns asked. "The photo means something?"

"Yeah," Stephanie answered numbly. "It's an exact match to the one he described."

"Well, congratulations, my dear. You proved me wrong. I guess he was just describing details from old files he found somewhere. Though," he muttered mostly to himself, "he might not be aware he is doing it. I was certain he believed what he was saying."

"He does believe it," Stephanie corrected. "He'd have to, Bullet." Stephanie tapped the little green image on the screen with her index finger. "These are autopsy photos. He couldn't have read about this. We don't release these to the public. Ever."

Stephanie tossed one of her overly masticated pencils into an old coffee cup on her desk and watched it ride the inside of the rim before accepting its fate and settling into the dregs leftover there.

"You don't seem pleased. I was under the distinct impression you wanted this case resolved," said Dr. Burns.

"What I want is the truth, Bullet, and, if anything, we're farther from that now than when we started."

"How? You said you were sure he was out of the country when this poor girl was killed. It is the right girl, isn't it?"

"It is, and he was. No doubt about it, at least according to the Army, but what about that tattoo?"

Dr. Burns again strained his eye against the image. "And you are certain that these pictures are not available to the public under any circumstances?"

"Yep," she answered. "So he knew her. Had to. These aren't exactly the kinds of pictures that make the evening news when a girl goes missing, you know?"

"So the only way that he knew about the tattoo …" the doctor began.

"Was the good, old-fashioned, horizontal way. Which, of course, is extremely unlikely since he was out of the country for almost four straight years before she died."

"Perhaps he was acquainted with her from before?"

"Unlikely," Stephanie grumbled. "File says she's from Arizona. Moved here when Grayson was in Fallujah, but it doesn't matter. She was only twenty when she was killed. Unless she got the tattoo illegally as a minor, ran into him while she was in Iraq, also illegally, during a war with no passport or while he successfully went A.W.O.L. and snuck back to the states and then back to Iraq again ..." she left the rest of the sentence hanging as she thrummed her fingers on her desk.

"There are a million explanations as to how he could know about her tattoo, and please do not even get me started on how faulty memories can be. There is simply too much about the human memory mechanism that we don't understand for us ever to rely too heavily on it."

She smiled, glad to be the one grilling him for a change. "And the other unreleased details of her killing?" she asked. "He got about ten more of those right too."

Dr. Burns acknowledged her point with a somber nod. "So, you have managed successfully and simultaneously to establish beyond all reasonable doubt that he both knew the victim and did not know the victim. Maybe yours isn't such an exact science either."

"You know, Bullet," she observed, standing and stretching her tense shoulders, "this is why everyone hates shrinks. Or at least why they hate you."

Seeing her tension, he rose to stand next to her and reached out to rub her shoulders for her, a gesture he knew would have gotten most other men badly wounded. Dr. Burns had expected no thanks, and he received none, but neither did she flinch under his touch. Progress.

"For the record, I thought they all hated me because they were jealous of my boyish good looks," he said. "You going to see Grayson again?"

"Eventually," she agreed. "But first I want to check some things, see if I can establish a paper trail of all of his whereabouts for the last couple of weeks. Believe it or not, you hack, you actually gave me an idea." She grabbed her jacket off of the back of her chair and slipped her arms through, flipping her hair back and out of the way of the collar.

"Well, I'll try not to break my arm patting myself on the back," he deadpanned, peering at her over the top of his lenses as she gathered her things.

"Don't worry," she called, hustling toward the exit. "If it turns out I've wasted this entire day, I might do it for you."

CHAPTER THREE

The black-and-white clock above the grey metal door had ticked off the seconds and minutes and hours of the day until it read 1:21 p.m. Still, Robert Grayson sat on the hard, wooden chair in the interrogation room, handcuffed and alone, shifting his weight periodically from side to side. The room was as hard and isolated a place as he could remember being, with nothing to do and absolutely no way to get out. It was the most he had relaxed in some time.

Now that he was safely off the streets, for surely they would arrest him soon, he was able to put his guilt aside long enough to focus on closely examining each of the murders. With each hour that passed, the images came back to him with greater and greater clarity, but they were not yet fully complete. Sometimes, one would show up with all of its gruesome images and sounds and smells intact and in perfect clarity—but for only an instant. Then, before he could capture it, it would fly again out of some window he had left open in his mind. Because of this, and after many assurances they would be used only for their intended purposes, he had convinced the doctor to leave him paper and a pencil. He was determined to record the details of all of the killings he could recall. There was no telling when another window might show up, and he wasn't sure whether the memories that were leaving would ever return.

Confessing, taking these notes, they were important, but they were only a distraction really. Robert knew there could never be absolution for what he had done, those terrible things for which he still had no explanation, but putting some focus, some purpose to the memories helped a little. And he could perhaps give some measure of closure to the girls' families. That was something at least. So far, he had partial notes about eight of them. Eight. How could it be so many? Eight young women would never go home to their families. Eight young women had died at his hands, alone and afraid and in agony. He let the number sink in. Eight. It was warm in the room, but Robert shuddered each time at the thought of them.

The worst part wasn't even the gruesome memories themselves. He had seen more than enough death to make him at least partially numb to the cold skin and lifeless eyes that haunted him now. The worst part was, as he took his notes for the crying families of his many victims, he would occasionally catch himself smiling. His stomach would roll, and he would lean over in search of the trashcan the detective had placed at his side at his own request. His throat was raw and burning from the repeated retching, but if the thought of enjoying each of those young women's deaths made him sick, why would he have killed again and again? Brutalized them and worse? The more he thought of it, the less sense it made. The only thing he knew for sure anymore was that before this was finished for him, before he met whatever fate he deserved, there would be more than eight of them.

As if answering some ghostly bell, another new face rose from the ever darkening quagmire of his mind.

Nine.

Just as the image arrived, the room's only door opened and Stephanie stepped through, temporarily dispelling the girl's ghost.

Unaware of her transgression, Stephanie crossed the room quickly to smile at Robert and ask permission to share the table. "Mr. Grayson, I'd like to ask you some more questions, okay? If you can help me now, I think this may be almost over, at least the worst of it."

"Fine," Grayson mumbled. His back was curved over even more than it had been that morning, and his shoulders slouched to the point of appearing detached.

Talking and waiting and writing had slowly worn him down further, not only because of the monotony of the tasks, but also because they required him to stay focused on his darkest thoughts, thoughts he knew he needed to relive in order to find closure, but terrible, dark thoughts he would rather have denied. He felt at times that reliving these memories in anything other than short bursts risked driving him mad either from the pain or from the pleasure, and as he had recalled each new victim, he had found the line between the two becoming increasingly blurred.

"It may sound strange, Mr. Grayson—"

"Call me Robert," he interrupted, taking his eyes off his lap for only a second before unsuccessfully attempting something like a smile. "After everything I've told you, I think I can just be Robert."

"Okay, Robert." Stephanie didn't acknowledge his smile. It was hard enough playing both sides of the legal fence without exchanging pleasantries with a man who was still a suspect in multiple murders, even if only officially. "I know it may seem strange, but I'd like you to tell me everything you can remember about the last few days, everything *not* related to any killings. Can you do that?" she asked.

He rocked forward and then back again in his chair as he

considered her request. "I guess, but why not about the killings? What does the other stuff matter?"

She repeatedly tapped the end of her pencil against her yellow tablet, sending little vibrations thrumming through the surface of the table. "Listen, a lot of these questions are going to seem mundane. Call it a hunch for right now if you want, but I just need you to walk me through everything you did."

"Alright, but it's a short walk. I went to work, bought a few groceries, met a buddy at a bar near my apartment, all the stuff I normally do."

"That's it?" she asked. "Nothing special or different?"

Stephanie could hear Robert's foot sliding back and forth across the concrete floor.

"No, other than the homicidal rampage I went on, but you don't seem to want to talk about that."

Stephanie was unsure whether his response was an attempt at dark humor or just meant to rush her along. She ignored it.

"How about on Thursday?" she pressed, pushing across the table an evidence bag that held a single piece of paper, a receipt dated Thursday she had found in his apartment.

He looked down at the bag and shifted again in his seat. "You've got that paper. You already know where I was."

"Maybe. But I need to know that you know."

Robert continued to squirm under Stephanie's gaze. "I realize how weird it may seem to be embarrassed about going to a place like that after everything I've already admitted to, but …" He swallowed drily. Stephanie produced an unopened water bottle and placed it next to him and indicated he should drink. Robert took it in his hands and felt its damp coolness, but he left the bottle unopened. He picked at the label with his thumb for a moment before finishing his second confession of the day.

"So, yeah, I guess I went to one of those new memory transplant places, Happy Memories, the one over by the Galleria."

"And what can you tell me about the memories you purchased?"

"Nothing," he huffed, rolling his eyes. It was the first time he had displayed any emotion other than remorse. "I gave them my money, and they claim they gave me somebody else's experiences, their good memories, but I don't know which ones really are mine and which are paid for."

Stephanie frowned. "Can't you remember what you chose?"

"I got a special deal," he said, attempting quotation marks with his cramped fingers. "Some kind of new program where the memories are completely random. No way to tell which ones are paid for, so they all seem real. The trouble is, now I don't even know if it worked. I should have just said no again."

"Again?"

As Robert made his way deeper into this conversation, Stephanie could see the veil that had shrouded him all day beginning to part. He even managed to hold a genuine smile for a moment. "I said no at first, but a few days later some guy called me back. He told me that since I was a vet and all, he wanted to make a special deal for me. He told me about this package they had. It was less than a quarter of what they quoted me the first time, so I reconsidered. Waste of money, I guess."

"You know the guy's name?"

"The salesman? Hard to forget. Stephen. Same as my dad."

"Stephen got a last name?"

"Sorry," he said, shaking his head. "It was something different though. Not like Brown or Jones or anything."

"That'll work. We can find him if we need him," she said, scribbling a note on the back of her legal tablet. "Next question, and I know it will seem strange so just hear me out, but if you don't know what memories you got, how do you know what's real?"

Robert's lips pressed together and curved into a heavy frown.

"Like these murders, for example?"

"I get it," Stephanie tried. "If I were in your shoes, that question could seem a little … insensitive. I'm just asking you to think about it."

"Insensitive?" Robert raised his bound hands as far off of the table as the cuffs and chains would allow to show them to Stephanie. "I don't think you have to worry about protecting my feelings, Detective. Look, I can't explain how I know, but those memories are real. Besides," he leaned back and looked up at the tiled ceiling for the hundredth time that day, "they aren't exactly happy, are they?"

"No," she agreed, "but I don't think they're yours either, and I can prove it, at least with one."

Robert's head tilted slightly and his brow furrowed, but he said nothing.

Stephanie took his silence as his consent to proceed, so she pulled out the report she had tucked between the pages of the legal pad and slid it across to Robert. He opened the file and attempted to read the technical and legal jargon it contained before quickly handing it back, pointing to it.

"I don't know what you wanted me to see there. It just said something about blood."

"It is about blood, animal blood, specifically a bird of some kind. My lab guys think it's chicken. They'll know for sure soon."

Confusion was written across Robert's face like it was a billboard.

"It's the blood that was on your hands," Stephanie told him. "The literal kind, and it wasn't human, Robert."

He looked at his hands. The blood had long since been cleaned away, but there were some stains soap and water would not remove.

"So *that* blood wasn't human. That doesn't mean I didn't kill all those girls, and I appreciate what you're trying to do, Detective—"

Stephanie cut him off with a practiced glare and another

plea for patience while she finished explaining her theory. It took several minutes, but she was able eventually to convince him at least of the incongruity between the timing of the girl's death and his whereabouts.

"You really think it might have been someone else?" he muttered. "But why give me the memories? What would that accomplish? Your tests could be wrong, you know. About the blood and about when the girl died. You might not even have the right girl. Any of those things is more likely than what you're suggesting. Right?"

"The victim is a perfect match. On every count. And one test might be flawed, but our guys use multiple means of determining time of death, and they all agree. And from what I understand, it's pretty damned hard to confuse chicken blood with human blood. Mr. Grayson—Robert," she corrected, "I won't lie to you. I can't prove you're innocent of this crime. I know it would be easier for you if I could, but I can't, and I can't explain what someone else's motive might have been for implanting these memories." Stephanie paused long enough to avoid tripping over her words. "I can't even say for sure that's what happened. What I *can* do is tell you that there is evidence, lots of it, that would keep any court in this land from being able to prove that you *did* do it. Let's focus on that for now," she said, leaning across the table ever so slightly.

Robert said nothing at first, and his silence looked as if it could transform to anger at any moment. He didn't give a damn about what courts could prove. He cared only about what was true, that he was a monster. That he might instead be the victim was too far removed from possibility even to consider.

"Even if you were right about one, it doesn't mean I didn't do the others," he said.

"That is possible," she agreed, sitting up stiffly to reestablish the distance between them, "though it's extremely unlikely. Tell you what though, if it turns out you're guilty, I'll put the cuffs back on you myself. Maybe even treat you to some good old fashioned police brutality. How does that sound?"

It was Robert's turn to ignore a bad attempt at humor. Instead, he looked closely at her with unblinking eyes and asked, "If there's even a chance I am what I think I am, why would you want to help me?"

Stephanie had expected this question. She'd even asked it of herself. "I don't. I want to help the families of these victims find *real* closure, and I want to help put the real killer away so he can't hurt anyone else. If we arrest you, the search stops before it even started. And for the record, have you heard me say that I'm sure you're innocent?"

Robert didn't know whether her candor was only an act meant to gain his compliance, but with her words, the tension in his body downshifted a single gear. Stephanie took this as a sign that she should continue.

"But I am sure you don't fit the profile of any serial killer I've ever heard of, and our shrink doesn't think you fit these crimes either. Add to that the fact that you've got the tightest alibi anybody could ever have dreamed of, and that memory transfer is all that's left."

A long silence passed between them as Robert considered her words. The knot of guilt and self-loathing that reached down into his soul receded just enough for hope to seep in and fill a few of the empty spaces. He wasn't yet a believer, not even close, but Stephanie had opened a door to a world in which he was something more than a deranged animal, even if it was only a crack.

"What if you're wrong? What if you're helping to turn loose a killer? How would you know?"

Stephanie pushed a lone paperclip around the corners of her legal pad with the end of her pencil as she considered his words. "I wouldn't," she admitted. "Not for sure, at least not yet, but I am a detective, and I'm pretty good at it. Have a little faith for now."

"I don't know. I'm pretty sure one of us is grasping for straws. I'm not sure I can handle it if that person ends up being me."

Stephanie gave no reply. His opinion couldn't alter the direction of the investigation, so there was no need to convince him of anything, really. Besides, helping him was only a byproduct of her main goal—to find the truth.

Robert broke the silence. "I don't have any faith left. It's all buried out in the sand in the Middle East." He stopped short for a moment and gathered himself. "But maybe I could try the benefit of the doubt. For now."

She shrugged. "Whatever. They amount to the same thing as far as I'm concerned."

Robert considered her argument one final time. She was wrong of course, but maybe it was worth at least seeing where things went. Maybe there was some chance, however small, that she wasn't even crazier than he was.

"So, what happens next?" he asked at last.

"The work begins," she answered. "For both of us."

CHAPTER FOUR

However much confidence Stephanie might have had in her theory, Robert still spent the next three hours alone in his cramped gray holding cell while the detective jumped through the various legal hoops required of her. Despite his alibis and lack of any physical evidence against him, Robert stood upon the most unstable of legal platforms, one Stephanie's bosses were reluctant to be under if it came tumbling down.

Robert had smiled a little when Stephanie apologized for the process. "Just like the Army," he told her. "Take your time. I'll be fine."

But Stephanie had her doubts. There was no telling what kind of condition Robert was really in, where his breaking point might be. After a brief but tense meeting with her boss and the D.A., she had spent the bulk of the time she was supposed to have been using to secure his release speaking to Dr. Burns, and while he was fairly confident that Robert would be able to hold it together for the time being, there were, he had been quick to point out, no guarantees when it came to the human mind.

"Would you care for some advice?" Burns had asked her.

Stephanie knitted her brows. "I'm trying to think of an answer to that question that might possibly change what happens next."

Dr. Burns, as usual, ignored her barbs. She wouldn't have come if she hadn't wanted his opinion. "His biggest problem right now is that he doesn't know what's real and what's just in his head. Don't keep him in the dark about any of it. Involve him in some way if you can so he can see the progress being made. And remember that he's accustomed to facing his problems head on, fighting them. Maybe that's what he needs here."

"And if that causes him to have some kind of psychotic break?" Stephanie wondered aloud.

Dr. Burns twirled his favorite pen between his fingers and thumb. "I've thought about it extensively. I think it's doubtful at this point. In any event, what's the saying, my dear? Hope for the best—"

"But plan for the worst," Stephanie finished. "Thanks, Doc. As always, you're about as useful as a match in a house fire."

Stephanie paced the precinct halls for several minutes to blow off some steam and returned to Robert shortly after the dinner she had arranged to be sent up to him had arrived. Already though, the only signs of the meal were the empty wrappers and the satisfied look Robert wore. Perhaps he'd be in a decent mood, she hoped.

"Everything okay?" he asked, wiping the greasy remains of his cheeseburger from his fingers with a paper napkin he had managed somehow not to consume.

Stephanie held up the keys to his cell and jingled them in response. "We're good to go."

"Then why do you look nervous?"

"It's nothing serious. How was your meal?" she asked, changing topics as she unlocked the door. "Sorry I could only do fast food. Trust me. It's better than what you would have gotten otherwise."

"Are you kidding? It was delicious," he replied. "I've been so screwed up the last few days I don't even remember my last meal. Plus, you do realize I ate nothing but Army food for years, right? I could eat that whole thing again and think it was a T-bone steak."

Stephanie smiled at his joke before she realized he was serious. "We can pick up something else on our way out if you're still hungry," she offered.

"Thanks," he said, slipping through the door as soon as it was wide enough and giving Stephanie a meaningful look. "And not just for the food."

"No problem, but don't thank me yet. If I'm wrong about you, I'll be the one who has to arrest you and put you back in here for good. And I will do it." She added after the briefest hesitation, "So don't prove me wrong, okay?"

Robert could read the seriousness carved into her face, especially in the way her dark eyes fixed onto his. She was not someone you messed with, but her confidence allowed her to convey it without being cold or distant. In fact, he admitted to himself, she was actually quite beautiful. Her dark hair and vaguely almond-shaped eyes suggested just a hint of eastern blood in her, perhaps Persian. In another life, he'd have been instantly attracted to her. But, at least for now, he couldn't imagine being intimate with any woman without it making him ill all over again. Too bad.

"Fair enough," he finally answered. "So, where are we headed? I'm kind of hoping your plans involve me going home and getting a shower and some fresh clothes, but I get the sense that might not be the case."

"No, we can do that." She hesitated. "But we need to talk first."

"Now I get the sense I'm the one who should be nervous. Why don't you tell me what's going on?" he asked, folding his arms across his chest and shifting his weight to one leg. "Remember that I owe you, and I want to help. Whatever it is, just tell me."

"Okay. Mostly, it's the D.A. I think he buys my theory about what happened to you, but he's still nervous. Since we're in uncharted waters here, he has a lot of authority to set precedent."

Robert nodded. "I take it this particular precedent being set is something you're afraid I might not agree to."

"Actually," she said, "you don't have to agree. I'm sorry to say, you're being placed in police protective custody on the grounds you are mentally incapacitated and might be a danger to yourself or others. I fought for you, but this is the best I could do." Which was not exactly true. The D.A. had indeed demanded protective custody, which was a stretch legally, but Stephanie agreed wholeheartedly that Robert should not be let loose on the general population until they knew more about his mental health. Burns had said to tell him the truth, but she couldn't see what good could come from making an enemy of Robert.

"Protective custody? You mean locked up? Then why did you just let me out? And didn't you just promise me I could go home?" The more he thought about it, the more upset he became. Without thinking about it, he shifted his weight back to both feet and took a step toward Stephanie.

She immediately stepped back and shot a hand out to signal stop. The other hand drifted toward her service weapon at her hip. "Whoa, Robert, I remember. We are leaving, just like I said. And you *can* go back to your apartment. You can even stay there, okay?"

If Robert noticed her movements or thought them threatening, he said nothing about it. "But?" he asked instead.

"But," she answered, watching him for any more signs of danger, "you can't stay by yourself."

"So I'm going to have a babysitter?" Robert thought it over only briefly before nodding. "Okay. A sitter it is." He slipped both hands in his pockets and shifted back, leaning against the painted cinder block wall.

Stephanie's eyes registered her surprise. "Wait. You're okay with this? I kind of figured you'd be, you know … pissed."

"Part of me is," he agreed, rubbing the back of his neck with his hand, "but another part of me is relieved. Sorry, I think you're probably a great detective and all, but I'm just not as convinced as you are about my innocence. If you are wrong about me, I'll feel a lot better with a cop tailing me twenty-four hours a day. Plus, at least I don't have to stay here. No offense, but your coffee sucks." For the first time since he had come into the station, he grinned at Stephanie.

She watched him a second longer, then allowed her hand to leave her hip. "Come on," she said, gesturing with a jerk of her head as she began walking. "We need to get you home. We have an early start tomorrow."

"There's that word 'we' again," he said, falling in step beside her. "Does that mean you're my babysitter?"

She scoffed. "Not even close. You'll have to make do with a nice uniformed officer spending the evening with you tonight."

"Okay, but at least don't forget that second cheeseburger you promised."

"Wouldn't it be a third cheeseburger, technically? There were two in that bag I sent you."

He opened one of the glass double doors leading out of the holding area and gestured Stephanie through ahead of him. "See? I told you that you were a good detective."

———

The day, as awful as it had been, had ended on a high note for Robert. By the time they reached his apartment, he was feeling better than he had all day. Stephanie stayed for a few minutes until he settled in, and they talked about normal things not related to the case until his sitter arrived. By the time she had gone and he was ready for bed, he felt more relaxed and better fed than he had in days. Above all, though, he was exhausted. He needed sleep.

But that night, Robert found that sleep did not come easily, and when it did, it came at a heavy price. All the relief he had gained during the day was washed away in a flood as old and new memories came to him in his dreams like nightmares, except nightmares aren't real. What came to him was something else. There was no name for what he experienced that night; real memories of real victims whom he knew he had killed, yet there was also the detective who believed he had not. He had wanted so badly to believe her, but the many dead girls who visited him in his dreams reminded him of the truth.

The first one he had killed had been a simple thing, unsatisfying really. Hardly worth remembering. He had merely shot her, but he had learned. He had been much more thoughtful with the next one. He had carefully slit her throat. Better. The next, he had strangled with barbed wire. Less elegant than the razor had been, but not without its appeal. It was not until he had begun experimenting with his bare hands that the purity of the act was made real for him. With that one, as with each subsequent one, he had temporarily but unmistakably been elevated to a higher plane. The sensation had been indescribable and pure. He had, for one fleeting instant each time, experienced immortality. In those moments, his had become the religion of death, and he its highest and truest prophet.

CHAPTER FIVE

"You're early, Detective," Robert grumbled at 6:58 the next morning, pushing open his apartment door and turning back to his kitchen without waiting to see if Stephanie followed.

Stephanie had promised Robert she would pick him up at 7:00 a.m. sharp to head back to the station for an interview she had arranged with the Happy Memories salesman Robert had dealt with. She arched an eyebrow but entered the apartment and let the officer on duty take his leave. "And you're surly in the mornings."

He poured himself a generous cup and offered the same to her. "Only on the mornings when I'm headed back to jail after only one cup of coffee."

"No, thanks," she said. "And at the risk of putting you in an even worse mood, you need to make yours to-go."

Robert transferred the coffee into the Styrofoam cup from last night's second dinner. He inhaled the aromatic steam rising from the cup before carefully sipping the hot liquid and nodding appreciatively to himself. He was not thrilled to be returning so soon to a place he'd been held captive at for fourteen hours, even if it had been by his choice, and he'd be damned if he'd do it without better coffee than the station had provided yesterday. He'd agreed to assist with the investigation in any way necessary, but there were limits.

Stephanie looked at her watch for the second time in under two minutes. "Ready? We need to leave unless you have a thing for sitting in rush hour traffic." Something about the way Robert was leaning his backside against his kitchen counter suggested he didn't intend to budge anytime soon. "You've seen Houston traffic, right?"

"I don't know. Might be better than hearing what this guy has to say. What if you're wrong? I'm not sure what I'm willing to believe yet, but at least right now there's a chance I'm not what I think I am."

Good question, Stephanie thought. She wished she were better at these types of delicate situations, but she had always felt most comfortable with problems she could point a gun at. Conversations like these were more Dr. Burns' area of expertise. "I have no idea what you're going through," she tried. "I do know it has to be rough though, but let's not go through this again, okay? Last night you believed in the evidence. Nothing has changed, has it?"

"One thing did," he answered. "I slept. Or tried to." Robert looked up from his coffee cup and smiled weakly at Stephanie. "When I close my eyes, I remember everything. I see their faces in my dreams, the way their eyes were begging for mercy, the way they—" He slammed his coffee down, much harder than he had meant to, on the counter and jammed his hands in the pockets of his faded jeans to stop them from shaking. "I even had to sleep with the lights on last night just to get through the dreams," he admitted, embarrassed for himself. "Quite the he-man, huh?"

Stephanie looked Robert over from top to bottom as if he were some kind of a puzzle that she might take apart and then try to reassemble for no other reason than the challenge she knew it would be. And that's what he was, she realized, a puzzle. It wasn't only the obvious contradiction of demanding to be locked up one day and then being reluctant to even go near the precinct the next. He also was a hardened veteran of many grueling military campaigns who had reenlisted multiple times, yet he seemed to be a gentle soul incapable of hurting anyone, least of all a woman. And he was, she admitted, despite his question to her, practically the archetype of masculinity. His years of athletics, military service, and hard work in the factory where he was employed had kept him lean and muscled. His dark, tousled hair that matched his tanned complexion and his impossibly rugged jaw all suggested that he really did look this good every day when he rolled out of bed; yet, despite hitting the genetic lottery, he seemed to keep himself drawn in, displaying none of the confidence, even the arrogance, that he could easily get away with if he chose. The detective in her was alert that there was a definite mystery to be unraveled about him that had nothing to do with the case.

"Believe me, I've heard a lot worse," she consoled.

"You wouldn't say that," he told her, straightening himself and tapping his index finger against his temple, "if you could see in here."

By 8:00 a.m., Stephanie was seated in one of the station's interview rooms, looking across the table at Stephen Hennerman, the head of sales for Happy Memories. Robert Grayson was in the adjoining room looking at the proceedings through the two-way mirror, alert for any discrepancies between his own experience and Hennerman's account.

"Mr. Hennerman, thank you for coming in to meet with me,

especially this early, and I'm sorry about the accommodations. Let me repeat on the record that you are in no way suspected of any wrongdoing. We're only meeting in here because there won't be any interruptions this way. Ready?" she asked, smiling.

He returned the gesture easily, his perfectly straight white teeth gleaming back at Stephanie. He reminded her of one of the *after* pictures from her father's dental practice. "Sure, but like I said on the phone, I don't know how much help I'm going to be. You said you had some technical questions, but I'm in sales. I know just enough to be dangerous," he told her with a wink that said any modesty he might display was as decorative as the expensive silver necktie he was busy adjusting. His blue suit was finely tailored and fairly fashion-forward. Probably Zegna, she thought, though she was less of an expert on men's fashion than on women's. His shoes, though, were unmistakable—Stefano Bemers. Hand crafted, each pair taking up to three months to make; thus, the $2,000 price tag.

Growing up working in her mother's boutique in River Oaks, the Beverly Hills of the south, had taught her a thing or two, though she had never embraced couture the way her mother had hoped she might. She had more easily adapted to a snug shoulder holster than to a Kate Spade handbag, but she had gained enough of an appreciation to know that his outfit cost far more than she would bring home this month.

"Don't worry," she said, keeping her own smile in place. "I can assure you that you know a lot more than I do. After all, I read in your background that you've been with the company since almost the very beginning. Besides, I just need someone who can give me the big picture for an investigation we're involved with. I don't think it's anything serious, but we have to do the due diligence stuff, you know?"

"Sure," he told her. Stephanie's assurances melted the invisible metal rod that had held him straight, and he settled back just a bit into his seat. "What would you like to know?"

"That's easy." She grinned, affecting an almost school girl eagerness to learn. "Is it real? We've all seen the ads, but what you guys do seems, to be frank, impossible."

His chest puffed out noticeably at her challenge. "Though we've been around publicly only a short time, we spent years in research and development perfecting everything. Now, we have the tech to take a memory from one person and implant it into someone else. It isn't easy, but it's not impossible either. Not anymore."

"Seriously? Any memory I want?"

He shook his head. "No, not any memory. It's not really very different from an organ transplant in that we find suitable donors, though in this case they are handsomely rewarded, and we match them with ideal buyers. The matches are sometimes hard to find, but when we do, it's completely authentic to the new owner."

"And, judging by the name, you guarantee the memory will be something they'll like?"

"The memories being sold, as well as the people buying and selling, are thoroughly vetted before any transaction takes place. People get exactly what they pay for."

"Forgive me, Mr. Hennerman, but that wasn't a yes. Are you saying that if I wanted to buy someone's bad memories, I could do it?"

"No. Our clients are guaranteed a *happy* experience every time. No exceptions."

His answer had been emphatic, but a slight shift in the pitch of his voice caught Stephanie's ear. "So there's no chance I could get the wrong memories? Something the seller didn't mean to get rid of or that the buyer didn't want?"

Hennerman dismissed the detective's question, suddenly paying more attention to a stray hair on his suit jacket than to her. "I told you, absolutely none. That process is monitored by man and machine from start to finish. Both would have to malfunction simultaneously and repeatedly in order for that to occur."

He had corrected his pitch and slipped subtly into the role of confident-to-the-point-of-being-bored salesman, but a nerve had clearly been struck. The question now was how much pressure to apply and where. She decided to keep things friendly, at least for the moment.

"Okay. Next question. How complete is the new memory? Like, do I just remember the parasailing I did or is it the whole day at the beach? Do I remember the entire vacation? The decisions leading up to purchasing the vacation? There has to be some practical limit, right? And wouldn't my brain have to be able to reconcile any disconnect?"

"Well done, Detective," he said, appraising her for more than her looks for the first time. "Most people don't think it that far through, but, yes, there is a very real limit. Fortunately, our minds don't record even our own memories perfectly, so there are always gaps. Our system exploits that natural tendency and gives just enough information for the mind to accept the necessary parts while leaving out critical details that would cause a conflict. Your own brain fills in any necessary gaps."

"What kinds of details? Dates maybe?"

He began tapping the table with a perfectly manicured fingertip as he spoke. "Sure. We have to keep the dates fuzzy. I should interrupt myself to tell you that we're getting into some technical areas here that I'm not really qualified to explain, but I think you get the point; we give the client exactly enough to make the memory work for them and no more."

"I understand completely," she told him. Time to turn up the heat just slightly. "We actually use a similar technique when interviewing murder suspects. We might present a scenario that's just plausible enough to be true as an excuse to get someone to talk. As long as you don't provide too many details, they usually go along with it. I guess some people just believe what they want, huh?" Stephanie paused for half a beat to let the tension build before laughing it off. "I guess that's good for both of our businesses."

Hennerman nodded slightly but said nothing and made no attempt to join in her laughter.

"Just one last follow-up on this part. When you say you make the dates *fuzzy*, could you just change them if you wanted to?"

"Making actual changes is impossible. We've tried to spice up the memories by adding details. We thought we could charge an even higher price," he admitted, "but the subject's brain rejected them every time. The best we could do is to blur out the details we didn't want."

"So there are things that can't be recalled, but whatever the customer remembers is completely accurate?"

"One-hundred percent," he agreed.

"Okay, that takes care of the buyer, but what about the sellers? I've read that you're very selective about the people from whom you'll take memories. Why is that?"

Hennerman looked at his watch and frowned before answering. "Several reasons. One, it's expensive for us to retrieve a single memory. The right donor has multiple memories they can sell so that the cost of acquisition is kept down as much as possible. Once we hook you up, we can take as many memories as you want to sell, but our costs remain fairly fixed. More memories," he said, tapping his head with his index finger and then switching to rubbing his fingers and thumb together, "more profit."

"How much are we talking in terms of cost?" she asked.

"Sorry. I signed a nondisclosure. I guess you could subpoena that," he suggested.

"Yes, I could," she told him, locking eyes for a moment before remembering that she was the good cop today. "But I doubt that will be necessary," she added, putting on her smile again. "What other reasons are there? You said there were several."

"Well, second, we aren't jackals. We aren't going to take every happy memory from someone. Sometimes our sellers are pretty desperate people. If we'd let them, they'd sell everything."

"So your best clients have had these full, amazing lives, but now they're destitute?"

"Actually," he countered, "and I'm not supposed to say even this much," he nearly whispered to her, leaning in, "many of our clients don't need the money at all. They're after something else entirely."

The cocking of Stephanie's head asked the obvious question.

"Well, other than money there are two basic factors that motivate people to come to us to sell," he said, holding up two fingers and counting off on them as he spoke. "New first experiences and guilt."

Robert watched their cat-and-mouse game unfold from his side of the mirror and wondered how much of it Stephanie was directing or even aware of. He hoped for his own sake that it was far more than it seemed. Nothing he had heard so far indicated there was even a shred of credibility to Stephanie's theory.

"New firsts I get," she said, interrupting Robert's grim thoughts. "I want to experience something and have it feel the way it did when it was new."

"Indeed," Hennerman agreed. "Many of our clients have pushed a given envelope as far as it will go. They're looking for ways to … keep things fresh, shall we say?"

"Right, but what about guilt? I thought you dealt only in happy memories."

Hennerman chuckled slightly in a way that Stephanie knew was somehow meant to be dismissive. She made a private note to check his file for unpaid parking tickets before he left.

"Don't be naïve, Detective. Something about which we feel

guilty now might well have been the basis for one of our happiest memories at the time it occurred. But," he conceded, "you are correct in that we no longer perform those transplants. It turns out that people need a certain amount of shame in their lives to keep them on the straight and narrow. We found that removing that burden often changed people's personalities—and not for the better," he added, pausing longer than he had to this point. "Sorry." He was suddenly aware of the gap in the conversation. "It's just that certain family members complained. It got messy, so I begged the owner to stop."

Stephanie faked an impressed whistle. "You got him to stop? No disrespect, but you're only the head of sales. You must be pretty influential there in other ways."

"Oh, not really, but as you said, I've been with the company since the beginning. In fact, it practically started in my apartment. Our founder already had the theories and the research, but we did our first actual transplant in my living room. Those were good days," he recalled, and, for the first time, Stephanie thought, his smile seemed genuine. Just as she thought it though, it vanished. "But then, you didn't ask me here to get the full company history. Please continue."

"Okay, back to the clients. Did you replace the old memories for the people who needed ... what was it?"

"Shame," he answered, shaking his head. "We tried. For reasons we could never discover, these things go only one way. Trying to undo the process causes ... complications."

"Are you saying that once I have a new memory, there's no way I could remove it?"

"Short of having a large chunk of your own memory wiped clean, sort of like reimaging a computer, no."

Stephanie swallowed hard, knowing Robert could hear every word of this interview. She'd have to wrap it up soon and try to get to him before he lost it.

"Okay, so how long ago did you stop?"

"Doing removals only? Almost four years. It was during the beta testing. Ironically," he said, again leaning in to invite her confidence, "the removal of those types of memories is what our founder actually had in mind when he began the company. Clean Slate, he originally called it. Didn't work, though, or not without the consequences I mentioned, so he shifted focus to the good memories, and we became what we are today."

"I see. So the technology *does exist*," she stressed, "for me simply to go have an unwanted memory removed and to give myself this 'clean slate'. People would probably be willing to pay a lot more for absolution than they are for a few fleeting memories of hang-gliding in the Bahamas," she offered, arching an eyebrow and watching his reaction.

He nodded. "Quite a bit more, but, like I said, it isn't good for them, and offering such services would likely attract a clientele that is less than desirable for our image. Besides, we're hardly hurting for cash doing business the current way," he said.

Stephanie stifled a grimace. Smugness was oozing off of this bastard like cheap cologne off a teenage Lothario. "So no one at your company could possibly be motivated to do a little side business? Maybe some salesman who lacks your obvious talents and who sets his moral bar a little lower?"

"Your flattery notwithstanding, I can't imagine who at our company would be so foolish or desperate. But it doesn't matter. To prevent such temptations and, more importantly, corporate espionage, no one person has more than one-third of the knowledge needed to perform that task. Keeps everyone honest, and it's a common corporate practice. KFC, Coca-Cola, even Play-dough—they all do it."

"Yes, but in each of those cases, one person originally knew the secret formula before dividing it. Your company is still fairly new. Someone there knows how the whole thing works, start to finish," she pressed.

"Of course. Our founder, Dr. Mead, would be able to do that if he were so inclined, but again, I can't imagine why he would. In the last year, Mead has made more money than he could spend in fifty lifetimes, and he's the darling of the technology world. I bet he's on the cover of five magazines right now, and that's just in the U.S. Not to mention that we'll likely go public in the next year or so. When that happens, he'll have a pile of cash he won't be able to see the top of." Hennerman was unable to suppress a self-indulgent grin. "We all will."

Stephanie abruptly rose and gathered her notes, nodding perfunctorily and extending a hand to the startled salesman as he also came to his feet.

"I've taken plenty of your time today, Mr. Hennerman. I'll let you get back to work. Thank you for your cooperation."

"My pleasure," he offered, buttoning and smoothing his coat front. "I'm sorry I wasn't more help."

As a uniformed officer entered the room and led Stephen Hennerman away, Stephanie turned to the mirror and risked a barely perceptible nod to Robert, thinking to herself, *Actually, you and that fancy suit of yours were more help than you could imagine.*

CHAPTER SIX

"That go about like you expected?" Robert asked from the spot where he leaned against the wall with his arms crossed. The question and the posture were meant to show his displeasure at the news Hennerman had delivered. If Stephanie picked up on either, she gave no sign; instead, without pausing, she simply grabbed him by the elbow and pulled him along with her toward her desk so hurriedly that he found himself taking longer and longer strides to keep up.

"I *would* say that that must have gone worse than I thought, but I don't think that's possible," he said, allowing himself to drop down into the chair that adjoined her cluttered workspace.

"Wrong. It went better, much better. And I'm hoping that we have some added good news from some of the information I requested," she said absently, scanning her desk for the desired files. "Ah-ha. Here we go."

Stephanie slit the top of a large manila envelope and poured the contents, a stack of computer paper, printed photos, and a standard looking thumb-drive, onto her desk. Quickly gathering the papers and scanning them one after another, she nodded to herself as she found each important detail in turn.

"Are we gonna pretend he didn't say that stuff about these memories being permanent?" he pressed her unsuccessfully. "And what is all that?" Robert tried to ask, but she stopped him with a raised finger, never breaking her concentration or rhythm. After a prolonged silence during which she never looked up or otherwise acknowledged him, Stephanie dropped the papers and told him simply, "It's the rest of your get-out-of-jail-free-card."

"More exonerating evidence?" he asked, gesturing with a thrust of his chin to the pile of documents and photos.

"From a friend at Quantico," she nodded. "Two more cases. Just like the other one, you nailed details that were never let out to the press or public. And just like before—"

"I was overseas when they were killed," he finished for her, running his fingers over the soft edges of the papers.

"Yeah," she said, cocking her head slightly. "Forgive me, but this is kind of a big deal, Robert. You know we have the death penalty in Texas, right? Well, you aren't going to be facing that now, or even prison time. I kind of thought you'd be more excited by this."

"It's great," he said without looking up from the papers. "Three murders I probably didn't commit."

"Not probably," she corrected.

"Fine, but even if you're right, I've now given you details about nine killings, and I'm not sure there aren't more." He rose from his chair and began pacing slowly in front of the desk. "And no offense, but no matter what the evidence shows, I still remember literally choking the life out of each of these women. And much worse beside that. And on top of that, I just found out that I have the good fortune of living with these memories forever, so I guess I am a little short on cheer at the moment."

He stopped pacing long enough to grip the back of the chair in his powerful hands. Stephanie watched as his knuckles turned white under the pressure. His eyes closed, and he began to rock gently on his heels to at least try to control his breathing and heart rate. Stephanie knew the signs of a migraine well enough to see them in him, and it looked like it was going to be a monster. Though she knew it to be futile, she tried to take his mind away from the growing pain.

"Robert," she said, standing and walking the short distance to him, "I don't know you well, and I don't know what you're going through. I won't pretend to. But I do know people, and I know the law even better."

Robert's stance relaxed slightly, but his hands did not let go their grip. "So I guess now you're going to tell me that if I have faith in the system, it will eventually clear me of any wrongdoing and everything will be fine, huh?"

Stephanie ignored the challenge and let him talk, figuring it might be good for him.

"Sorry," he offered. "This is harder than it looks."

"Don't be. I'd say you're holding it together pretty well, all things considered. But I do recommend that you put this between your teeth," she said, extending one of her pencils to him.

"What for?" he asked, accepting the item and noting with a frown the many teeth marks already present along the soft wood.

"Helps with headaches."

"I don't have a headache," he lied, trying politely to return the apparently often-used tool.

"Yes, you do," she said, pushing it back at him. "And even if you didn't, you will after I get through."

One look at the seriousness etched into her face overcame all the anxiety the potential germ factory in his hand might have caused. Robert dutifully placed the pencil between his teeth and waited for the rest of the day's good news.

"Robert, that guy is lying. I'm not sure yet about which parts, but I have guesses. We aren't going to take the word of a liar that you can't get rid of whatever they put in your head. Not yet, anyway. Besides, he didn't say you couldn't get rid of the memories. He just said there would be a price to pay. It can't be worse than the one you're already paying, can it?"

Robert considered her words. Maybe she was right. "How do you know he's lying?" he attempted to articulate around the pencil. When he was very young, his grandfather had kept a few horses. Sometimes he would see them saddled up and with the bits in their mouths. He knew how they felt now.

Stephanie's nose wrinkled as she searched for the right way to explain her thoughts. "I don't know if you could pick up the vibe through the mirror, but that guy was all about bringing home the cash."

Robert nodded and removed the newly dampened pencil from his mouth. "Obviously."

"Do you mean to tell me," she said, "*that guy* went to his boss and told him to stop selling something that was marketable and that maximized profits just because it was bad for people? And that crap about calling you in and offering you a special rate because of your service? No way did that happen," she insisted. "That douche nozzle would sell Krazy Glue covered hand grenades to school children for the right price. Count on it."

Robert blinked hard at Stephanie but soon found that he could not suppress his laughter. The sense of humor on display was so out of character for the Robert she was getting to know that Stephanie couldn't help joining him.

"It's nice to see that you can do that."

"Nice for me too," he agreed. "I guess I haven't had anything to laugh about lately. Not sure it's a good sign that it took exploding children to do the trick, but I guess it's a start."

"It is supposed to be the best medicine," she reminded him.

Robert wasn't so sure, but he didn't want to ruin the lightness of the mood by disagreeing. He took the safe path and steered the conversation back to something simpler. "So what do you think that Hennerman guy is trying to hide?"

"Not sure yet, but I'll bet you a nickel it's somehow connected to you. How many secrets can one company have after all?"

Yeah, but secrets are like earthquakes, Robert thought. *It's not the number of them that gets you. It's the magnitude.* "No idea," he offered instead, "but I'm hoping you plan to find that out soon."

"Not me," she corrected. "Us. We've found a thread. The next step is to start pulling at it and see where it snags. Wherever that is, if it does involve you the way I think it does, you might be the only person who'll notice it when it happens."

Robert's eyes went wide. "Me? I'm glad to help, but I'm on house arrest, remember? And for good reason. Besides, I've told you everything I know in all that paperwork you gave me, and I gave that shrink pretty much my whole life story."

"Protective custody," she corrected. "And you've only told me everything that you *know* that you know, and I agree there's nothing there. No offense, but, on the surface at least, there's nothing special about you."

"Thanks for that," he said, feigning hurt. "For a second there, my ego was really starting to get out of hand."

She brushed his objections away with the back of her hand. "I just mean that there isn't any obvious reason why he, or whoever, would've chosen you, but that doesn't mean the reason doesn't exist. I need to find out what you know that you don't think is worth remembering. And you'll still be under protective custody. Mine."

"So let me see if I have this straight, *Detective*. You actually want to rely on my memory, the one we know has been tampered with, as the cornerstone of your case?" Robert pretended to look around the room for something. "Do I just start by screaming and throwing things around, or do you think I need to kind of build up to that point? I've only been crazy for a short time."

"Looks like your sense of humor is returning in spades. Good. I think you're going to need it."

Robert rolled his eyes and huffed. "Who's being funny?"

He has a point, Stephanie conceded. *But didn't Bullet say to keep him involved? This should certainly count.* "Okay, so it sounds a little unorthodox, but I'll at least feel better if you're where I can keep an eye on you. And the closer you are to the case, the more likely it is you'll remember something. I know it's hard having to deal with what you're going through, and even though I still think what Hennerman said about you keeping those memories forever is bullshit, it does look like you will need to keep them at least for a while longer. Think you can handle it?"

Robert brought the pencil she had given him to his nose and took a whiff. He appeared to think over her question carefully before finally nodding and putting the pencil back between his teeth. "One question doh. Do dese come in any udder flavors?"

CHAPTER SEVEN

Stephanie's actual plan, as it turned out, was somewhat less absurd than Robert had thought. They started by again going over photos of girls who were possible matches for the murders Robert remembered. They reviewed countless images of one grisly death after another before Robert finally could take no more. He begged off on the excuse that his headache was getting worse, but they both knew it was more than that. Each picture represented a nightmare that had played out for the victim and for her family. Even if none of them turned out to be ones Robert remembered, each was still a reminder of the kind of pain and horror for which he felt responsible. After three rounds and as many hours, Robert finally identified two more girls.

"Still no names or faces, I take it?" Captain Bates asked Stephanie while Robert was on one of his innumerable coffee breaks.

Stephanie shook her head. "No, ma'am."

"He give you anything besides a match on the pictures?"

"Cause of death. This one," Stephanie indicated a photo, "was the barbed wire girl he wrote about in that journal he gave us."

She laid another picture next to the first. "This other one here the killer choked with his bare hands."

Captain Bates rubbed her temples with both hands, then opened a desk drawer and removed a bottle of aspirins. She shook the little plastic container before unscrewing the lid and popping two in her mouth and swallowing drily. "Okay. I'm going to pretend you are not riding around getting chummy with the only viable suspect in a multiple homicide investigation while I tell the D.A. that we are making zero progress toward finding any other leads. In return, you *are* going to find me something. Soon."

Accordingly, Stephanie scooped Robert from the break room the instant she left the office and deposited him into her car to begin the next phase of the plan.

"I don't mean to sound like I'm complaining," Robert said yet again from his spot slouched deep into the passenger seat of the unmarked sedan, a white Ford Crown Victoria, whose front windshield the pair had been staring out of all afternoon while Hennerman's car remained parked at his office.

"Could've fooled me," Stephanie replied without looking over at him.

Robert ignored her and continued. "I'm grateful to be through with those pictures. I really am. But you don't have anything I could do that would be easier on my ass?"

"Well," she quipped, "you aren't in prison. From what I hear ..."

Robert shifted in his seat at the unspoken image. "Ouch. Okay, I got it. But seriously, nothing else?"

"Like I said the ten other times you asked, I truly do not. Look, you obviously don't run in the same social circles. Your addresses are on opposite ends of town. You don't belong to a gym or go to church or any other establishments where social status and income aren't as likely to be limiting factors. And neither Stephen Hennerman nor any member of his immediate family has ever served in the military. There is simply no obvious explanation as to why you have been targeted, so we have to go where he goes until we find something. Understand?"

The knowledge that she was correct didn't stop Robert from a small amount of sulking. "I still don't see why I have to be here with you all day. You said this was probably a long shot anyway."

"It is, but it's better than doing nothing. And I thought you military types were tough," Stephanie said, looking at Robert over her sunglasses. "You mean to tell me this is less comfortable than the inside of a Hummer?"

"It isn't about comfort. It's about being bored to death. And we rode in Hum-vees and M113s, not civilian Hummers. Besides," he said as he adjusted the car's already overworked AC, trying to coax just a little more cool air from its depths, "I was getting paid to do that, and if I had refused, somebody would probably have shot me."

"Yeah, well, somebody here might shoot you too if you don't stop complaining."

They might not have to, the way you drive, he thought. "Anybody ever tell you that your bedside manner could use a little work?"

"Those are doctors you're thinking of. I'm allowed to be as direct and disagreeable as I want as long as I remember to turn off the dash camera first."

Robert shot her a sideways glance. "Most of the time, I'm pretty confident you're just busting my balls, but sometimes I'm not so sure."

The rest of that day and most of the next two were spent watching Hennerman drive to work by 8:00 a.m., remain there until at least

5:00, and then head back to his high rise condominium.

After watching Hennerman drive his silver Mercedes SLK through the gated entrance to his condo on the third night, Stephanie admitted defeat.

"Thank God," Robert muttered as she put the car in drive. "Maybe I can finally get some sleep now."

"That's practically all you've done for three days," she told him. "Trust me. You snore."

"I do not," he objected. "Much. Anyway, I meant sleep in a bed."

Stephanie gave him a puzzled look, though she suspected she knew the reason for his insomnia. "I've had you home by eight every night. You still having the dreams?"

Robert nodded. "It's always the same. I'm dealing with everything during the day, but the nights are ..." He paused to choose his words carefully. He didn't want the detective worrying about him when she should be focusing on the case.

"Harder? I could have Bullet prescribe you something if you want," she suggested.

He shook off the idea. "No thanks. I can't just take pills forever. I have to learn to deal with this on my own at some point. That might as well be now."

"Yeah, but—"

"I said I've got this," he answered a little too loudly, cutting her off and instantly feeling guilty for doing so. He knew she had only been trying to help, and he could ill afford to alienate anyone right now, especially her. "Sorry," he offered weakly. "Maybe I'm not quite as okay during the day as I thought. But I will be. Especially now that we're through day camping in your car."

"No problem," she assured him. "I get it. And it may help your state of mind to know that we have not been wasting the last three days, despite your in-no-way-repetitive-or-whiny objections."

He ignored that last part. "We haven't? Maybe I *was* sleeping then 'cause I missed something."

"You didn't miss anything, and that's the whole point." Stephanie continued on quickly before Robert could voice his confusion. "There was nothing to miss. Nothing at all. Three days and nights, and Mr. Suave went to work and then went home alone. No visitors. No fancy bars or clubs. None of the things that all that money he makes could buy. He strike you as the kind of guy who likes to spend his evenings alone with a good book?"

"Not much point in owning those fancy suits and that car if all you do is go to work and straight home again," he agreed. "You think he's hiding something?"

"Or afraid of something," she said.

"Time to turn up the heat on him?"

"Stop watching cop shows. And no, we'll keep him on a low boil for now. What do you say we pull on a new thread instead?"

"Unravel the whole sweater if you want," Robert encouraged. "As long as we don't have to do it from anywhere near this car."

CHAPTER EIGHT

A plum. Sometimes, he thought the color was more like a grapefruit, but this time it was definitely a plum. Of course, he considered as he had stared into the girl's pleading, wide eyes, maybe it was because her skin was much darker than the others. He had given his special gift to one other black woman, but her skin had started as a rich mocha color. Ultimately, her face had turned more burnt orange than grapefruit or plum. What did they call that color? Not orange ... sienna. That was it. She had turned burnt sienna. He had thought it quite beautiful at the time, but it paled compared to this.

Too, he thought, it could be because that other woman had been African American, while this one was purely African, a recent immigrant here on a student visa. He had at first thought her accent was Nigerian, but she had told him that she was from Cameroon. Later, he would look up Cameroon on a map and be pleased to see that he had essentially been right. Cameroon and Nigeria are neighbors. How different could the accents be? He decided it had actually been rude of the woman to correct him when there was really no way anyone could have been expected to hear the difference between those two accents.

Maybe, he decided, it had been her rudeness that caused him to rush the job, to withhold some of the beauty that could have been hers if she had just been nicer. Of course, he had still completed the act that was required, but it had been only a clinical thing. He wasn't even able to pleasure himself now as he thought of her. That had never happened before. Still, her death had been pure and holy and, therefore, a gift. He had witnessed to her about the sacredness of life in the only way a person could truly understand it—by taking it away between his two squeezing, choking hands. And she had loved him for it. Yes, he decided, she had eventually loved him for his gift the way that all of them had, so he determined to grant her forgiveness for her rudeness as he began to rub himself to the memory of her face, her exquisite plum-colored face.

"What's up?" Stephanie asked when the uniformed officer answered Robert's door the next morning. For the last few days, Robert had greeted her at the door with fresh coffee each morning. It had become something of a routine for them.

"He won't come out of his room," the officer, a petite but tough looking blonde in her late twenties, had told Stephanie.

"Is he awake?"

"Yes, ma'am, or I would have busted in the door. He'll talk to me some, but he said he wasn't coming out until you got here. I figured it was better not to upset him."

"Okay, thanks. I got it from here," she said. The young officer nodded but didn't budge from her spot. She seemed to be waiting for something. "Umm ... good work," Stephanie added. "You were right not to get him agitated."

Satisfied, the officer nodded, tipped her cap, and left.

Stephanie padded the short distance across Robert's cheaply carpeted living room to his bedroom and was about to call out when the door eased open a crack. All the lights, even the one in the closet, were on. Robert peered at her through the artificial brightness. He wore badly wrinkled track pants that were threadbare in most places and an old plain tee shirt that should have been converted to a dust rag years ago. He looked like hell, Stephanie thought.

"She gone?"

"Yeah. It's just me. You want to tell me what's going on?"

Robert opened the door the rest of the way, turned his back on Stephanie and her question and walked over to his bed where he fell onto his back.

"Talk to me," Stephanie pressed, crossing over to stand near his bed but not crossing the line of joining him on it. This case was complicated enough.

Robert said nothing. With each silent second that passed, Stephanie's concern grew more and more real.

"More dreams?" she asked. "Maybe it's a good sign. Maybe these things are working their way out of your system, you know?"

Robert rubbed his face with both of his hands and finally sat up. He reached over to his nightstand and retrieved yesterday's paper and handed it to Stephanie, who took it without question and began scanning the headlines.

"I read the paper yesterday. Did I miss something important?"

"Not the articles," Robert told her. "Look at the back. In the margins."

Stephanie flipped the paper over and found the handwriting there scrawled in the margins in black ink.

Her feet go down to death; her steps lead straight

to the grave.

This is what the LORD says: "Those destined for death, to death; those for the sword, to the sword; those for starvation, to starvation; those for captivity, to captivity."

Those who walk uprightly enter into peace; they find rest as they lie in death.

The words repeated several times as they made their way around the border of the paper, framing the articles in their macabre verses.

Stephanie tugged at her ear as she thought about what this could mean. "You wrote this?" she asked, already knowing the answer.

"All of it," he confirmed. "It's from the Bible."

Stephanie forgot her earlier instinct to avoid his bed and took a seat next to him. "Robert, with everything you've been through, I'm guessing it would take more than a few Bible verses to shake you up this badly. These are all connected to the girls somehow, aren't they?"

"Probably," he agreed, leaning his head forward and resting his powerful forearms across his knees. "I wouldn't really know though, Detective, because I don't remember writing them. Not one single word."

"Oh," she managed.

Robert laughed bitterly. "Oh is right. But it gets even better. You know how I know they're from the Bible?"

Stephanie remained silent. Robert had a point, and the fastest way to get to it was just to let him talk.

"I looked them up." Robert pantomimed typing on a keyboard. "I had to look them up since I'd never heard of them before. See where I'm going with this?" he asked, his legs beginning to bounce on the balls of his feet. "Not only did I perform the neat trick of writing a bunch of Bible verses about death sometime last night without remembering doing it, but I did it without ever having read the Bible."

The pair looked at each other wordlessly for a brief eternity before Stephanie could stand the silence no longer. Knowing she would be rebuked, she still tried to offer some comfort by reaching out her hand and rubbing his shoulder tenderly. She was not prone to initiating contact with other people, unless it was in the process of Mirandizing them, but she couldn't think of anything to say, and doing nothing felt even worse. She was surprised when he did not immediately reject the gesture.

"I know this must be bad," she finally offered. "But in one night you've come up with more information about the killer than I've been able to gather using all of my other resources put together. I'm going to have someone analyze those verses, and that's going to put us one step closer to this being over, one step closer to catching the killer and getting you free of his thoughts. *His* thoughts, Robert, not yours. You know that, right?"

Robert chewed his lower lip and nodded unconvincingly.

"His thoughts maybe," he said, patting her hand before rising to walk toward his bathroom door where he turned around to face her again, "but *my* handwriting. This means I act out things he thinks about, Stephanie, things he's done probably. We both know it's only a matter of time until I take it up a couple of notches."

"That's why you have the officer with you," Stephanie started to say, but she got no farther than a couple of words before Robert entered the bathroom and closed the door on her. As soon as Stephanie heard him enter the shower, she snatched up her phone and dialed the station. After three rings, someone picked up.

"Hello?" a familiar male voice said.

"Bullet, it's Stephanie. What's your day look like?"

"Not too bad, I've got a meeting at ten and some paperwork to take care of. Why?"

"I'm gonna need you to clear your schedule. I'm bringing Robert straight to you. He's in bad shape, Doc."

"Okay," he agreed hesitantly. "You think it'll take all day?"

"No. I've got another project for you though, and I need it done today."

"You don't ask for much, do you?"

Stephanie clicked off the line without responding. She dropped the phone back in her purse, stared at the door, and listened as Robert moved around behind it. He might be right, she knew. If he could act out one memory from the killer, why not others? It was an option Stephanie had not wanted to consider but had always known was there. The Robert she knew was a good man, but there was someone else inside his head now. If he managed to take control …

"Believe me, Doc," she whispered to herself, "if you even knew the half of it, you never would have answered the phone."

CHAPTER NINE

It had taken some convincing, but on the drive to the station, Stephanie had finally convinced Robert to speak with Dr. Burns again.

"It would be pointless. I already told him everything," Robert had complained.

"Yeah, but there are new developments, aren't there? I'm going to need his help developing a profile of this killer, and I'd like him to get the information about the dreams and the Bible verses first-hand. You'd be doing me a huge favor," she said, giving him her best over-the-top doe-eyed look.

"Stop it," he chastised. "You're about as helpless as a grizzly bear. But okay. You made your point."

After arriving at the station in near-record time, Stephanie had stashed Robert in Dr. Burns' office and given him the rundown on the night's events.

"Give me a few minutes to get some stuff together. I'll come find you when I have it," she told him. "And Bullet, thanks for your help. With everything."

Dr. Burns watched her for a moment as she sat and began

plinking at her computer's keyboard before he nodded to himself and walked back to his tiny office to check on Robert.

Stephanie went to H.M.I.'s website and printed all of the pertinent information she could find about Dr. Lawrence Mead, which was very little. She then switched to a general Internet search of his name, remembering what Hennerman had said about all the magazine articles. She could find data going back about three years on him, but almost nothing before that. What little existed before that time frame was purely academic, papers he had published and so forth, plus the typical biographical data. Mead had a wife, two kids—one boy, one girl—was originally from California but educated mainly on the East Coast, etc. Whoever the brain behind the memory switching technology was, he had burst onto the scene from relative obscurity.

Frustrated by the little data she could find, but content that she had found all there was, Stephanie switched her search to the Bible verses Robert had written. None of the verses was familiar to her, her own Biblical education having ended after her confirmation at thirteen. What the Episcopal Church had managed to get her to absorb before that had been more along the lines of the "big picture" parts of Christianity. Miracle birth, Jesus grows up, more miracles, Jesus dies, another big miracle. Perhaps, she considered ruefully, she could have paid a *bit* more attention in church all those years ago. Thankfully, the Internet provided what hours of misspent Sunday mornings had not.

Proverbs 5:5—"Her feet go down to death; her steps lead straight to the grave."

Stephanie scanned the surrounding verses. She did not need to be an Old Testament scholar to decipher this one. All of the lines were about avoiding the temptation of women, especially adulteresses. The verses went on to say that if a man fell for one of these women, he would reach the conclusion on his deathbed that he had wasted his life and had refused counsel from older, wiser people.

It makes sense, Stephanie thought. This killer would hardly be the first to think of women as a symbol of wickedness and temptation and to attempt to remove that temptation from the world in order to save men from such an outcome.

Jeremiah 15:2—"This is what the Lord says: Those destined for death, to death; those for the sword, to the sword; those for starvation, to starvation; those for captivity, to captivity."

Again, the surrounding verses were about failure to obey and the punishment one receives for such sin. In this case, there was nothing about women. It was all about Jerusalem, specifically about some guy named Manasseh, son of Hezekiah, king of Judah, and some unspecified thing he did in Jerusalem. There wasn't a ton of other information about him, but that made no difference to Stephanie. Whatever he did, the message was clear—you get whatever you have coming to you. No exceptions.

Finally, Isaiah 57:2—"Those who walk uprightly enter into peace; they find rest as they lie in death."

Stephanie puzzled over this one for some time. It seemed in sharp contrast to the other two verses. Those were all about wickedness and punishment. This verse was actually quite comforting. Stephanie once again scanned the surrounding lines to find they were much more consistent with the message from the other verses. They were all about bad deeds and punishment.

Perhaps that was the point, she reasoned. The contrast. The first verses were the rules and the consequences, but there also had to be a reward, didn't there? The killer probably believed that he was doing the Lord's work by removing temptation and that he would find rest and peace as his reward when he died. It was impossible to know for sure if any of her assumptions were correct, but she would check them with Bullet shortly. And even if they were only assumptions, they at least felt like progress. *Not terrible*, she thought, *for two hours' work*. Stephanie stretched and decided to take a break and find Dr. Burns. She needed to deliver on her promise to him about the other favor she needed.

Although Dr. Burns' door was closed, which always meant he was not to be disturbed, Stephanie knocked gently. A chair scraped noisily across the floor and footsteps made their way to the door. Opening it, Dr. Burns motioned for her to stick her head inside. There, sprawled out on the doctor's undersized, rock-hard excuse for a sofa, was Robert, fast asleep and apparently, at least for the moment, at peace.

"What did you give him?" Stephanie asked as soon as they were back out in the hall.

"A rather elephantine dose of anti-anxiety meds combined with a sleeping pill. I wouldn't normally mix them, but you saw for yourself the shape he was in. He didn't want to say it at first, but he hasn't slept in several nights."

"I know," she nodded. "He was lights out most of the time in the car while we were together. How's he doing otherwise?"

"Otherwise?" Burns shrugged as he folded his arms across his chest. "Much worse than I had hoped. His blood pressure is sky high for one thing. These memory lapses, or whatever they are, concern me, to say the least. But those aren't even the worst parts. He is suffering an identity crisis for which there is no precedent. I can't begin to predict how this will affect him long term, but my guess, and that's all it is, is that it's going to get worse and worse until it reaches a breaking point."

Stephanie chewed the inside of her lip as she took in the news. She'd known already Robert's situation was far from ideal, but the way Bullet described it, she wasn't sure whether he'd be better off in some facility somewhere. Then she imagined herself in his place for a moment and abandoned the idea of cooping him up somewhere. At least for now.

"I get it, Doc. I'm on the clock. I don't suppose you could be specific about what that breaking point might look like or when it might arrive?"

He smiled sadly. "Not even remotely, dear. That's what no precedent means, but imagine this. Tomorrow morning, I walk into your apartment and tell you that you're not a police officer. Everything you remember about being an officer is a lie. I can even wave a magic wand and prove that I'm telling the truth. You are actually, I don't know, a baker. Now, let me ask you, do you feel like a baker? Does my telling you you're not a highly trained, capable homicide detective change anything at all for you about your sense of who you are? Are you going to be able to walk into a bakery and start living that life just because I *told* you that everything you think about yourself isn't real?"

Stephanie swallowed drily. "Jesus, Doc, we should switch places and maybe let you start doing the interrogations."

Dr. Burns put an affectionate arm around her shoulder and briefly laid his cheek against the top of her head. He was at the top of an incredibly short list of people for whom she didn't return the gesture, but neither did she pin his arm behind his back and sweep his legs from under him.

"Sorry, kiddo. You know I always shoot straight, especially with you."

Stephanie did know it. It was how he had earned the nickname he so despised.

"You're saying that no matter how much evidence I provide him, he's always going to believe he's a killer?"

She felt his head nod before he let her go.

"At least on some level. How long do you think it would be before you found yourself in a police station trying to live what you thought was the *right* life?"

"Wait. You're saying he'll become a serial killer? That can't be right," she insisted. "I know people better than that. Besides, what about all that guilt he feels? That means he doesn't *like* the memories the way a real killer would. Doesn't it?"

"Maybe," Dr. Burns said. "But he's no ordinary person anymore, and you can't treat him as if he were. I'm not saying what he's going to do next, but I'm saying you shouldn't make any assumptions either. If he finds himself in the wrong situation, that other side of him is going to come out. I just don't know what that situation might be or when it will happen."

"So what, then? Just keep him doped up until we find a way to undo whatever has been done to him?"

"If that were an option, I can't say I'd be totally opposed to it. One, we don't know this damage can be undone, do we? And two, those medications ease his other symptoms by lessening the guilt you mentioned. If you are right, the guilt may be what he needs to keep hold of his sanity, no matter how it affects him in the interim. Either way, he needs to work those issues out very slowly and with professional help, which I can't give him forever."

Hennerman's words from the interview room came back to Stephanie then. *"People need a certain amount of guilt to keep them in check."*

"Yeah, but surely just until I can find—"

"You're being blinded by something again," Dr. Burns interjected, giving her a look that bordered dangerously on sympathy. It was like her father was staring at her, only worse. "That anti-depressant takes away some of the bad feelings he associates with the killings," he hurried on before she could interrupt again, "but it does nothing to take away any of the *good* feelings."

Stephanie's head popped back. "The good feelings? What are you talking about?"

Bullet's eyes widened. "He hasn't told you." It was not a

question. "Stephanie, he got these memories, we assume, from *Happy* Memories, Inc. He didn't just get the images associated with the murders, he got all of the pleasure that the killer associates with them, too. He enjoys thinking about those girls just as if he were really the killer."

"No," she said, shaking her head curtly, "I would have seen it. He doesn't like those memories. He doesn't even like talking about them."

"No, he doesn't," Dr. Burns agreed. "But not because he doesn't like them. It's because he hates that he likes them so much, which does nothing to improve the overwhelming sense of guilt he's experiencing. I'm sorry, sweetie. I wish I had better news, but he has a long road ahead of him however this turns out, and you might too."

Stephanie set her jaw and looked past the doctor at the closed door, imagining the anguished man sleeping on the other side of it, and said, "Then I guess we'd better get started on the other thing I need from you."

Dr. Burns' patient smile returned as always. "I was wondering when you'd ask."

CHAPTER TEN

At exactly 11:00 a.m., the special phone Stephen Hennerman always carried did what it usually did at this time every day. He took a deep breath before reaching into his jacket pocket to retrieve the phone.

"Yes?" he said.

"Don't sound so glum, Stephen. I've called with good news, after all."

Hennerman didn't bother stifling a groan. He could hear the pleasure in the caller's voice as he spoke. "That would be a first."

"No, truly this time. You are no longer being followed. You are free to resume doing whatever you wish."

"If you say so," Hennerman replied. He knew better than to grovel or to try and provoke the other man. He certainly knew better than to ask to be released from his servitude. Events would unfold precisely as he dictated. They always did and, unless he quit caring about the lives of his ex-wife and child, they always would. "Is that all?"

A pause. Hennerman could picture the man on the other end as he stuck the knife into his ribs and enjoyed twisting the handle.

"Well, now that you mention it, there is one little thing …"

"What do you know about Lawrence Mead?" Stephanie asked Dr. Burns on their way back to her desk.

"The H.M.I. guy? Just the usual, I guess. Invented the memory switch technology. Filthy rich, and he's going to get more so from what I've gathered."

"That's about all I found too," she agreed, settling into her chair and picking up the pages she had printed. "But what about what he does? Or, more specifically, how he does it? What do you know about that stuff?"

"This isn't what you want to hear, but even less than I know about the man," he answered, taking his usual seat.

"But somebody has to know something. I mean, he can't just mess with people's brains without someone knowing what he's doing and how he's doing it, right?"

"You'd be surprised. Not everyone considers what he does a medical process, but since he's licensed to practice, that's really a moot point. It would be different if the process were chemical-based, but since it isn't, the F.D.A. has no reason or right to explore, and as long as he doesn't invent any new machines that are considered medical devices, there's no oversight from the A.M.A."

"So no one is even looking into this stuff?" she sputtered, tossing the papers on her desk.

"Quite the opposite. Everyone is talking about it. There are tons of theories, some facts, and lots of people who would kill to know how he does it so they could have a piece of his market share. So far though, he's kept it locked down tight," he said, pantomiming the turning of a key. "Of course, once the company goes public, all that will change," he added.

Stephanie perked up. "Why will it change then?"

"Well, investors aren't going to dump hundreds of millions of dollars, which he will get, into something so unknown. Once they become owners, they'll expect to know at least the basics."

"And he'll have to tell them?"

"Not the small guys, the individual investors, but the big boys, the corporations who own corporations who'll be buying it. He'll have to give them something. From there, the necessary information can probably be extrapolated, and it's off to the races for the competition."

"I didn't know you knew about all this stuff," Stephanie said, nodding her head in a gesture of respect. "Maybe you should look at my pension account."

"I didn't until recently, but it's relevant to my profession in this case, so all of the medical journals have been covering it. You see, once the competition finds out how it works, the doctors are the next to know. Rival companies will want the data independently verified. The entire medical community is chomping at the bit," he grinned. "Myself included."

"Do you have any guesses? I mean, what do you shrinks think you know right now?"

He rocked his head side to side a few times and one corner of his lips curled as he thought. "Lots of guesses, but little that we know for sure. How technical an explanation do you want?" he asked, looking over the rim of his glasses.

"Let's keep it below my headache threshold, if possible."

He smiled and slid one of her stray pencils across her desk at her. "Just in case," he apologized with a shrug. "Basically, Mead's early research, what we know of it because very little was published, focused on the concept of heredity and its role in shaping people as individuals. He was interested in finding out which personality traits and even tendencies were most likely to be passed on from one generation to the next. It was interesting but pretty mundane. Lots of people had looked at it before him. But one day," he snapped his fingers, "he suddenly changed gears and began focusing on the area of genetic memory. Apparently, he wanted to find out if there are memories carried by our genes and passed on from generation to generation. With me so far?"

Stephanie hesitated a second before nodding.

Dr. Burns caught the slight delay. "The answer to the question you're asking yourself right now is, 'not that crazy'. Does that surprise you?" he asked.

"Seriously?"

"I'm not saying he was right," he nearly blurted. He was practically bouncing in his seat as he spoke. "But I can't prove him wrong either. Neither can anyone else. In fact, the question has actually been around a long time, and there is some fairly compelling evidence to support the idea, at least in animals, but no one has had the means to test the hypothesis. We *think* that maybe he found a way."

Stephanie picked up one of her pencils and glared across the desk. "Bullet, I swear to God that I'm going to use this on one of us in the next minute if you don't start making sense. Why do you only *think* he found a way?"

Bullet sat back in his chair, spreading his empty hands before him. "Because that was when he quit publishing. Two years later, H.M.I. was founded. You know the rest."

Stephanie shook her head and let the pencil fall onto her desk. "Yeah, but that ain't saying much."

"All in good time, my dear. I know patience is not your strong point, but you'll just have to wait along with the rest of us to fill in the gaps."

Stephanie smiled and shot Dr. Burns a glance that made

him want to find an exit. They both knew he wouldn't like what was coming. "But what if I didn't have to? It would make all the difference in the world in this case."

Silence. *Fine then*, Stephanie thought. *The direct route it is.* "Doc, I know you won't like this, but I'm going to have to ask you to come with me to do an interview."

Dr. Burns didn't bat an eyelash. "You know I don't do that, not even for you."

Stephanie clasped her hands together in a gesture of prayer and laid them on the desk. "It's important, Doc. Please."

"I don't help you catch criminals, Stephanie. I never will. I am a doctor, and my job is to tell you whether suspects are competent to stand trial and to get help for those who aren't. You find the bad guys. I help the ones who need help without making any moral or legal distinction. Period."

"I understand your little code or whatever it is," she said, brushing off the notion with a wave that earned her a disapproving glare. "But this interview isn't with a criminal, not as far as I know anyway, and you *would* be helping someone who needs it—Robert."

"Wait. Are we talking about who I think we are?" Dr. Burns asked.

"We are if you mean Dr. Mead. Please, Bullet, it's the fastest way I know to get to the truth, and according to what you said earlier, time is of the essence for Robert. Please."

His eyes narrowed slightly as he fought to think of reasons he should turn her down. "I wouldn't be any help. My knowledge of all of this stuff is purely theoretical. Besides, what interest do you have in the technical matters?"

"None, but I do need an excuse to go and see him without revealing Robert or my investigation. Those are my big guns, and I may need them later. What I need is to give him an opportunity to lie, Doc. If he does, he's part of what's going on there."

"You don't know that for sure. He could just be protecting other secrets."

."I don't think so. Anyway, I'm willing to take my chances. How about you? You get to be the first in your field to interview him. That's a lot of publishing cred." Stephanie wrinkled her nose and added. "Or whatever kind of credibility it is you people have."

Dr. Burns thrummed his fingers across Stephanie's desk and pretended to think it over. "Fine," he told her, holding up his index finger, "but, your offensive phrasing aside, this is your one time to ask me this. You sure you want to use it for this case?"

"Positive. And thank you, Doc. I mean it."

"Don't patronize me by acting as if I had some choice in the matter," he chided her. "I'm a sucker for you, and you know it. Speaking of which, you might want to hurry and take advantage of my weakness before our patient's meds wear off."

"How much time do we have?" she asked pensively.

"Three or four hours, I would think. Everybody metabolizes differently."

"That's plenty. I'll put a uniform outside your office door, and we can head over to see Mead now."

"What makes you think you can even get in to see him without a warrant?" he asked, rising. "I'm sure he has at least a couple of secretaries to get past and probably more security than you can shake your Taser at."

Stephanie smiled and said, "You've heard of the good cop bad cop routine right?"

"Yes," he said slowly, suddenly not sure he wanted to know the answer.

"Well, there's a third—the cop who could ruin your company if word got out that an investigation was under way to find out if your technology actually turns your customers into stark raving mad killers, thus destroying your life and everything you've ever worked for."

"Oh," he said. "Is that all? I never heard of that one, but then, it must be hell to fit on a business card. And look at the progress you're making. In your plan, you didn't even threaten to shoot anyone."

Seemingly in one fluid motion, she grabbed her keys from her desk drawer, indicated with a jerk of her head that they should get moving, and patted her holstered Ruger .40 caliber with her other hand for emphasis.

"Oh, it's still an option," she said with a smile, "but I thought I'd try my friendly approach first. Like you said—progress."

CHAPTER ELEVEN

It took a bit more persuasion and far more time than Stephanie had imagined, but she did get her meeting after she managed to get in front of one of Mead's senior security staff who understood the financial ramifications of her threat to take a sordid investigation public.

Dr. Burns noted with some pride that Stephanie had asked nicely, twice, before she had pulled out the metaphoric big guns. Even then, she merely suggested that leaving homicide investigators in the lobby of H.M.I.'s executive level offices might not send the right message to the troops or to the reporters who would, coincidentally, be arriving shortly.

Soon thereafter, the pair was seated in comfortable chairs in an oversized corner office that resembled a luxury suite more than it did a workplace. A middle-aged secretary poured steaming coffee from a silver urn into china cups and set it before them and then informed them curtly, but without being rude, that Mead would be with them as soon as possible, which might be some time. She turned and left, closing the office door behind her without waiting for a response from either of them.

Dr. Burns turned and looked at Stephanie as if to ask if this had been the reception she had had in mind. Stephanie, however, was already up and had her back turned to the doctor as she took in the room's details.

"Don't even look at me like that, Bullet," she answered him. "We're in, aren't we?"

The doctor threw up his hands in mild defeat and let the matter drop.

Stephanie accepted his surrender with a nod as she surveyed the room, noting that everything about the place reflected the wealth of its owner without actually reflecting any particular style or theme. Overstated opulence might be the best description, she thought. Even though Stephanie had been raised in River Oaks, the wealthiest section of Houston, a town rich with engineering and oil money, she had never seen anything like this office. She took out her phone and began snapping pictures.

The desk was clearly mahogany, and all around the edges was a fine inlay she was sure was actual gold. The pen set on the desk was Mont Blanc. The brass and silver desk clock was stamped Chelsea on the underside of the base. Though she hadn't heard of the clockmaker, she bet herself that a quick Google search would reveal it to be among the finest, and costliest, in America. On and on it went. Lladro porcelain and first edition, leather-bound books on the bookshelves, among them a Bible so old it looked as if Gutenberg might have had a hand in its printing. Oversized, museum quality paintings hung on the wall, the frames of which alone she was sure cost more than her car.

"Dr. Mead certainly isn't playing his finances close to the vest, is he?" Dr. Burns asked her. He had not moved from his chair, but his eyes took in all the same little details of the room that Stephanie's had.

"I bet the bathroom has pieces of the Magna Carta to wipe

your ass with," she agreed.

"Charming," he said, grimacing.

Stephanie completed her turn around the office, returned to the large desk, and was just beginning to examine a small picture, presumably of Mead's wife and daughter together, when the door opened and a man matching the pictures of Dr. Lawrence Mead entered the room. He was of medium height and build with graying hair and a matching beard, but his steps were quick and his eyes showed none of the signs of age or weariness from which the average working fifty-something man typically suffers. *Money*, Stephanie thought, *might not buy happiness, but it sure as hell doesn't seem to hurt anything either.*

"Detectives, so sorry to keep you waiting," Mead offered with a smile, extending his hand to them both.

"It was no trouble. I'm sorry to have to bother you like this, Dr. Mead," Stephanie responded. "And I'm the detective, Stephanie Monroe. This is my colleague, Dr. Benjamin Burns. He's consulting on a case I'm working on."

He gestured them back to their chairs as he unbuttoned his Valentino suit jacket and seated himself behind his enormous desk. "This would, I assume, be the same case that caused you to question one of my people already."

Stephanie wasn't sure whether to be surprised that Hennerman had reported their meeting, so she gave no reaction. "Correct. We're in the very early stages, so I'm not at liberty to discuss much, but your help would be invaluable."

Mead offered no response, much less his help, but neither did he object, so Stephanie continued.

"Um, right, so I'll come to the point then—"

"Forgive my rudeness, Detective," he interrupted. "I spend my days around nothing but computer experts, engineers, scientists, and the like. The social niceties sometimes end up taking a backseat with that crowd. It's a bad habit I've picked up. How can I help?"

Stephanie noted that though his apology sounded sincere, his face offered no insight as to whether he truly meant what he said. *I wouldn't want to play poker with this guy,* she thought.

"No worries, Doctor. I'm in something of a hurry myself, so I'll try to be brief, but it's a rather complicated situation. We have a suspected murderer in custody. All of the evidence shows me he is the killer, and I even have a confession from him. Everything is as rock-solid as it gets."

"Sounds cut and dried," Mead said. "But I'm sure you would not be here if that were the case."

"Exactly," she nodded. "The problem is his confession. You see, he's a client of yours."

Mead's right eyebrow arched dramatically at the news.

"I can't say the name, of course," Stephanie offered by way of apology, shrugging. "Innocent until proven guilty and all that crap. You know how it is."

He brushed off the apology with a wave of his hand. "No, it's fine. I understand. How can I help?"

"We picked him up on something unrelated, but I guess he figured we were on to him for something a lot more serious. Before we could charge him, he confessed. It was from his confession that we uncovered all of the physical evidence. It's pretty disturbing stuff."

Mead's head bobbed as he listened. "This evidence you're speaking of, do you mean bodies?"

Stephanie nodded before saying, "Yes, but even with the bodies, the D.A. has doubts as to whether his confession is going to be admissible since he'd just had his brains scrambled by your company. His words," she interjected quickly, "not mine. He's just concerned that a jury won't hold our guy accountable if he was incapacitated in some way when he confessed, and, much as I hate to admit it, we'd never have found everything else if he hadn't volunteered the information. If we lose the confession …"

"You'd lose everything that came with it," he finished. "But that doesn't make sense, Detective," Mead said.

Stephanie did her best to feign an apology. "I know. It's a terrible system, but it's all we've got."

Mead gave a quick shake of his head. "No, no, I mean, nothing that my company does would explain someone confessing if he didn't want to. My system doesn't affect the parts of the brain associated with decision making. Whatever he told you, I assure you he told you of his own free will."

"I'm sure that's true, Doctor, and, even if it weren't, I wouldn't care. I mean, this guy is a first rate dirt bag. The stuff he did …" She shivered slightly. "But the problem is the D.A. has to be able to *prove* what you say about what your system is true. Right now, any first year defense lawyer could pilot a cruise ship through the holes he could poke in that confession." Stephanie made a point of sighing and shaking her head. "Nothing like this has ever happened, and we need your help. Without it, a guilty man is going to go free, and I would hate that almost as much as I would locking away one who is innocent."

Mead tapped the ends of his fingers together, making his own show of thinking over her request. "I'll be happy to confer with my lawyers to determine what information we can release to you that might help prove your case, but if what you're asking is for me to walk into open court and reveal my company's secrets, that I cannot do under any circumstances," he said, shaking his head emphatically.

"I get it. I really do, but if we don't come to some kind of … arrangement, I'm afraid that the D.A. is going to have no choice but to subpoena all of your records and research. A team of people, most of them outside contract workers, would spend weeks going over all of your research. With that many hands in the information cookie jar, a few crumbs are bound to get lost."

Mead blanched visibly at the picture Stephanie painted for him.

"Exactly," she said. "I know how much you want to avoid that, and, believe it or not, so do I. What I want is for us to reach a mutually beneficial arrangement. I need answers quickly, and you have secrets that are unrelated to this case that you need to protect." Stephanie paused to allow him to imagine millions of dollars fleeing out the door and back into the warm, safe pockets of investors before she continued. She scooted to the edge of her seat, leaned in toward Mead, and spoke softly. "What I propose is this—explain to me in layman's terms as much as you can about how you do what you do. Dr. Burns' job will be to determine if what you say would be something a jury could understand and use to get a conviction; furthermore, nothing you tell me will be used in court against our suspect unless you approve it. Agreed?"

Mead almost came out of his seat to jump on the offer. "I have your word on that last part?"

"Absolutely," she agreed. *Can't use evidence against a suspect I don't have, asshole.*

"You too?" he asked Dr. Burns, who had missed the subtlety of Stephanie's promise. He had been caught up watching Stephanie work. In all the years he had known her, he had never seen her in her element before.

"Hmm? Oh, yes, most definitely."

Mead shot his cuff and looked at his watch, a Rolex, Stephanie noted. *Of course.*

"Twenty minutes," he said. "Any more than that and we'll have to reschedule."

Stephanie laid her phone on the desk, pulled up the voice app, and hit record.

"Then I guess we'd better get started."

CHAPTER TWELVE

"What would you like to know first, Detective?" Stephanie put on an embarrassed smile. "We might as well skip all of the most technical parts. I'd never understand them anyway, I'm sure. Why don't you just start with what it is you do here?"

"Alright. At our most basic level, we simply take a memory that exists in one place and move it somewhere else."

"You're too humble, Doctor. You make it sound like no more than rearranging furniture," Stephanie suggested.

"A touch more complicated, perhaps," Mead said, smiling slightly, "but that's not a terrible analogy."

"Really?" Stephanie answered, surprised. "How so?"

"Moving a sofa isn't hard to do. Anyone can accomplish that if they have the tools—strength, leverage, whatever. Knowing the perfect place to put it is another matter. It takes an expert to identify the one space that is an exact match between the room and the sofa. That's really the magic in what we do."

"Surely finding and removing a memory can't be nearly as simple as you make it sound. We are talking about people's brains, after all."

Mead nodded. "To be sure, but we mapped the entire human genome years ago, Detective. We've cloned sheep and a host of other animals besides. We're no more than a generation away from creating true artificial intelligence. A species capable of such feats should be able to accomplish anything, don't you think?"

"Maybe," Stephanie conceded, "but how do you actually go about extracting a memory and inserting it somewhere else? And how can you know it doesn't have any adverse effects on either of the parties involved?"

"Perhaps your friend here could help with this," he said, indicating Dr. Burns. "I don't know what kind of doctor you are, but I would wager you know a thing or two about the human brain or else you wouldn't be here. Am I correct?"

"Certainly," Dr. Burns agreed without elaborating. He was in shrink mode now. Say as little as possible as long as the other party is willing to talk.

"Then you can confirm our brains function in a manner very similar to a computer. There are spaces where memories are stored, just like on a computer. And, just like on a computer, there are even spaces dedicated to long-term memory and spaces where recently acquired information is kept for easy recall. Am I correct so far?" he asked.

"That's the prevailing theory," Dr. Burns agreed.

"Okay. And, again, just like a computer, you can have the world's most sophisticated C.P.U. but, if you don't have a way to read the output, it isn't worth much to the user. That's where my research really focused in the early years, and it's still how we find the memories we need." Mead practically glowed as he spoke.

"A monitor," Dr. Burns said, shaking his head in disbelief before looking at Stephanie. "He invented the equivalent of the computer monitor. A screen that sees everything the brain sees.

Incredible."

Mead said nothing at first, but his grin showed that Dr. Burns had hit the proverbial nail on the head.

"That was phase one," he finally agreed. "We could *see*, for lack of a better word, all the memories a person could recall, but it was similar to looking up a file on a computer when you don't know where the file is stored. You know it's there, but the amount of data that has to be sifted through in the human mind is almost beyond reckoning, far more than any computer is capable of holding."

Stephanie sat taller in her seat and shifted a little. She was unaccustomed to being left out of an interrogation she was running. "So you needed one serious search function to make your system work," she said.

Mead nodded again but did not look at her or otherwise acknowledge her presence. He obviously relished having the upper hand.

Enjoy it while you can, pal, she thought.

"Exactly. We knew memories didn't stay put once the mind stores them. They are transient, so to speak. Once we developed a way to predict where a given memory might be located, it was relatively easy to download the sequence of electric impulses that make up the memory. We were moving so fast in those days," Mead recalled.

The way he spoke of his company in its fledgling days reminded Stephanie of the way most people thought back on a child's birth or the day they met their true loves.

"Pardon me for a minute," she interrupted to play her part. "Doc, how are we doing so far? Is this something a jury could run with?"

Dr. Burns played along. "Maybe, but we're beginning to get into an area that sounds more like science fiction than science."

Stephanie frowned at the news. "Dr. Mead, perhaps you could

just give us some idea of how much of a technological leap all of this was?"

"That's an excellent question, but one without a clear-cut answer, I'm afraid. Think of it like the Wright brothers. What did they invent, Detective?"

"Flight," she answered. *Duh.*

He held up a finger and wagged it at her. "That's correct but only in a sense. Flight has existed since the time of the dinosaurs. The Wrights simply formed a machine from existing parts that could replicate what nature had achieved long ago. You see, once they understood the concept of lift, it was only a matter of time until they achieved flight. To the uninitiated, it must have looked like magic. To those who knew the math, it was the satisfying but foreseeable conclusion to one of nature's grand designs."

Visions of Mead's finger dangling limply from his hand as he groaned in pain danced through Stephanie's mind. Bringing Dr. Burns had been an even better idea than she had realized. She swallowed a few choice words and instead simply said, "I see. So are you suggesting that nature had already achieved what you do? And that this technology is our destiny?"

"I know that it's hard to think in those terms, Detective, but again, at the most basic level, yes," he nodded. "First, we shared stories using sounds and then words. Somewhere along the way, we learned to draw images to share ideas. The written word came next, and then the printing press. After that, cameras, then audio and video recorders, then we developed a way to digitize it all and send those things back and forth electronically to each other on the same device you're using to record this conversation. The sharing of ideas and memories is hard-wired into our DNA, as is the need to do it as efficiently as possible."

Stephanie hated herself for it, but she was impressed. "Okay. Let's say a jury accepts this as the next logical progression. There is still a serious difference between the technologies you mentioned and your own. Those are all copy-and-paste. Yours is cut-and-paste. Why?"

Mead stiffened ever so slightly in his chair. "I wish I knew. The brain is far more complex than a computer. I'm confident that we will be able to make a copy someday, but, for now, we must make do with simply moving the original."

"Surely you have some idea?" Stephanie pressed, delighted that she had made Mead nervous.

He checked his watch again. "I'm afraid that we are beginning to run short on time," he said, though they were nowhere near the twenty-minute figure he had quoted Stephanie earlier. "And we really are getting into areas I'm no longer comfortable discussing, but let me leave you with this. What we do is perfectly safe. We didn't invent one new thing in order to accomplish what we do. We merely perfected the use of tools that already existed, that have been used on humans for years, even decades in some cases, to do something new, something extraordinary, all by discovering what a memory truly *is*. And none of that," he insisted, "would ever cause any type of modification in someone's behavior. That confession you have is sound. I'd run with it."

I'm sure you'd like that, she thought.

Mead stood and gestured to his watch apologetically. "If you'll excuse me, I truly am quite behind schedule now."

Stephanie ignored his request and remained seated, giving him a neutral stare that neither invited discussion nor prompted an argument. "My time isn't quite up, Doctor, but I promise I'll be brief. You said earlier that knowing where to put the sofa is what makes you different. What did you mean?"

Mead at first considered remaining standing, but instead he sighed heavily and sank back into the soft, rich leather of his office chair, which somehow felt slightly less comfortable than it had just a moment ago.

"Certain memories from one customer can't go to just any other customer. If you had a strong fear of flying or heights, for example, your mind would reject the notion that you went skydiving and enjoyed it. We didn't realize at first that compatibility was an issue, but it turns out that it's the most important factor in a successful transfer."

"Of course," Dr. Burns said. Stephanie looked over at him to continue, but he appeared absorbed in his thoughts, absently tapping the sides of his glasses.

"Just for argument's sake, how do you know this doesn't change a person's mind in other ways?" she continued. "How does a jury know that a criminal wasn't prompted to turn himself in when he wouldn't have otherwise done so? I mean, your assurances aside, getting a jury to believe that is the most critical part of our case."

"There's precedent. Before I even got started, scientists had already implanted false memories into patients with no harm or any kind of change in personality. We actually thought about going that route, but the level of detail needed to convey the emotion associated with the memory was just too much to try to create from scratch. And in our own records, this part of which I'd happily supply you, there isn't a single complaint by any of our clients. Surely, that should satisfy your jury?" he asked, his impatience now making it impossible to hide his frustration.

"Let's hope so," Stephanie agreed with a smile, retrieving her phone and turning off the recorder. "I'm sorry to have taken so much of your time, Dr. Mead, but this was more helpful than you can imagine."

"My pleasure. If it's okay," he said, hitting a button on his desktop phone, "my secretary will show you out."

"Of course," Stephanie agreed, already heading for the door before the secretary could arrive. "And by the way," she added, smiling and gesturing to the framed photo of Mead's wife and daughter, "I meant to compliment you on your beautiful family."

"Hmm? Oh, yes. Thank you. They're quite the pair. This place keeps me away from them far more than I'd like, but I do it all for my girls," he said.

"Yes," Stephanie agreed, smiling and looking around at the room's extravagant furnishings one last time. "That must be it."

CHAPTER THIRTEEN

Robert was shaking off the cobwebs of his deepest sleep in weeks when an officer he didn't recognize came into the doctor's room to check on him.

"Detective Monroe around?"

"Not yet, sir. Anything I can get you while you wait?"

Robert stretched his large frame and rubbed his neck where the end of the sofa had pressed against it. "I'll take one of these sofas to go if you have any extras."

The officer smiled. "I guess it must agree with you. I've checked on you three times. This is the first time you've moved."

Robert nodded and looked around. "Guess it does. It looks like I commandeered the doc's office. Hope he's not too upset."

"I don't think it was a problem, sir. Dr. Burns is out too. They should both be back soon though. You want some coffee? Or maybe a newspaper?"

"Actually, if the doctor is really out, I think I'll just lie back down."

"Roger that. If you need anything, I'll be right outside."

As soon as the door closed though, Robert rose and stretched again. He turned to take in the couch on which he had slept, reasoning that it must have been a good deal more comfortable than it looked or else Robert was far more tired than he had realized. Probably it had been both, he thought. Then he remembered the pills. Happiness through pharmacology wasn't something Robert put much faith in, but Dr. Burns had insisted that he take the pills or else submit himself to twenty-four hours of psychiatric evaluation. The coffee, he knew, would be terrible. Faced with limited options, Robert had taken the pills and, he had to confess, felt almost human for the first time in as long as he could remember.

He was taken from his thoughts when Stephanie walked through the door and found him standing in the middle of the darkened room.

"Hey," she greeted him. "How are you feeling?"

"A little better, thanks to the doctor," he allowed. "And you, I guess."

"Me?" she asked, flipping on the light switch after gaining Robert's permission.

Robert shuffled his feet a little until he caught himself at it. He opted for shoving his hands in his pockets instead. "Yeah. You brought me here, right? You made me see him when I wanted to handle it my way. All your idea, and you were right. Thanks."

Stephanie couldn't help noticing that he looked embarrassed. Accepting help was tough for some people, especially for people in certain professions like soldiers. And cops, she grudgingly acknowledged.

"Don't sweat it. All in a day's work, right? Hey, you wanna work off some of your debt?" she asked.

Something about the way her eyebrows arched caught Robert off-guard. He gave her his best hesitant smile. "Are you trying to take advantage of me, Detective? I was recently drugged, and I hear the law frowns on such things."

She tried to give him a hard stare. "They frown on beating suspects too. Which do you think I'm considering at the moment?"

"Those have to be separate things? I'm pretty open-minded." His sense of embarrassment immediately returned, stronger than before, and his face glowed beet-red. "Sorry. I don't know where that came from," he stammered.

"Wow. No worries. I guess you really are feeling better, huh?" Despite the complexities of this case and the many reasons that she should keep her distance, Stephanie found his ability to handle and even to return her dark sense of humor refreshing and maybe just a little attractive. Shaking her head and smiling, she said, "Actually, what I had in mind was to get your feedback on an interesting interview I just had."

"With whom?" he asked, glad for the distraction.

"The C.E.O. of Happy Memories, Inc. Dr. Lawrence Mead."

Robert's own eyebrows arched considerably at the name. "You weren't kidding about interesting. Well, I don't know what help I can offer, but I'm happy to take a look."

After joining Stephanie at her desk and listening to the recording twice, even making a few notes the second time, Robert sat back and rubbed his face with his hands before offering his thoughts. "It's fishy," he said.

"Fishy," she repeated. "Any chance you could tighten up that analysis for me?"

"He's just off somehow. I interrogated a lot of people when I was in the Army. Mostly, it was people I was accusing of wanting to blow me or my friends off the face of the earth. I learned pretty quickly to be direct with them, even rough at times. I'm willing to bet you know why I did it that way."

It was a safe bet. She had employed the same technique many times. "You were looking for a specific reaction that an innocent person would probably have."

"Exactly. You told me you bullied your way in. The innocent ones I dealt with either yelled back because they knew they had nothing to fear or just went silent and complied to get it over with as fast as possible so they could get on with their day. Mead wasn't angry or business-like, not at first. It's like he remembered to act that way after first showing you a lot of kindness. Doesn't fit," Robert said, shaking his head.

"That's not all that doesn't fit," she said, leaning forward. "In any investigation, you have knowns and unknowns, right? The knowns so far look like this." As she spoke, she began to count off her points on her fingers. "One, someone at H.M.I. is lying to us. Two, someone at H.M.I. is probably involved in covering up the identity of a serial killer. Three," she said finally and with some hesitation, "there's a timeline in place that doesn't make sense."

Robert cocked his head. "Which is?"

"Which is that I can't find a victim who died any more recently than roughly three years ago, but you had that bad voodoo put on you just a few days ago. Why the gap?"

Robert thought silently for a minute or so, closing his eyes and rocking gently back and forth in his chair. "Well," he observed, "it could be simply bad luck that we haven't found newer victims. There are killings I can remember that we haven't accounted for yet."

"And *all* of the ones you remember whom we haven't found are from the same time period?" Stephanie's forehead drew up in wrinkles at the thought. "That's too big a coincidence for me. If we haven't found those other girls, there's a reason for it. But keep going."

"The killer could have gotten better at hiding or disposing of the bodies," Robert suggested.

"Obviously, but how and why? His other disposals were just body dumps in fairly secluded areas. Nothing sophisticated about it. Serial killers don't change their M.O. without a strong reason, like fear of getting caught, but we didn't even know he existed three years ago."

"We also know that he hasn't changed the way he kills. I'd remember that, but I don't. Once I started strangling the girls, he never went back, so—"

"He," Stephanie interjected.

"What?"

"You said once *I* started strangling. You meant once *he* started."

"Sorry." Robert twirled his index finger around his temple. "Things are still hard to keep straight sometimes."

Stephanie nodded and uncharacteristically glanced down briefly. "Yeah, I get that now. Bullet had a talk with me, tried to get me to understand maybe just some little part of what you're going through. I mean, I already knew it was tough, but, after talking to him … well, I don't know how you're doing it. Sorry I didn't get it sooner." Stephanie looked up to find Robert's eyes locked onto her. When she met his gaze, they neither looked away nor spoke for several seconds as something real but intangible, an understanding of mutual trust and respect, passed between the two of them.

Robert broke the silence. "No need to apologize. I still have my doubts, and there are certainly moments when I have visions I don't think I'll ever un-see, but until you straightened me out, every moment was like that. It was hell, Stephanie, seriously. And you saved me from it, or at least from some of it. I'll never be able to pay you back for that."

"No problem," she said quickly, hoping to move on before any more awkwardness could creep its way into the moment.

Robert understood and offered a crooked grin. "Back to the case?"

"Definitely," she nodded, relieved. "Okay, the easiest explanation for the timeline gap is that there are still victims out there we just haven't located for some reason, but given the consistency of this guy's methods, that's really unlikely. So, what else could account for there being no bodies? Other than there being no bodies, of course." She threw on the last remark as an afterthought and laughed weakly at her own bad joke.

Robert, though, didn't join her. Instead, her words had brought him back to a time he had spent considerable effort distancing himself from. "Back in Iraq, and especially in Afghanistan, if our enemies started behaving differently, it was always either because we caused it or because they were getting help from someone else."

"Are you saying you still think it was some kind of outside pressure? It would have to be something pretty profound. I've never heard of a serial killer who just stops killing. Ever."

"Maybe," he said, but his voice held no conviction. "You said you're sure an investigation didn't cause whatever this change was. Couldn't someone else have been investigating him though?" Robert asked. "Something you don't know about, maybe?"

Her shoulders popped up almost imperceptibly in barely a half-shrug. "Anything is possible, but I've found nothing to that effect so far. And I pulled favors with every agency who could possibly have been looking into something like this. If I've missed anything like that, we'll never find it."

Robert nodded. "Fair enough. We'll treat that possibility as either a no or an unknown. Nothing left to do but stay with the knowns."

"So, what's that leave us with?"

"Well, if we accept the idea that the killer got help from someone, either the good kind of help that got him to quit killing or the bad kind that helped him cover his tracks better, then we can make the assumption that it's gotta be the same person who gave me the memories, right? Unless there's a team of people out there suddenly willing to help serial killers." Robert was getting excited now and got up to pace as he thought it through. "And if Mead is the one lying and the one with the know-how to use the technology, doesn't it make the most sense that he's the one covering for somebody?"

"Correct," Stephanie said, gesturing him to sit back down. "But we're a hell of a long way from proving anything like that. If it even can be proven. Does that machine of his keep records? Can they just be erased? I have no idea, and we'd have to have enough evidence to get a subpoena before we can even try to find out."

Robert finally paused his walking and rested his hands on the back of the chair to consider her words. His weight shifted to the balls of his feet like a prizefighter coming into his stance. He hated to admit it, but he was back in his element now, unearthing bad people who were experts at not being found, and his pulse raced at the prospect of the chase. "Okay, we think we know what happened, when it happened, and how, but proving those will be tough."

Stephanie nodded. "Or worse."

"Or worse," he agreed undeterred. "So what about who and why? There can't be that many people he'd do something like this for."

"A best friend?" she offered. "Family member? Somebody who would confess to him. Have to be somebody close."

"Which would make his reason for helping something noble but twisted. Maybe. But what if it's the opposite? What if somebody coerced him?"

It was Stephanie who rose from her chair now. "How?" she asked, her voice more animated than it had been. Answers were still in short supply, but she knew they were at least finally asking the right questions. "His tech removes memories completely. The killer wouldn't remember he had anything to hide or any reason to coerce anyone into anything. No, Mead, or whoever, joined forces with this asshole. No other explanation."

Robert rocked his head back and forth as if he were attempting to shake something loose. "Okay, so someone close. That can't be that big of a haystack," Robert insisted.

A frown settled onto Stephanie's face. "The pile of suspects he'd be willing to do something like this for might be tiny, but that doesn't help us much."

"Because," Robert interrupted, "thanks to Mead's invention, he probably doesn't even know he is one anymore." He looked crestfallen.

Stephanie reminded him, "Hey, don't get down on me now. We've come farther in the last five minutes than we have in the last week, and a lot of it is thanks to you. Besides," her eyes suddenly widened, "we may not have to find the needle in this case."

Robert tried to catch her meaning but came up short. "Sorry?"

Stephanie fell back into her chair, leaned back, and locked her hands together behind her head. "Mead's greatest assets in this game are that he is the only one who knows what he's done, which we can't change, and he probably can't be linked directly to the killings, which we also can't change, and, finally, he believes those killings have stopped. As long as all those things remain true, he's in the clear forever."

Before Stephanie was even finished speaking, Robert caught on. The wide grin that materialized across his face looked like it might not ever come off. "So since we can't change the first two things you mentioned …" Robert started.

Stephanie nodded slyly. "We change the third. Where's the first place you'd go if a secret you needed to stay buried suddenly turned up?"

"I'd check my burial site," Robert answered. "And fast."

CHAPTER FOURTEEN

Dr. Lawrence Mead regarded the younger man sitting across from him with great curiosity, as he always did. He had been sitting, watching while the boy, which Mead still considered him after all these years, played one of his video games. Mead had tried to find the appeal in such games, but they were as much a mystery to him as the young man himself. The boy claimed to like the challenge of the games, but Mead himself couldn't understand how it could be considered challenging if you were allowed to keep starting over with no consequences. They were a distraction, he allowed, but they were hardly a challenge.

"I've met a woman who seems extremely interested in our situation," Mead said through the bars that held the other man captive, the same bars that had held him captive for the last three years. Though the room in which he was housed could hardly be called a cell, he was still a prisoner. He had television, video games, books, magazines, music, and nearly anything else he requested that did not allow him contact with the outside world, but there was no doubt he was a prisoner.

"What kind of woman?" he asked without prying his eyes

away from the screen where two ridiculously dressed characters, a man and a woman, were battling it out for survival one impossibly acrobatic maneuver after another.

"A policewoman. A detective, actually. She came to my office with some story about needing my help with an investigation. She was lying, of course." Mead leaned back against the divan he kept just out of arm's reach of the bars. One leg crossed over the other, he played absently with one of the tassels on his overpriced Italian loafers as he spoke. He appeared no more concerned than if he were discussing the outcome of the other man's game.

The prisoner clicked a button and the onscreen combatants paused in mid-air. He laid the controller on the ground between his feet and looked over at Mead. "Does she know what you've done? Does she know about ... about me?"

The doctor inhaled deeply, paused a moment, and exhaled slowly through his nose as he thought about what he should share. Not everything, certainly. Very little, really, he decided. Better to keep him in the dark for now. Soon enough he'd have to set him free, especially now that the police were involved, and then he'd know for sure fairly quickly if the years of treatment had done any good at all. If not, well, better not to wander too far down that road until absolutely necessary. So much depended on his years of hard work finally paying off, after all.

"She doesn't *know* anything."

The prisoner's eyes narrowed, and he glared like a hungry lion at Mead.

He smiled back at the man. "Oh, she suspects something, naturally. Wouldn't have come to see me otherwise. The important thing is that she can't prove anything. And she never will, so don't worry."

The younger man returned his eyes to the television where his male character had been in the process of delivering a series of wicked punches to the female character's face. Her head was snapped backward, and there was blood spraying from her head and pooling on the ground behind her. It was meant to be so lifelike. He knew it to be anything but. He had seen the kind of real damage that a man's hands could do to a woman. It wasn't like this stupid game at all. His hand wandered slowly down to retrieve his controller, but he didn't immediately resume his game. Instead, he looked back at the doctor again as he sat there reflecting his gaze through the bars.

"Even if you're right, even if she doesn't arrest you, you know you can't keep me in here forever. Eventually, I will get out. What will you do then?"

Mead stood, straightened his tie, and looked down on the prisoner one final time. "That's an excellent question, and one we'll answer when you're ready. Not before. Good night," he said, but the young man had already turned his attention back to his game.

"Mr. Grayson, I feel the department owes you an apology," Captain Bates began. Robert and Stephanie had whisked themselves into her office to present their plan, confident that it was, at least, better than no plan at all. Stephanie's boss did not seem to share that opinion. "Very often in police work, our detectives will try to come up with a plan based on some sort of logic that is generally grounded in evidence and police procedure. Oh, and that doesn't drag an innocent man's name through the mud."

Robert felt embarrassed for Stephanie, but one glance at her showed him that Stephanie looked for all the world as if the captain did this to her on a daily basis. She looked almost bored, Robert thought.

"Captain Bates, if I may, I know how it sounds. It's a longshot, to put it mildly."

Captain Bates came up out of her chair and walked around her badly worn metal desk so that she was standing directly in front of Stephanie. "No, Mr. Grayson, me getting to retirement before Detective Monroe finds a partner she can tolerate is a longshot. This is worse than that. This is the Cubs winning the next three World Series. This is our freeway construction ending next week." She seemed unable to come up with a less plausible scenario than either of the first two, leaned her backside against the top of her desk, and threw up her hands in defeat. "And tell me this. How are you planning on drawing out an accomplice, assuming that Mead even has one, when, according to you, he might be the only person in the world who actually knows that Mr. Grayson is innocent?"

It was Stephanie's turn to try to calm her boss. She sat up slightly but otherwise made almost no movements. When she spoke, her voice was as soft as velvet.

"Look, Captain, I get what you're saying. But we think Mead believes he's stopped the killer for good. If we claim that we've found new bodies that match the M.O. exactly, that we even found a fresh body in one of the killer's old gravesites, Mead will have to find out for himself if it's true. Whatever his reason for helping this bastard, he knows he's potentially put himself in a deep hole. He'll have to start checking the old sites, sites we've never released to the public. We catch him at one, it's at least enough evidence to get a search warrant of his records."

"Which you have no idea if we can even actually understand, correct?" Bates asked, but it was clear to Robert that she was at least listening now. Maybe the Cubs had a shot.

Stephanie nodded. "True, but that doesn't matter. He won't take the chance. You know the D.A. will offer him a deal to roll over on the killer, and his lawyer will sure as hell know that."

No one spoke for a moment as Captain Bates thought over her options. Her forehead was creased, and her feet were tapping alternately as she worked the problem over. Finally, she asked, "Do you really think this will work, Stephanie?"

Robert, who had barely moved since he had first gotten shot down by Stephanie's boss, was ready to hear her assure her boss that all would be well.

Stephanie sighed. "Honestly, Captain, I have no idea. You're right. It's a longshot, but I know it has a better chance of working than wasting our time doing nothing. If Robert's willing to go through with it, I don't see that we have another choice."

Captain Bates' eyebrows shot up. She looked from Stephanie over to Robert. "Mr. Grayson, what do you say? Are you sure you're willing to go through with this plan? We'll try to protect you as long as possible, but eventually the press and the public will demand a name. You sure you want it to be yours?"

Robert looked at Stephanie, who nodded to him, and then up at Captain Bates. "Captain, if it has even a chance of bringing this thing to a close for me, you can release my name now if you have to. I don't know how many more of these nights where I wake up seeing myself killing these girls over and over I can take. And this thing with the Bible verses? What's next? Do I start acting out something else he's done? How long before—" He stopped his sentence midway, unable to finish the thought. He felt a reassuring squeeze on his hand and looked over at Stephanie. He smiled and nodded his thanks. "Believe me, I'm ready."

Captain Bates gave them a curious look before reluctantly nodding. "Okay. We'll try it, Detective. But what about the logistics? If we end up having to use his name and claiming that he's been in jail all along, he can't very well have been seen at his apartment this whole time. We have to stash him somewhere, and the department's coffers aren't exactly overflowing."

Robert groaned. He hadn't thought of this. If the captain was saying that a hotel wasn't an option and neither was his own place, that only left staying in one of the small cells here at the station. The terrible coffee alone was enough to give him cause to reconsider.

"Why doesn't he just stay at my place?" Stephanie offered.

Robert and Captain Bates shot her equally curious looks.

"Why not? People can keep an eye on him there as easily as they did at his place. I'm not married, so a strange man about my age moving around in my apartment would just be seen as a new love interest at best."

Robert wanted very badly to object, but the thought of putting off this plan's one bright spot was more than he could take. Besides, he reasoned, it *was* the only way they could collaborate on the case at night while she worked during the day.

"Mr. Grayson?" Captain Bates asked.

Robert put considerable effort into making certain his nod would appear nonchalant.

Captain Bates wiped the palms of her hands against one another and let out a deep sigh. "Very well. For the record, I'm not sure you staying at a detective's house is such a good idea, but then very little about this plan strikes me as making sense. It's going to take me a couple of hours to organize a press briefing. You two should use that time to think this over."

Robert waved off the warning. "That won't be necessary, Captain, but, again, I appreciate your concern."

"In that case, Mr. Grayson, congratulations. I am about to make you one of the most notorious serial killers in Texas history."

A surprisingly short time later, Stephanie and Robert watched from the station television as the D.A. gave a press briefing to a packed sea of reporters who hung on his every syllable. Stories like this didn't come along often, and when they did, news ratings went sky high and papers sold like they did before the days of the Internet. The D.A. issued just enough misinformation and legal jargon to make three points clear: A killer, who had confessed, was in custody; the details of his crimes were of the most heinous caliber the D.A. had ever heard; and the killings spanned a multi-year period that included one or more slayings within the past month. His office's top priority was to bring swift closure to these awful crimes and nothing less than even more swift and terrible justice to those responsible. Additional details would follow soon, including some details on the locations of the bodies.

Stephanie glanced occasionally at Robert during the spectacle. If hearing himself discussed in the terms the D.A. was using bothered him, he didn't show it. He watched on as impassively as if what was happening to him was as routine as a haircut.

He's giving up so much to make all of this happen, Stephanie thought, *and his only reward will be possibly to get his job and apartment back.* She was unsure whether to admire him or pity him. He deserved better than sympathy, she decided, so she broke the silence.

"You're doing a good thing here, Robert. Not everybody would in your place."

"Hey, I'm only agreeing to help you bait the hook," he answered without turning his gaze from the television. "You still have to catch him and clean him."

She nodded once. "I will, and then I'm going to fry his ass too."

CHAPTER FIFTEEN

Stephanie spent nearly all of the next several days either staked outside of Mead's office, his suburban mansion, or at her desk reviewing again and again the details of the killings and of H.M.I. and its founder while other officers covered Mead. She went home each night only because she knew Robert's days were spent staring at a television or beating himself up over the crimes he was forced to relive every time he closed his eyes. It was not good, she repeatedly told herself, for him to spend too much time alone with his thoughts. The easy solution would have been for him to go out and get some fresh air, maybe call on an old friend, but there was nothing about this case that involved doing things the easy way. If the police did end up having to use Robert's name with the public, Captain Bates had been correct that he could hardly have been seen wandering around the park or movie theaters while he was supposedly in custody.

"If you end up having to go inside, we'll make sure the sheriff knows to keep you safe," she had told him over a late dinner after the third night of coming home with nothing to report except that Mead seemed to live as domestic a life as Stephen Hennerman did.

"Nice of you to say, but if I have to go inside, I think we both know how that plays out. To everyone who'll see me, I'll be a serial killer and a rapist. In that order, by the way. But don't worry about me just yet," he assured her. "I'm doing fine here. Your place isn't exactly a step down from my bachelor pad, you know."

Robert was right on that count. Stephanie's apartment, while small, was well appointed with plush furniture and what Robert guessed were fairly expensive paintings and even a small, abstract sculpture. He'd had a poster of a former Houston quarterback on his bedroom wall. Its primary function had been to cover a long crack that needed to be repaired but that Robert had been too lazy to deal with properly.

"Don't take this the wrong way, but detective work seems like it must pay better than I thought. Unless you're on the take," Robert joked. He couldn't imagine a scenario any farther from the truth. True, Stephanie worked from a set of rules known only to her, but he sensed they were all centered around putting bad people away as efficiently as possible. He respected her for her commitment and for her willingness to bend rules to get the job done. He had been there himself many times what seemed like a lifetime ago.

Stephanie didn't answer right away. She looked around at the art and the furniture just as Robert had done and wished for the hundredth time that none of it was there.

"Actually," she finally said through a thick scowl, "I am. Just not in the way you mean. This stuff is all from my parents. I couldn't afford half of half of it."

"You don't seem like you like having it all that much," Robert observed. "Why keep it?"

Stephanie sighed heavily before taking a long pull on her Lone Star beer bottle. "I don't know. Maybe because they were all gifts. Some gifts are harder to get rid of than others."

Tell me about it, sister, Robert thought, but he opted to let it pass. Even with all of the time he had spent around her lately, Robert knew almost nothing of her personal life, and he sensed that she might be about to share something about herself that was worth knowing if he could keep her talking. She wasn't the only one who had experience interrogating people, after all.

"Is that the only reason?" he asked.

She eyed him over the top of her bottle. "You're pretty good at this, Robert. You'd make a decent cop if you ever decided to come over to the dark side."

He smiled and made a mock toast with his own bottle. "And you're even better at deflecting. Now tell me."

Stephanie lowered her empty bottle onto the table and folded her hands together in front of her mouth as if she were about to start praying. "I can't really. I'm not even sure myself. I guess it reminds me of what I don't want to be when I grow older, patterns I don't want repeated."

Robert shoved the paper plate of barbecued chicken and potato salad remains away from himself and folded his own hands to match Stephanie's pose. "You realize we've just crossed an important bridge, don't you? I suppose you know what this means."

Stephanie's eyes narrowed at Robert. "I truly do not, but I'm dying to hear what *you* think it means," she answered after depositing her empty bottle onto her plate and stacking them on Robert's. "Right after you do the dishes," she added.

Robert scraped his chair back across the fake wood of the tiny dining room floor and gathered up their trash. Three long strides took him to the kitchen, where he deposited the remains of dinner in the trash and then turned back to smile at Stephanie. "The dishes, madam, are done. Now, what I had in mind was that you and I would just talk. Not about Mead or the case or anything like that, just normal small talk that you make when you meet someone new and interesting." At the last minute he added, "And beautiful."

Robert paused to see if his statement might get a blush out of Stephanie, but he had known she would never make it that easy on him. Plus, he wasn't sure she had ever blushed, wasn't sure she was even capable of it. It was one of the things he liked about her.

"Come on," he urged. "You know practically everything that's happened to me since I was eighteen, but I barely know you at all outside of this case. Let's just take one night off and swap embarrassing stories from our misspent youths." Robert tried to give her his best puppy face, but based on her confused look, he guessed he didn't quite have the knack for it.

Stephanie rose to her feet as she carefully weighed the pros and cons of his suggestion. She was happy to discuss something else for a change, but exchanging personal stories with a ruggedly handsome and emotionally vulnerable man in her living room was a potentially hazardous river to cross. One look at the pain and weariness in Robert's eyes though, and she knew she had no choice. He felt alone, disconnected even from himself, and it was obvious he needed to talk to someone who could understand at least a little of what he was experiencing. "Okay," she relented, "but I'm definitely going to need another beer. My youth was more misspent than most. And you're going to have to go first."

"Me?"

"Hey, you're the one who wants to play this game," she shot back.

Robert smiled, a move he hoped didn't look half as forced as it felt. What could he tell her that she didn't already know? She had researched practically his entire life.

"Come on. Too late to be embarrassed."

"You know, realizing you have no story left to tell is more embarrassing than anything I could actually tell you," he admitted.

"How about you let me be the judge?"

He caught her meaning easily. "My most embarrassing moment?"

Stephanie raised an eyebrow at him, a look that told him to quit stalling and get on with it already.

He cleared his throat and smiled again, this time easily. "Alright, then. I was seventeen and interested in very few things that didn't involve sports or girls. To that end, my favorite haunt was the gym at the community college near my parents' house."

Stephanie gave him a wolf whistle. "You little underage Romeo. Stepping up to the college girls early, huh?"

Robert blushed almost all the way up to his temples. "I guess. But there were plenty of girls my age there too."

"And those were definitely the ones you were there to meet."

Robert ignored her jibe and continued. "On this particular day, there was a young lady of what you might call uncommon beauty on the treadmill. I watched her the whole time I warmed up and even for a while when I went to pound the weights. She was killing it the whole time. Not jogging, you know? Like, running to beat the band for at least half an hour. I staked out a spot by the fountain figuring she'd have to stop soon, but this girl was in the zone."

Stephanie practically squealed. "I sense that your teenage hormones are about to get the better of you."

"Shush. Anyway, I gradually made my way to the treadmill right next to hers. I figured I'd start running along with her and maybe strike up a conversation when she cooled down. The trouble was, I was strictly a sprinter. No long distance running ever. But, figuring I was in great shape—"

"And a guy," she interrupted.

He grinned again. "Hey, I was a kid! Anyway, yeah, I tried to match her. Worked for about ten minutes. At the end of which time I had gradually been losing a little ground to her with every step. And I was trying so hard not to stare at the beauty next to me that I just locked my eyes on the television in front of me."

Stephanie could see where this might be headed and covered her mouth with both hands. "Oh, no," she said.

"Oh, yes," Robert said, nodding. "Stepped right off the back of the machine at full speed. Launched myself into the front of the treadmill behind me so hard I almost knocked it over. And it gets better. In my rush to act as if nothing had happened, I tried to jump back on the horse I had just fallen off of. Ever try that with a moving treadmill?"

By now, Stephanie was laughing so hard her sides were hurting her. Most people tried to maintain a little decorum when they heard this story, but the little amount Stephanie had to begin with apparently was simply not enough to hold her in check.

Robert let her have her moment before adding, "I found out later she was some big track star. And married to some guy who ran on the Olympic team. It was all for naught." He shook his head in a mockery of sadness.

"Are you kidding?" she asked, wiping tears from her eyes. "That's one of the best stories I ever heard. That's hardly for naught."

"Yeah, well, it was certainly a learning experience for me. I let my ego convince me I was something I wasn't, and I paid for it by getting that ego thoroughly trounced. I promised myself that day I would never let that happen again. I guess anything you have to go through at seventeen is worth it if you can learn that kind of lesson that early in life, huh?"

There was a pause before she nodded and wiped her hands absently and unnecessarily across the legs of her designer jeans. He searched her face for some clue to what he might have said, and in that moment he saw in the face of the strongest woman he'd ever met a profound and tangible sadness. All of the humor of a moment ago evaporated, and Robert looked for some way to repair the damage he knew he had somehow caused.

"Stephanie, I'm sorry if I said anything wrong."

She brushed off the idea with a shake of her head. "Not your fault. It's just what you said about being that age and learning things about yourself."

"Something happened to you when you were seventeen."

"Yeah, but it's not the kind of story you want to hear, trust me."

"Why don't you let me be the judge of that?"

"Seriously?" she asked. "It's not a funny story like yours."

He shrugged. "Doesn't have to be. It just has to be yours. If you feel like telling it, I'd like to hear it."

For reasons Stephanie could not explain at the time, the objection she was about to offer died in her throat and before she knew what was happening, she found herself agreeing.

CHAPTER SIXTEEN

Fresh beers in hand and sitting on Stephanie's sofa at a distance from one another close enough to be called friendly but too far to be called intimate, Stephanie began her story.

"I grew up in an affluent part of town, River Oaks, to be precise."

Robert whistled appreciatively.

She nodded. "Exactly, and it was just like you'd imagine it, except my parents couldn't quite afford it, not really. They drove luxury cars, but they were always second-hand, and they were leased. We lived on the right street, but in the smallest, oldest house and only because one of dad's poker buddies from the bank gave them favorable terms on a loan."

"Keeping up appearances?"

"And how," she agreed. "My father would have been content with less, I think, but he eventually got caught up in the image and the lifestyle as well. He's a dentist. Plans to retire next year, though I doubt they've saved a penny, so who knows? My mother owns a successful but small boutique in River Oaks. There are good years and bad, but it mostly does well."

"So the money goes out as fast as it comes in?"

"Like you wouldn't believe. In fact, they'd likely be truly wealthy if they just lived in a typical white-collar neighborhood and invested their money like normal people, but Mom didn't want that, and my dad has always done whatever it takes to keep Mom happy. What Mom wanted was to invest in her store by building the image of a successful boutique owner. She thought the rich folks were more likely to buy from one of their own. Guess I gotta hand it to her. She was right about that."

Something about the way she said 'their own' gave Robert the distinct impression that Stephanie didn't quite fit in with the rest of her family. He knew how hard being a black sheep could be. His own parents had nearly lost their minds when he had joined the military. It was months before his father, a former San Francisco peace-knick, would even speak to him. Robert snapped back to the present and realized Stephanie had paused. It must have been obvious that he was lost in his own thoughts. He apologized and asked her to continue.

"Anyway, other than a couple of really fiscally irresponsible parents, it was still a good life. My older sister and I had everything we wanted, and my parents, to their credit, didn't shuffle us off to boarding school like so many of our friends' parents did. When we were old enough, we even got to work in the family businesses. My sister tried both on for size, and, no surprise, found a clothing store to be infinitely more interesting than our father's posters of various kinds of gum disease and tooth decay.

"Caroline, my sister, is three years my senior. I idolized her. She's beautiful, she got good grades, and, most importantly to my mother, she was incredibly popular with Mom's friends and especially with their sons. When Caroline went to work at the store, I knew that's where I would go as well even though I'd rather have spent the time working with my dad. When I turned fifteen, I followed right along in her footsteps. The first couple of years, it was fun going there after school and on the weekends. We were never too busy, so I was able to keep up with my schoolwork, the one place where I matched Caroline at that time, and still learn all about the store. I wasn't as interested in fashion as my mother or sister, but I pretended to be for their benefit, at least at first. I think they both knew the truth, but like the rest of our lives, as long as everything looked alright on the outside, that was good enough."

Stephanie could see Robert hanging on her every word; yet, she could not help but stop and close her eyes as she recalled those days. Though she had devoted a considerable portion of her adult life to blocking out any images associated with those times, they were as clear to her now as if they had happened yesterday.

In Robert's limited experience with Stephanie, she was not given to theatrics, so he gave her time to collect her thoughts. While he did, he toyed absently with the label on his beer bottle, peeling it down in one long section with his thumbnail and pressing what he could back into place before removing it for good. By the time he had the bottle completely bare, Stephanie was ready to continue.

"One day after school, my mom left my sister and me alone to watch the store while she ran to the bank to make a deposit. By then, I was seventeen and my sister was twenty. We were more than capable of running the place for as long as we needed to, so my mom was often on these bank trips for a couple of hours or more while she snuck in a few extra errands. And by errands, I mean martinis at the country club.

"Anyway, my sister's boyfriend at the time had stopped in to pay her a visit. Mom didn't usually go for that, but he was charming, good looking, and from one of the wealthiest families in town. My mother was thrilled that Caroline was dating him and was always pestering her about how serious things were getting. Caroline would tease our mother about wanting to hear wedding bells, but I think it was the cash register ringing that she was hearing. I didn't blame her, though. If you had to marry off your first-born to someone, this guy was as good as it got, at least on paper." Despite her best efforts, Stephanie lost the smile she had been pretending as she spoke.

Robert reached out and put a hand on Stephanie's arm, giving it a reassuring squeeze. "Look," he interjected, "I can see Prince Charming is about to get a pretty ugly makeover. You don't have to share anything you don't want to, but I'm here if you want to finish."

Had it been anyone else, Stephanie would have thought he was trying to get out of having to hear her problems, or else trying to play the sensitive guy angle to better his odds of bedding her, but as she looked in his eyes, she could see he meant exactly what he said. Nothing hidden and no ulterior motives. She patted his hand and nodded her thanks to him.

"The thing about this guy, he was even nice to me—something her boyfriends weren't always known for. He treated me like an adult, and let me tell you, when a hot twenty-one-year-old guy treats an awkward seventeen-year-old girl like she's special, like she's his equal, he can just about do no wrong. Or so I thought at the time."

Stephanie's voice had increasingly taken on a detached quality as if she were describing the events from some old movie she had seen years ago rather than personal details of her own life. Her eyes were locked onto the now-empty beer bottle at her feet, but they were seeing through the amber glass and ever deeper into that past she had not revisited often with anyone, least of all a man whom she would, under other circumstances, consider a potential romantic interest.

Robert could guess where this story was headed at that point and wanted again to tell her she didn't have to finish, but he had learned well enough lately what it was like being treated like a victim. He bit his tongue and let her roll on unabated.

"After he'd been at the store with us for a few minutes, he claimed not to be feeling well and asked Caroline to go to the drugstore for him. She didn't want to leave me in charge of the store, but he convinced her I could handle it. He told her I was practically an adult. He was talking to her, of course, but I think we all knew that his words were really for my ears. I could tell Caroline didn't want to leave us, but I didn't know why then. Now, sometimes I wonder if a part of her suspected."

She shrugged the thought away and continued.

"Anyway, as soon as she was out the door, he asked me to show him the backroom. I knew he'd seen it dozens of times, so of course he obviously had something else on his mind, but I didn't care. I honestly thought he just maybe wanted to talk to me. Another part of me knew he wanted something else, but I still went with him. It was naïve, but I don't think I imagined how far he would take things. When he kissed me, I was conflicted, but I let him do it. It felt so nice, and it was like I was finally beating my sister at something. Her alpha male boyfriend preferred me to her. He even whispered that in my ear. How much prettier and more mature I was, stuff like that.

"It wasn't long before he was progressing to other things, things I wasn't ready for yet with him, but I couldn't bring myself to say anything at first. He was older, so I figured maybe this was just normal. Plus, we'd known each other for a while, so maybe he thought I should feel more comfortable with it all. After a minute, I did try to stop him, but he didn't even slow down. When I tried to move his hands again and tell him I wasn't ready, he told me that he had misjudged me, that I wasn't as mature as he thought. Those words crushed me, but they did help me to see the situation for what it was.

"I turned and tried to walk out of the room, but he reached out and grabbed me by my hair and jerked me down. I never imagined he would do something like that, to hurt me like that. I tried to stand up, to run out, but by then he was squatting with his knees on top of me." Stephanie unconsciously allowed her hand to drift to her chest as she spoke. "I could barely breathe. He was so heavy. He just stared down at me for a moment with this really blank look. He wasn't even blinking or anything, and then he hit me across the face, hard. I was so shocked that I didn't feel the pain at first. When I did, I knew that there was no way out, no one to scream to, so I just let go and let it happen as quickly as possible."

Stephanie inhaled deeply and held it for moment to calm her rapidly beating heart. When she slowly let her breath out, she looked up at Robert. He hadn't moved, hadn't spoken. By now, the few people she had ever had to tell this story to had interrupted her a dozen times with "I'm so sorry" and "How awful for you", and, her favorite, "It wasn't your fault". Robert was one of the very few men she had ever met who seemed capable of just listening without needing to come to her rescue.

"You aren't saying anything," she observed quietly.

He shrugged. "Not my place. So what happened next?"

She tucked her feet up under her, her shoes long since forgotten somewhere, and settled into the cushions. Now that the worst part of the story was over, she felt strangely relaxed. "Nothing for a while. He pulled his pants back up and thanked me. Told me that he knew I had it in me to see it all the way through. He told me not to tell anyone, warned me that high school kids just love to gossip and that they'd never understand what we had. When Caroline got back, she knew something had happened. She was pretty upset. She accused me of all kinds of things, none of which I confirmed or denied. I felt so confused and so guilty. I just couldn't think straight for a while."

Robert only nodded. "Did you tell anyone at the time?"

Stephanie shook her head. "Not right away. It took me about three weeks to come to grips with the fact that it had actually happened, you know? My grades dropped. I quit seeing my friends or even leaving the house except for school. I quit working at the store with no explanation, which pissed my mom and sister off to no end. My family thought maybe I was on drugs, so they finally confronted me with an intervention. I almost told them I *was* on drugs just so they'd send me away somewhere, but for whatever reason, I told them the truth. Thank God, they sent me to see a psychiatrist to help work things out, which did help eventually. Strangely, it also became the basis for the longest friendship I've ever had," Stephanie said, finally allowing a hint of a smile to form at the corners of her mouth.

Robert's head cocked a little to the side. "You became besties with your shrink?"

"I know. It's weird," she said, grinning at the thought. "You know what's weirder? You know him."

Robert straightened his head back quickly. "Dr. Burns?"

"The very same. He's my dad's patient, and he has a small practice outside of his work with the police. Or at least he did at the time. He still sees a few patients on the side, mostly cops who don't want their visits to be on the record, that kind of thing, but a few other people too. He's actually a big part of the reason I became a cop."

"He thought maybe bringing justice to others might help you," Robert guessed.

Stephanie's eyes widened and she shook her head emphatically. "Burns said he thought putting a gun and a badge in my hand was just about the worst idea he'd ever heard. He still says that all the time, actually," she added. "No, he had lots of pictures on his walls of cops and lots of cool stories. It sounded like just about the farthest thing in the world from dentistry and high fashion, plus my family hated the idea, so I ran with it."

Robert laughed and shook his head. "Was there ever a time you weren't hard headed?"

"No, but Burns assures me there's still time."

"So what ever happened to him—Caroline's boyfriend?"

She shrugged. "Karma, I'm guessing. Two days after he raped me, he got behind the wheel of his fancy sports car after he'd been drinking. Wrapped the entire front half of it around a concrete divider on the highway. I'm told his casket had to be closed. Tragic really," she said, her voice devoid of emotion again.

Robert nodded knowingly. "Of course you'd cleaned up any physical evidence by that point, and there was no witness to question …"

She picked up her beer bottle and made a mock toast to his guesswork. "Very good. My family, of course, told me just to let it go. More specifically, my mother told me. I was worried they wouldn't believe me, but it was actually worse. They believed, even Caroline, but Mom felt that pursuing the matter after his death would just look like we were trying to trample on his memory. She urged me to think of his family and all of the grief they were still experiencing, how they were innocent in all of this and how it couldn't do any good now anyway. We all knew what she really meant—the rich in this town stick together. If I came forward with what happened, the other families would stop shopping at Mom's store, even if they believed me."

Would they have believed her? Robert wondered, but even as he did he knew that Stephanie's mother had been right about one thing. It wouldn't have mattered.

Stephanie could see that Robert was struggling with what to say. It was difficult to find the right words, she knew, so she supplied them for him. "No one buys haute couture from the rape salon. During one of her unusual bouts of martini-fueled honesty, my mother actually said that we might as well rename the store that if I pursued the matter. And that was pretty much that."

Robert considered telling Stephanie that her mom sounded like a real winner but decided that she probably had reached that conclusion on her own long ago, so he settled for quietly setting his own empty bottle on the floor next to Stephanie's as he considered the ramifications of everything she had just told him. He looked up to see Stephanie watching him thoughtfully. "What?" he asked sheepishly.

"Nothing," she lied, smiling at him.

"Can I ask you something?"

"Sure," she answered.

"Why did you tell me? It couldn't have been easy."

Stephanie considered many answers before deciding on the easiest and most honest. "I'm not completely sure. Maybe I just thought you needed a reminder that after bad things happen, we can still find peace."

Robert gave a deep sigh. "That would be nice. Have you? Found it, I mean."

Stephanie's smile was a mixture of sadness and hope. "I'm not sure, but like Bullet says, there's still time. Speaking of which, it's your turn. I go, you go. Remember?"

He nodded and leaned back into the plush cushion of the sofa and stretched his legs out before him. "I remember, but it's pretty late. You want to pick this up tomorrow?"

"Nuh uh. No *way* are you getting off that easy. We're pretending we're adults after all, so spill it. And you'd better make it a good one."

Robert had been ready to tell Stephanie a lie by omission about his past, but after she had bared her soul to him, he knew he could hold nothing back now. He thought about another beer to bolster his courage, but he doubted it would help. Instead, he took a deep breath, looked at Stephanie again, and for the first time, he told the story of the man he wished he had killed and the little girl he wished he hadn't.

CHAPTER SEVENTEEN

"I joined the Army right out of high school like a lot of guys. It seemed like a logical choice for an athletic guy with no particular inclination toward college or a desk job. I figured it was that or I'd end up working construction or something somewhere, so I enlisted the week after I graduated. I didn't plan on staying long, but I figured it was at least a good start."

"Was it?" Stephanie wondered aloud. She remembered his outstanding military record as well as its abrupt conclusion.

"For sure," he smiled. "I was a three-year starter on the varsity football, basketball, and track teams at my school, so I pretty much breezed through all of the physical stuff the Army demanded. It was actually kind of fun. And I guess I'm a lot smarter than I look because I tested pretty high on the ASVAB. That's the entrance exam. I was a category two. Damn near made category one, which would have meant just about any duty post in the world doing any job I wanted. Still, with my scores, I had a lot of options, but I chose to join the infantry."

Robert smiled, more to himself than to Stephanie, as he recalled those early days.

"A few of the guys who knew my story thought I was crazy for choosing infantry, but I loved every minute of it. The more the officers demanded from me, the more I gave. The challenge was like a drug for me, you know? And I was good at it, too. All of it." Robert swallowed hard, and his smile vanished.

Evidently, not all of his memories of his service days were pleasant ones, Stephanie thought.

"Eventually, my reputation got to the point that officers were seeking me out and offering me some pretty cool jobs with elite units. It took a while before I settled on one specialty that sounded like a perfect fit." He paused in his telling to stare at his hands, which he had clasped together as he spoke. He looked up to see Stephanie watching him, following every movement he made with her well-trained eyes. "Ever had to kill anyone, Stephanie?" he asked.

Her eyes snapped up to meet his. She shook her head. For all her bravado, she had only had to draw her service weapon once and had never had to fire it.

"It isn't like you think, or at least it wasn't for me."

Half curious, but also half afraid to know the answer, Stephanie asked, "What was it like for you?"

"Smoking, actually."

"Come again?" Stephanie puzzled.

"You know that smoking is eventually going to cause you problems if you live long enough, but you're enjoying it so much at the time that you just ignore that little nagging voice in your head. One day, you decide to start listening, but by then, you're either addicted or the damage is already done, so you just keep doing it until something makes you stop."

The way Robert settled back into his seat suggested to Stephanie that, at least for the moment, he was through talking. "That *something* you mentioned—I'm guessing you're talking about the guilt you felt, that you still feel now probably. Robert, I'm sure it's normal to feel guilt over those deaths—" Stephanie began.

He cut her off with a look that made Stephanie immediately fall silent. Instantly, Robert regretted the action and tried to smile at her and apologize, but the smile would not come. Still, Stephanie signaled him to go on.

"You're right about the guilt. I think it would have been normal, but I never had any. Not even once. I … I didn't stop killing because I felt guilty, Stephanie." He looked down and swallowed drily before continuing. "I stopped killing because I didn't."

Stephanie was unsure how to respond. Her instincts screamed at her that she needed to connect with him, to reassure him that he wasn't some kind of monster, but a whispered, "*Oh*," was all she managed.

Robert gave a small nod but did not look up. "You see it, don't you? If I feel bad, something's wrong with me because soldiers aren't to blame for shooting other combatants. But if I don't, I'm a monster. Clever little catch-22, huh? No emotion is the right one, so all emotion must be bad. Only one solution in that case—you shut everything down, quit thinking about it, and move on the next mission." He risked a look up away from the floor and at her. If she was afraid of anything he had said, she wasn't showing it.

Stephanie measured her words before she opened her mouth. Her voice needed to be even so that no trace of pity could creep in. Not that she didn't feel sympathy for Robert, but knowing him, he would see it as a weakness and might shut down.

"But you didn't do that. I've seen your record," Stephanie confessed. "I know you got out when you were close to being able to retire. Did the guilt catch up with you at some point?"

He rolled his shoulders half-heartedly. "Not at all. Back then, when I killed people, I was absolutely sure it was the right thing to do. And worse than that, I didn't just accept the killing as a necessary evil. Way back in some dark corner of my brain, a part of me enjoyed it, or at least enjoyed the knowledge that the killer inside me was ready for action if it came to it."

Dr. Burns had warned Stephanie that Robert was dealing with some pretty heavy baggage from his past, but she'd had no idea the elephantine nature of it until that moment. Robert was still looking into her eyes, seeking signs of judgment or worse, of fear. She still wasn't sure how to absorb these revelations, but she also knew that Robert might not even mean everything he was saying. There was no telling how much the memory transplant had affected him. Besides, the good feelings he had were probably from knowing he was protecting his country and his way of life, not from the actual killing. More importantly, whatever he said about a lack of emotion on the topic, he had stopped taking lives. That had to count for something.

"Stephanie, I've looked at myself in the mirror the way you're looking at me enough times to know that you're trying to make some decisions about me, about what kind of man I am. No," he insisted before she would have to lie and deny it, "it's good that you're doing it. But if you're going to do it, you need to be able to do it properly. That means telling you everything. If you still want to know."

Jesus Christ. What am I supposed to do—say, 'no thanks'? The man in her living room had just told her how much he had enjoyed killing people, and then had dropped the bombshell that there was more. *How many secrets can one guy have?* Stephanie realized suddenly that she hadn't answered Robert's question yet. She nodded at him to go ahead.

"You said you saw my service file, right?" he asked. This time, he didn't bother waiting on an answer. "I hope whatever was in it was a good read, because there's a sure bet that at least part of it was fiction."

Alarm bells went off inside Stephanie's head. "Fiction? You mean you weren't really in any of those places you were supposed to be?"

Robert realized his mistake and shook his head. "Stephanie, everything I'm about to tell you from this point forward is classified. I am absolutely forbidden to tell you any of it. If anyone ever finds out, I could be brought before a firing squad. Like an honest to God old fashioned firing squad. Do you understand?"

She nodded.

"So when I'm done, if you think I lied about where I was, or if you think I'm a threat in any way, one call to the United States Department of Defense will have me out of your, and everyone else's, hair forever. Fair enough?"

Stephanie was intrigued, of course. She couldn't imagine that he had kept something from her that impacted the case, but she begrudgingly acknowledged that the national security oath combined with death penalty excuse was a pretty good one, so, despite her many questions and her newfound sense of unease, she emulated Robert's earlier wisdom of knowing when to keep quiet.

"As you already guessed, I had resolved to make some changes in my life, but that didn't mean I wanted out of the Army yet. I still believed in the mission, just not the means. So I joined a new squad that was attached to a regular infantry unit. Officially, we were front line support for U.N. troops assigned to watch the borders. Unofficially, we had a special purpose. We were the guys who came knocking when you were suspected of harboring or aiding terrorists. Or of being one.

"My job was to figure out who the terrorists were turning to for support, and then to get those people to give up what they knew. The good part was that we almost never got into firefights. The Army found that it made it hard to question people if you killed them first, which suited the new me just fine. The bad news is that we were very good at our jobs, and you definitely did not want me or my guys knocking on your door in the middle of the night."

He made this part of his confession plainly and without apology or bravado. It was a simple fact for him now with no more or less moral ambiguity than buying products you knew were assembled in third world countries by child laborers. There had been reasons that had justified the required actions at the time, even if those reasons now seemed insufficient.

Stephanie struggled with the desire to ask him whether he was talking about CIA stuff like water boarding. Robert could see the conflict in her eyes and wished that he could exonerate himself completely. He would have to settle for being honest with her.

"I never exactly tortured anyone, Detective, but I also never let someone I knew was guilty walk away from me without getting what I wanted. There's a line right there, and I'd say I straddled it pretty hard. I'm not proud of some of things I did, but the results we got saved a lot of lives, and at least I wasn't killing people."

Stephanie nodded her understanding. "I get it. But don't call me Detective, okay?" She had never made that request of anyone, and she wasn't exactly sure why she did so now. The formality of the title simply no longer fit. Not while Robert was baring his soul at great personal risk from the Army. Then she remembered something she had seen in his file, a part she suspected was every bit the truth. "You tried to make up for some of what you had done by helping the villagers when you could, digging wells and that sort of thing, didn't you?"

He nodded. "Fortunately, I was one of the guys who managed never to lose sight of that line between right and wrong. Some guys did, and once they crossed it, they almost never came back. And then," he added, calling up images from a long buried past, "there are those guys who started out on the wrong side of it."

Robert thought back to a time and place he had meant never

to speak about to anyone, a place he tried not even to think about to himself, though he failed almost daily. Not for the first time, Robert thought that the memories we want the least seem the most reluctant ever to leave us.

"This one time, we were on patrol in a little village on the outskirts of Afghanistan. Actually, calling it a village is being generous. It was a few huts, no roads, no markets or schools or anything. Just a handful of families grinding out an existence the same way they've done for thousands of years. We had gotten word that insurgents had been using that village as a supply dump and a rest stop."

Forgetting herself, Stephanie asked, "Were they?"

Robert nodded. "Probably, but we didn't find anything except a bunch of tracks leading out into the desert. It didn't matter though. Those people had no idea who they were helping, and they didn't care. They weren't anti-coalition or anti-insurgent or anti-anything else except anti-starving-to-death. Those fighters gave them some food and water in exchange for letting them park their trucks in the desert near the villagers' huts, something they could have done whether the people had taken their food or not.

"Even the least experienced of my guys would have known that there was no reason to shake anyone down there, but we had a young lieutenant with us, some guy who was looking to make a name for himself. It was his op, and more than anything else, what he wanted was a fight."

Robert closed his eyes, breathed deeply, and tried to slow his rapidly increasing heartbeat.

Stephanie took advantage of the brief pause to ask another question. "I take it you got one?"

Robert nodded slowly, his eyes opening and turning glassy as he drifted farther back to that night in the desert. "When we got there, there was no resistance. We just parked the vehicles and walked right in. The people totally ignored us. We asked a few questions, poked around, the usual stuff. It was clear that there was nothing there for us. We thanked them for their time and mounted up and rode back the way we came, but when we had made it about two clicks, the lieutenant ordered a stop.

"He decided that we were going back there as soon as it got dark. He got the idea that they were hiding something after all. We all knew better, even him, but he was the officer, so we went along. When darkness came, he chose two of us to sneak back in among the huts and keep watch while he interrogated some woman he had talked to earlier that day. He figured he could scare her into revealing something, but I guess no one told him that this was a woman who carved a living out of stone and sand, who had probably learned to kill before the lieutenant had finished grade school. She was less impressed with his efforts than he would have liked."

Robert looked needlessly over at Stephanie to make sure she was still following his narrative before going on. "The other guy and I were keeping watch while the lieutenant did his questioning behind a little pen that held a few goats or something. Things got rough quickly, which was no surprise with that asshole. We knew we didn't have long before her family and friends came looking for her, and we did not want a firefight breaking out in a village full of civilians. If that happened, the best-case scenario was that we'd all end up court-martialed. Worst case, either they or we would have all ended up dead out there in the sand. Those people absolutely do not play around when one of them is threatened.

"Anyway, we were getting pretty twitchy out there by ourselves, and we were hearing noises from the lieutenant's spot that weren't right. My buddy wanted me to stay put, but I couldn't. I had done more of those field interrogations than I care to remember, and I know exactly what they're supposed to sound like. This one was all wrong. I went around the corner of the little shed, and there he was. He was on top of her, his pants were part of the way down, and he had her pinned down on the ground. She was fighting like hell, but he was just too big."

He paused again to look at Stephanie.

"If you'd rather I didn't go on …"

She checked the urge to give him a harsh look, knowing his offer wasn't meant to reflect a perceived weakness on her part. "I'm okay. Please, keep talking," she insisted.

"Well, I don't know exactly what came over me, but when I saw what he was doing, I snapped. I was right back to the old me. I wanted so badly to shoot him, but I couldn't be sure that I wouldn't hit her in the process. Besides, a gunshot would have brought the whole village down on us, so I drew my knife instead. I would have laid him open like a fish too, but just as I was walking toward him, a young girl came out from behind the nearest house and saw me."

Robert swallowed hard and thought about asking for another drink, but he knew the futility of that path. Besides, it was nearly over now. "This girl was carrying a rifle, an AK-47." Robert pantomimed carrying the gun. "It was huge on her. She couldn't have been more than thirteen or fourteen." Robert again swallowed drily. "Imagine yourself in her position—two men wearing the same uniform, one raping a friend of yours and the other walking toward her with a knife. She reached the logical conclusion and raised the rifle to kill me."

Stephanie's heart ached for the good man who sat beside her. This time, it was her eyes that closed. "But she didn't because you're still here," was all she said.

"It's … it's not so much that I would have minded dying, as long as I could have killed that son-of-a-bitch first," Robert growled. "But if she had fired that gun, like I said, a war would have started in that village. So to save the rest of her people, I threw that knife and buried it right in her chest. I don't know if she even knew what happened. She just dropped. I must have hit her heart."

Robert was rocking subconsciously back and forth now, and Stephanie could tell that at least part of him wanted to stop. Perhaps, she reasoned, he was afraid that if he did stop, he might not be able to start again. She knew how he felt. Some dams, once they get broken open, are not so easy to close again.

"I guess the lieutenant heard her fall or something because after he knocked out the girl he had just raped, he stood up and came over to me to thank me. He *thanked* me. I think I was in shock. When we got back to the truck though, I got over it. I beat him so badly that I broke my hand on his head. My men pulled me off of him to keep me from killing him, but I came near enough. After my beating, he was no longer fit for duty, not that he ever was. I hear he still can't talk exactly right." He added as an afterthought, "I hope he always remembers why."

Stephanie knew that her words could not console him, but she could not resist at least leaning over and placing her hand on his arm. Robert glanced down at her hand and then into her eyes. The gesture, he could see, was meant to be intimate in a way that had nothing to do with romance and everything to do with a connection between two people who shared opposite sides of an experience that could never be forgotten or explained. He offered a faint smile to show his understanding and his appreciation.

"This is the part where the fiction in the file starts," Stephanie guessed.

"When we got back to base, I got locked up and the lieutenant got sent to the infirmary and then home. I would have been instantly court martialed for attacking a superior officer, but this guy had deep connections that ended up working in my favor.

If the Army had held a trial, I would have been given a chance to tell what I saw, and my buddies would have backed up every word even though they didn't see a thing. There was no way his guardian angel was going to let that happen, so I was told to finish out my time stateside and then to muster out. That's what I did."

Robert inhaled slowly and let out a heavy sigh. Speaking these forbidden words was something he had been sure would never happen, something he had sworn never to *let* happen. Until tonight, he had always known he would keep that vow. "Now you know partly why this has been ... difficult for me. I killed a lot of men, Stephanie, but she was different. I murdered that girl, and I have been trying my best to live with that. It's been hard, nearly impossible some days, but I've been trying. Now, I can remember all these others, and it's sometimes just a little more than I can handle. Especially because I can feel the ... the ..."

Stephanie had watched and listened as his words had tumbled out like water over a fall. She knew that sharing this part of his history with her had been nearly impossible for Robert, not to mention illegal, and she knew now what he held back. Taking a gamble, she helped him finish his confession.

"You remember the pleasure that the killer experienced when he killed along with your own mixed emotions over the lives you've taken. I know, and it isn't your fault. You can't help what someone else felt, and it doesn't mean you murdered that girl or that you enjoyed killing her. I promise."

Robert looked up from the spot on her carpet where he had again been focusing his attention. "How do you know? I never told you."

"Not exactly," she said, keeping Dr. Burns' role in her discovery to herself for now, "but as soon as you told me you'd had to kill a girl before, it made sense. And I have a little good news. I think it maybe explains the three-year gap in between the killings and you getting the memories."

The dark cloud over Robert parted, if just slightly, at the news. "How?"

She tried to smile. "Do you remember what Hennerman told me about how the memories being transplanted have to match up with the mind of the person receiving them? Like how I couldn't accept a memory of sky-diving and find it pleasurable if I have a fear of heights?"

He nodded mutely.

"Well, Mead needed to find someone whose mind could accept that he had killed those women, and it needed to be someone who could associate something positive with the deaths the way the killer had. I know you didn't enjoy killing her," she hurried before he could protest, "but you said yourself that her death saved the lives of a lot of people. Maybe that, plus how you felt about the other killings, was enough of a connection. Think about it. The normal recipients of these transfers don't have memories that match up exactly either. They just don't have anything that forces them to reject the memory as being impossible."

Robert thought it over. What she said made a perverted kind of sense, he decided, but it certainly didn't put him any more at ease about his past knowing he was an ideal candidate for memories like these. "So Hennerman selected me because he needed a certain kind of killer. I guess I should feel special."

"Hey, it's not like he could have started advertising his services to convicted murderers. They're kind of hard to find since they're usually either locked up or executed, and even if he could have, murderers aren't exactly trustworthy partners. The next best options would have been soldiers or police officers, people allowed to kill as part of their jobs. He'd avoid cops though. That just left vets like you."

"Even if that's true," Robert said, "and I'm just some unlucky guy who got his card drawn because of one event from my past, it wouldn't explain why he waited so long to do this. It's not like he knew about the girl I killed. That was just dumb luck. And never mind the biggest question of all. Why even give me the memories? That's the big thing I keep coming back to."

"I do too," Stephanie agreed. "Except I don't think he did wait three years. I think as soon as he had the tech down to a science, he probably started trying this special discount-for-veterans crap, especially ones who served on the front lines. I'll bet that was even on the questionnaire you had to fill out."

Robert thought back and nodded. "It was, for sure. First page."

"My bet is that he tried this dozens of times. With that monitor he invented, he could scan the customer's brain for a compatible memory. None of the other potentials was a match, but then he found you. Except that along with the ability to accept the killings as having a positive outcome, you were also dealing with a tremendous amount of guilt over a girl's death, something he'd have had no reason to look for in your past. One in a billion chance it worked out that way. If not for that one experience, you'd probably be on the run from us in Mexico or someplace."

Robert absorbed the information slowly. Dumb luck, or more probably, karma, had led him to be the winner of the absolute worst lottery in human history. What did it say about him that his mind accepted killing innocent young women as acceptable in certain circumstances? Was the death of that one girl more than just an isolated incident?

"But still, putting aside the fact that I'm apparently one step removed from being this generation's Jack the Ripper, why the hell would Mead do this to me? Why not just erase the memories and be done with it? What could he have to gain?"

For the first time, Stephanie scowled at Robert as words from her own past rang in her ears. She couldn't sound like Bullet, but she could deliver the same message he had given her when she had needed it. "Hey, drop that self-pity crap. Being capable of something, not that I'm saying you are, and actually doing it are totally different. We're all nothing more than the consequences of the choices we make. Some sick son-of-a-bitch chose to kill women just for pleasure. You didn't. Your choices, however awful to you, were made to save lives. Different choices because you're totally different men. As for why Mead would do this, I'm not sure yet, but I have a theory."

One of Robert's eyebrows arched noticeably, but he remained otherwise stoic as he considered her words. Perhaps she was right. There was no way to know for sure.

"What's the theory?" he asked.

Stephanie relaxed. "I think you were an insurance policy. Something Mead has done, probably removing the memories, has stopped the killer from being active. He's worried that at some point that won't work anymore. Hell, he might have done this before and seen him relapse. I think he wants somebody to hang the killings on if they ever start up again. One anonymous tip to us about you, we apply a few old school, backroom questioning techniques like the kind you probably used, and before long you're telling us what we want to hear."

Robert dropped his head and the corners of his mouth formed a long frown. He thought of the many suspected terrorists he had applied considerable pressure to over the years. How many of them had just said what he wanted to hear? "That is some seriously dark shit to rain down on somebody. That would really work?"

Stephanie wrinkled her nose and nodded. "Not fun to admit, but yeah, I think it would. We'd stop looking for another killer right away. Without physical evidence, maybe we don't get a conviction, but why would that matter to Mead? All he would care about is that it would be enough to keep us from looking for someone else. And even if we did keep searching, any ambulance chaser in the phonebook would be able to get the real killer off when he can point to another case in which someone confessed. That's all the reasonable doubt any jury would ever need. I hate to say it, but it's really pretty clever."

Robert searched quickly for holes in the theory but found none, so he gave a lame smile. "Except I went and confessed and threw off the whole thing because apparently I'm Mister Johnny Good-Deed."

Stephanie made a throaty laugh. Her eyes sparkled sometimes when she was happy, Robert noticed. He wondered if she were aware of it.

"Speaking of good deeds," she said, "I have yet another theory. I think that's what the killer thought he was doing, a good deed of some kind, and Mead knows it. I think it's why he keeps trying to help him. He knows that the killer doesn't think of himself as evil, so Mead doesn't want to see him punished. He wants him to stop, for sure, but he's trying to do it his way so the guy doesn't go to jail."

Cold trickled down Robert's spine, causing him to shudder. How could someone who's done the things this man did not see himself as evil? "Like some sort of prodigal son who he's trying to show the error of his ways?"

"I thought you didn't read the Bible?"

Robert shrugged. "I haven't, but I think everyone knows that one."

"Well, the real prodigal son realized what he did and came home to repent. I don't know if this guy …" Alarm bells suddenly resounded in Stephanie's head. She had missed something obvious from the beginning, and the realization made her slightly queasy. Still, she had to smile at the knowledge that she had just taken a huge step toward finding a killer.

"You are a genius, Robert, an absolute genius. I could kiss you."

Robert felt the skin on his cheeks warming. He hoped he wasn't turning as red as he felt. "Well, I mean, let's not rule anything out—" he started, but Stephanie had already moved on, seemingly unaware of what she had said.

She shot up off the sofa. "We need to get to my office, now. There's something there I need to see."

He rose reluctantly to meet her. "Oh, good. That's where I was hoping this was headed," Robert lied.

"Sorry it's not what you had in mind," she offered, "but it's very necessary. Besides," she added, flashing him her best smile, "if I find what I think I'm going to, maybe we can actually see about that kiss."

CHAPTER EIGHTEEN

For several years now, it had been the habit of Dr. Lawrence Mead to go to bed early in his own private quarters. Due to his somewhat recent and completely fabricated propensity to snore loudly, his wife was happy to allow the arrangement. After three decades of marriage to a man obsessed with his work, she valued her sleep over any romantic notions that might occasionally creep into her husband's head. On most nights, Mead used the privacy to slip through a secret, narrow passage in his closet and down to a particular section of his basement. Tonight, he'd had no reason to do so, and that troubled him greatly.

The room was hidden behind a false wall that Mead had constructed as the home was being built. He had taken his wife and daughter on a cruise for two weeks and paid the contractors double their normal rate to work around the clock so that the sound-proof room would be completely undetectable. Other than himself, the only other person aware of the room was the young man who normally occupied it, David.

The room was necessary in order to keep David locked away while the proper adjustments were made to his mind. Mead had tried first simply removing the memories he felt had caused David's problems in the first place, but the human mind was apparently more complicated than he had wanted to admit. He had cursed himself at the time for not understanding that better. He should have known. David was counting on him, after all. But he hadn't given up. He had next tried to implant memories that might help, but if anything, that had been even less successful. David had made almost no progress at all in the last three years, but, Dr. Mead told himself, thanks to his treatments, he had at least gotten no worse. The only redeeming thought in the nightmare that had been Dr. Mead's life for many of the past years was the knowledge that he would one day find what was needed. David would be cured of his ailments, and Mead would simply erase any memories of this unpleasant time of being held against his will. On that day, everything would be perfect. The true value of his real research would finally be realized.

Except that he might now never get that chance.

When Lawrence Mead had gone downstairs after dinner as he often did on the pretense of getting some last minute work in before bed, he had checked on David. Usually, he was asleep or reading or playing one of his video games. He would look at Mead with pleading eyes, but he had long since given up asking to be let out. If nothing else, progress had been made in that David at least seemed to understand why he was imprisoned, the necessity of it all. There was no longer the animosity between them that used to permeate everything. David had opened up and had even begun talking more during these visits. Lately, he had been almost chatty. Tonight, however, David had nothing to say. Of course, that was only because he was nowhere to be found. Where he should have sat, there was only an empty bed with an open cell door nearby.

Mead agonized as he walked the small space across from the cell where the divan lay knocked on its side. Had he left the door open? Had David somehow found a way to pick the lock? Either way, this was very, very bad, especially when the police were now involved. If they found David, which he allowed they almost certainly would eventually, they would find out about his own role in the killings. And he couldn't even imagine what they might do to David. Probably a lifetime of prison or even the death penalty, neither of which was fitting in this case. He shuddered. Still, David had made his choices, and now Mead had to make his own. If he could not save David from punishment, perhaps there was a way to improve his own situation.

His mind made up, Mead marched back upstairs to find a phone. He had calls to make, and time was growing shorter by the second.

CHAPTER NINETEEN

It took Stephanie almost thirty minutes of searching through her piles of notes and files to find what she wanted. During this time, Robert had little else to do but sit and watch her work. Her movements were quick, he noticed, but ordered. She was never frantic. She stayed in control and focused, never letting the urgency of her task distract her from the importance of it. *She'd make an excellent soldier*, Robert thought.

Stephanie read over her early notes, nodding to herself occasionally and, finally, fell back into the chair at her desk, her fingers making a staccato tapping across her laptop's keyboard as she called up the articles noted in her files and quickly scanned over them. Satisfied at last, she pushed back from the computer and shook her head in apparent disbelief, smiling simultaneously at her own ignorance.

"What did you find?" Robert asked. Stephanie was obviously pleased about something, but he was tired beyond the ability to care as much as he knew he should.

"A couple of things, but those aren't why I'm smiling. What I didn't find, on the other hand …"

"I'm worn out, Stephanie. Maybe you could share your good news?" Robert asked. "Some of us are a little slow to pick things up for ourselves."

"Let me start at the beginning. We know, or we think we know, that the killer is someone important to Mead, right? Still, we kept wondering why he would risk so much, all of his money, all of his success, to help a killer, even if the killer is someone important to him, when he knows he might get caught."

Robert frowned. "Yeah, but he knows we can't really prove anything. That's his ace in the hole, so to speak, isn't it? He's not truly exposed at all."

"Not in the legal sense. That keeps him out of jail, maybe, but to ruin his company, all I have to do is go public with a few logical connections and some evidence that could never be used in a court of law."

Robert worked the problem over in his mind as Stephanie laid the facts out for him. Whatever conclusion she had reached was still just beyond his grasp, but he sensed it was right in front of him somewhere.

"Okay, I agree that it never made sense that a guy with an ego like Mead's would take a fall like that for anyone, no matter what kind of court he has to face."

Stephanie gave a dismissive nod as if that fact were beyond discussion.

Robert finally gave up. "So what changed? What did we get wrong?" he asked.

"The timeline. He didn't put his company at risk by helping a killer. His company exists *because* he was helping a killer. Think about it," she urged. "What if he's known all along? What if it's the reason he started his research in the first place?" she asked, picking up one of her least chewed pencils and rolling it back and forth on her desk as Robert listened.

Robert again plodded his way through the marsh that was Stephanie's theory. On the surface, it made sense. Mead invents a process solely to help whoever it was, and then he realizes the commercial applications after the fact. Starting the company exposes his technology to the world, but it's sure to make millions. At least. And Stephanie had been right that it was a one in a million shot that the guy who'd inherit the killer's memories would also be suffering from an advanced case of guilt and involve the police at all.

Robert put his hands up in a sign of surrender. "Okay, you win. Your theory works," he said. "But until you know who he'd do this all for, it's still only a theory."

Stephanie brought her hand down on top of the pencil and smiled. She had clearly been waiting on this moment. "Maybe so, but remember what Hennerman told me in that first interview? The company didn't start out selling good memories to people—"

Robert closed his eyes slowly to better see the interview again in his mind. As he recalled the words, he gave a smile of his own. "It started out helping people get rid of bad ones." His eyes sprang open. "Like maybe killing a bunch of girls?"

"Or maybe just one at first," Stephanie agreed. "Who knows what the number might have been then? Mead knew somebody, somebody close to him who had done something terrible. He was doing research into the nature of memories, and I think he saw a way to help his friend out of a jam by wiping away his sins. Somewhere along the way, he meets Hennerman, or someone like him, who convinces him to profit from what he's made."

Robert was once again back on his feet and pacing as he thought. They were still dealing with miles of conjecture, but he could sense the spark in the air that came with getting closer to their prey by the moment. His body remembered the rush of the adrenaline that came with this part of the hunt even if his mind had pushed it away. Robert took a moment to recognize and even relish in his quickening pulse. He thought briefly of trying to slow it somehow but dismissed the thought as he realized he neither knew how nor cared to eliminate this feeling. He was alive again, and his senses were always sharper on the hunt. He told himself it would help him to think.

"Okay, but the technology took a while to get right, like all new tech. Hennerman said something about beta testing until a few years ago, didn't he? Maybe he wasn't quite helping the guy enough, so he goes on killing the whole time until three or so years ago, until Mead finally gets it right."

"And," Stephanie rushed to add, "because he had a human subject to test his work, he sped the process along way faster than it would normally have developed. All the more reason for the tech world to think of him as a genius."

Robert stopped pacing mid-step to look over at Stephanie. The grimace he wore was one she'd never seen on him. "But how did Hennerman find out about this operation? No way does Mead spill his secret to anybody without a powerful reason, the kind I wouldn't mind giving him at this point." His powerful hands closed tightly into iron fists and flexed back open again.

He's tired, she thought, frowning. *I've pushed him too far tonight. Better wrap it up.* "I wondered that too, and I get the sense that's going to end up being an obstacle we're going to have to climb if we ever want this case resolved."

If someone had asked, Stephanie would have said her words had felt innocent enough when she had said them. The truth was, they were so benign that she hadn't thought about them at all. She'd had no guard up, and so the words had simply come out. She also would have said that the instant the words had escaped her lips, she'd known she wanted them back.

Robert spun on his heel almost in a blur and closed the little space between them so quickly she'd had no time to react. "*If* we want it resolved? Do I look to you like a man who isn't committed?" He towered over her, sucking in great lungfuls of air between sentences, exhaling slowly, giving her time to respond. Stephanie declined the silent invitation, didn't even acknowledge she had heard him. She looked at him without giving the impression she was staring at him or looking through him, neither provoking nor ignoring him.

"Robert, I need to be able to stand up now. The way you're standing is keeping me from doing that. Are you willing to back up two steps?" Her voice matched her body language. There was no sign of fear or of anger. There was only the request, which he could grant or decline.

Robert looked down at the spot where he stood and then again at Stephanie. Her words had done their job as he seemed to realize for the first time where he was and how threatening his presence had become. His first reaction was to shove his hands deep into his pockets, hiding them away the way a child might attempt to hide the obvious evidence of some little crime. Then he faded backward silently, giving her far more room than she had requested. He tried to look back up at Stephanie, to form an apology that might begin to be adequate. He found he did not have the words. "I … I didn't …"

Stephanie rose slowly to her feet and kept her hands out well in front of her. "No, don't. Not only was there no harm done, but I'm the one who could see you were getting too worked up. I never should have pushed the pace so much. I sometimes forget where your limits are because you never let them show. We'll both do better next time, right?"

Robert's cheeks burned red, and he felt the perspiration sliding down his back and his palms. He didn't know what to say. He clearly had been about to hurt Stephanie, and there would have been nothing he could have done to stop it. That other mind had been in control. Somehow, he had let that other side of him, the monster, out of its cage.

"Right, Robert?" Stephanie repeated in a soft voice.

He looked up at her, barely making eye contact, and gave the slightest of nods.

"Want some good news to cheer you up? Come check this out," she told him, gesturing him over to her computer. She opened up the photos she had taken in Mead's office.

Robert let one foot almost slide forward, then stopped and seemed to root himself to the ground. "Maybe it would be better if I stayed over here," he mumbled.

Stephanie pretended a casualness she did not yet truly feel. "Don't be silly, Robert. It's fine. Besides, the cord won't reach over there, and you're really going to want to see this."

Slowly, he eased himself behind her chair just close enough to be able to see the pictures scrolling by on her screen until she stopped at the one she wanted.

"Who do you see in the photos on his desk?" Stephanie asked, tapping her pencil eraser against the spot in question.

Robert squinted his eyes. "A woman and a girl, presumably his wife and daughter. You think one of them is the killer?" Robert asked. "They can't be. I'm sure you remember that some of things I did," he closed his eyes and shook his head slightly to clear the fog, "sorry, that *he* did, could only be done by a man."

Stephanie handed him a copy of one of the first articles she had found online about Mead. She transferred the pencil to her other hand and pointed out one line in particular for Robert to see.

"Now, who do you *not* see in the photo?" she asked, grinning widely.

Robert looked from the article to the photos twice to be sure he was seeing them both correctly.

"Holy shit," he breathed. "The bastard has a son."

CHAPTER TWENTY

David Nathaniel Mead—male, age twenty-seven, parents Lawrence and Linda Mead, high school diploma, no college, no job, no known aliases, no known anything. He was easy to find once Stephanie had a name, but there was virtually no information on him that was helpful. She was able to determine only that David had been educated at more schools than she could count on both hands and that he had disappeared from the grid shortly after graduating.

Throughout the late night and into the early morning hours, all traces of their weariness forgotten, Robert and Stephanie poured over every piece of data they could find, exploring theory after theory for something that would help them prove what they now felt they knew for certain—that the younger Mead was their killer and the elder Mead the brains behind the cover up. By 3:30, both were exhausted and growing more frustrated with each passing minute. Robert twice refused Stephanie's requests to head home and let her handle the search for a while.

"We're *this* close," Robert said, tossing the file folder back onto Stephanie's desk and reaching for his coffee mug for what seemed like the hundredth time. "And yet, nothing you have here looks like proof to me. I still say you're just going to have to risk it and subpoena his machines and records."

"And *I* still say," Stephanie repeated, "that there is no promise that will do us any good. I won't base my case on the premise that he was dumb enough to keep records."

Robert rubbed his face with the palms of his hands as if he might scour the sleepiness away. "Okay, then what do we know for sure that you can use?" Robert asked.

Stephanie had been ready for the question only because she had been wondering the same thing. Producing her notepad, she began to read.

"One, we know who the killer is and what Mead's role was, but we can't prove anything." She looked over the top of her notepad to make sure Robert was paying attention. Seeing his nod, she went on. "Two, we know when he finally got the process correct and that someone, presumably Hennerman, convinced him to turn a profit off of his work. Three, we know he felt the need not just to wipe out his son's memories, but to transfer them to you, again, presumably, as an alibi."

"So everything we know is also paired with at least one pretty huge presumption, and you left out the part about there being no way you can even get a conviction without finding the son. Even then, it might be a longshot."

"Well," Stephanie said, throwing her notepad down on her desk harder than she had intended, "at least we know some things. It's a hell of a lot farther along than we were a few days ago. You could try looking at the bright side occasionally, you know."

Robert rubbed his eyes again and yawned. "Sorry. I'm just exhausted," he apologized. "You think Mead knows where his son is hiding these days?"

Stephanie picked up her own coffee mug and examined the

dregs at the bottom before deciding that her need for caffeine was not quite as strong as Robert's. "You can count on it," she assured him. "After going to all that trouble to get his kid fixed up, he's going to want to keep him somewhere safe."

"So close," Robert moaned. "And yet …" He sighed deeply as he accepted the fact that the case would not be solved that morning. He had known, of course, that it would not. Still, as the pieces had fallen into place, he'd begun to think ahead to a time without the dreams when his head might be clear again, when he might look at Stephanie without some part of him seeing her the way David did.

And exactly how much of David was there in him? The way he had behaved earlier suggested it was way too much. He hadn't even been aware of what he was doing. How many other times had that happened without him knowing?

"Stephanie, listen," he began. Stephanie tried to hold out a hand to stop him, but Robert shook her off. "I think I need to say this one out loud. What I did earlier, I'm sorry for that. I don't know what happened. I mean, we *both* know what happened—I just don't know why it happened then. Worse, I don't know what else I might have done if … if you hadn't been there."

"But I was there," she answered. She scooped up her keys, slung her purse over her shoulder, and walked to him. "And there's a reason I was. We expected this might happen, remember? Come on. It's been a long night and then some."

He couldn't help smiling. Her displays of rough cynicism and strength were always secondary to her kindness. He wondered how many people she let see that. "But what if I had hurt you?" he asked.

"Don't flatter yourself, big boy," she teased. "Now, come on. I need my beauty sleep."

CHAPTER TWENTY-ONE

Somewhere, through the deep dark veil of restless sleep Stephanie had lost herself in, she was vaguely aware of a telephone ringing. Summoning all of her will, she reached out through the darkness to grab the offending device and saw the station's number. Her phone didn't show the extension, so it was impossible to know who was calling unless she answered, but she knew it must be an emergency for anyone to call in the middle of the night. Except that sunlight was filtering in past her curtains. She had overslept.

"Hello?" she answered with an alertness she did not feel.

"Stephanie, it's Benjamin. I don't know where you are, but I think you're going to want to get yourself to the station as quickly as possible."

She was suddenly fully alert. Something in Dr. Burns' voice told her that this was not simply a suggestion. "What's happening?"

"Mead just marched in here with an entire team of lawyers surrounding him like they're Secret Service, and they all just went into Bates' office. Mead did not look well, either. I don't know what any of this is about, but it's a near certainty it involves you, or at least it should."

Stephanie made a mental note to take it a little easier on Dr. Burns. "You're the best, Doc. See you in thirty."

Stephanie threw cold water on her face, pulled back her dark hair and twisted it into a bun that she held in place with one of her pencils, and quickly threw on the first thing she found in her closet that wasn't too wrinkled.

She considered waking Robert to tell him she was leaving but decided against it. He needed the sleep, and she could always call him later with whatever she found out. It might be nothing anyway, she reasoned. He was most likely coming in to throw some weight around and claim harassment in order to slow the investigation. But for once, Stephanie hadn't harassed him at all, hadn't even seen him since their interview. Still, better not to get her hopes up.

Two minutes later, a text message from her boss lit up her phone.

"Get your ass in here now. Mead is here looking for you, and he has what looks like every lawyer within fifty miles with him."

With pleasure. Whatever he's got to say is probably bullshit, but at least I'm getting to talk to him again. Stephanie vacillated every two minutes for the remainder of the drive as to whether she should mention the son. It might spook him into letting something slip, but it might be just as likely to send him into even deeper legal cover from which he might never emerge. Her indecision left her feeling like someone was running an ice cube down her spine despite the already sweltering heat of the late-morning sun. Probably just the lack of sleep. She hoped it wouldn't show during the interrogation she had planned.

She needn't have worried.

Twelve minutes later, Stephanie, her boss, and the district attorney sat across from Dr. Mead, who was flanked by two of his legal advisors, who were in turn busy whispering things into

Mead's ears. Mead listened impassively. The entire scene reminded Stephanie of something out of King Arthur's court. Finally, Mead raised an authoritative hand, and his henchmen immediately went silent. The king was ready to speak.

"Detective, District Attorney Howard, I am here against the wishes of my legal team because I require your help with a matter of great importance, and since it is I who am asking you for something, I am prepared to offer something of value in return—the killer you seek, or at least his identity."

The ticking of the overhead clock filled the room with its quiet repetitiveness. Stephanie didn't bother denying that she'd never had a suspect in custody, but neither would she confirm anything for him.

"I take it by your silence that you are somewhat surprised to hear this," Mead offered with a nod. "No matter. The offer stands, and you can expect my full cooperation. On one condition."

The D.A. did his best to act as if this kind of thing happened every day. "And what might that be, Dr. Mead?"

Mead ignored the question momentarily and appraised Stephanie coolly from across the table. She was smart, attractive, and obviously capable at her job. Had life worked out the way he had planned, she was exactly the kind of woman he would have hoped his son might one day meet. As it was, he thought sadly, David was not yet exactly prepared to interact properly with women, especially ones as determined and intelligent as the detective. If only he'd had more time.

"Detective Monroe," he began, "I am, by most accounts, an intelligent man. Surely you realize your little charade in my office and then in the press would never have been sufficient to draw me out?"

Stephanie hadn't blinked since Mead had locked his eyes on hers, and she didn't now. "And yet ..." she stated, indicating his chair with a slight flourish of her hand.

He offered a stiff smile. "True enough. Here I am, my hat in my hand."

The other parties in the room sat silently as the obvious game of cat-and-mouse played out. They knew Mead, for all his willingness to help, had an agenda. Neither the D.A. nor Stephanie nor her captain was willing to risk interrupting the little drama until they had what only Dr. Lawrence Mead could offer, the killer in cuffs and behind bars.

Though she knew it was necessary to let him have his moment, Stephanie disliked being in the dark about what Mead wanted, a feeling Mead clearly enjoyed giving her. She decided she had nothing to lose by playing the only card she had. "Doctor, if you're looking to establish some sort of intellectual superiority or just a plain old upper hand in a negotiation, you can rest easy. It's pretty clear you have something you know we want, something you think we'd trade for. If I were a betting lady," she continued, "I'd guess you want to give us your son in return for leniency for yourself. Something like that?"

If Mead were even slightly surprised, nothing in his countenance betrayed him. Rather, he simply chuckled and then winced at the pain that it brought on. It had taken a fair amount of liquid courage to get this far, and though his hangover hadn't really begun kicking in yet, it was clearly going to be a rough one when it did.

"Detective," Mead began heavily, "I love my son with all my heart, but I have no illusions about him. He is what he is, and he needs to be confined until his condition can be cured, something I once thought I could do for him. I was wrong about that, and many young women paid a terrible price for my hubris. We all have."

"Not to mention one very innocent man who never should have been involved," Stephanie seethed.

Mead flinched. "Yes, Mr. Grayson. I admit, he is a part of

the reason I am here as well. I cannot explain what happened to him. A glitch in the system, perhaps? In any case, you are correct insofar as he should not have been involved. He has my sincerest apologies."

Dr. Mead seemed genuinely remorseful, though Stephanie couldn't say whether it was for his son's behavior, his own inability to cure him, or for what happened to Robert. Probably some of both of the first two, she reasoned. She wasn't buying the bit about Robert's involvement being accidental though. And remorseful or not, something else about him was … off. Maybe it was the way he freely offered up his son for sacrifice like they were some modern day Isaac and Abraham. Stephanie remembered the Bible verses Robert had written. She hadn't had time to think of them lately, and they'd seemed like a dead end anyway.

"Doctor, do you read the Bible often?"

Stephanie's question took Mead back in his chair just a bit, but he immediately recovered.

"I don't wish to complain, Detective, but mine has not been an easy life nor my son an easy burden to bear. I try to find comfort where I can, so, yes, I read the Bible sometimes. Is that relevant?"

Stephanie wasn't sure. She wasn't even sure why she had asked. It was David she needed insight to.

"It might be," she answered. "Does your son read it?"

Her boss and the district attorney were granting her a little leash to work with since Mead had asked for her, but their stares told her the slack was quickly going out of the line. She still had no idea why she was pursuing what she already knew, but she could hear her father's voice whispering at her to keep asking questions. One look at Mead, and she was glad she had, at least for once, listened.

Mead's upper lip trembled slightly, and he quickly removed his hands from the table and held them in his lap. Stephanie smiled. He hadn't wanted her to see them trembling. He ignored her question and moved ahead.

"I wish I came here offering happier tidings," he continued. "Had I done this any earlier, perhaps I could have."

Mead signaled one of his attorneys, who slid a legal folder across the table to the D.A. without speaking. Stephanie hadn't known lawyers were capable of going this long without saying anything.

"Here is what I can offer you. Inside that folder is my detailed account of everything I know about each of the women my son claims to have killed. David's methods were … visceral, I suppose. If you can find him and take a DNA sample from him, I would imagine you should have no problem matching him to these women. All I ask is that if the information I have provided you aids you in a conviction, you take the death penalty off the table for my son. He is, after all, quite sick."

Three voices began speaking at once with different versions of the same questions, but Mead waved each of them off. He looked only at Stephanie, who met his gaze as he knew she would, without blinking. Having apparently been appointed the *de facto* lead negotiator, she spoke for them all, asking the one question everyone shared.

"You said *if* we can find him. Dr. Mead, do you know your son's whereabouts right now?"

Mead sighed heavily and shook his head. "For the last three years, I've had my son locked in a room in the basement of my family home. There is, so far as I know, no way in or out that I do not control. Despite this, some time yesterday afternoon or evening, my son escaped." He let the gravity of his words sink in for a moment before adding, "And I have absolutely no idea where he might be. I am truly sorry."

Stephanie swallowed her desire to reach across the table and slap Mead hard enough to rattle his brain. Maintaining her illusion of calm, she asked, "Surely there is some place he would be drawn to? A favorite hangout or childhood haunt? A friend's house, maybe?"

Mead's hangover was settling in and was indeed gearing up to be of the epic variety, but still he wished for a last drink to calm his nerves.

"Detective, I'm afraid that David has no friends, nor does he have any place like you are suggesting. To say that he was different as a child is to say that the Titanic had mild buoyancy issues. Do you understand?" Mead leaned across the table to bore into Stephanie's eyes even further. "There is absolutely no predicting where he might go. To make matters worse, if, indeed, that is possible at this point, he has no recollection of any of his crimes, so he is unlikely to revisit any of those places except by accident. So," Mead continued as his lawyers tried unsuccessfully to whisper something to him, "if he is to be found, it will have to be one of you who does the finding."

Captain Bates muttered something under her breath as the D.A. shook his head. Stephanie remained motionless as she considered the implications of what Mead had said.

Mead only smiled sadly as he watched his words affect each of them in turn.

"Why come to us now?" Stephanie finally asked. "You knew I was never going to be able to pin these killings on your son without your help."

"Because, Detective, despite what you may think of me, I am not an evil man. I tried to help my son and to protect his potential victims from harm at the same time. As long as those objectives were possible, I was willing to do whatever it took. Things changed, obviously, when my son broke free. Now, my goal is to keep him off of death row and to keep as many women as possible alive for as long as possible."

"As long as possible?" Stephanie asked. "You think we won't find him in time?"

Mead closed his eyes and tried to soothe away his headache by rubbing his temples. Without being asked, one of his attorneys opened his briefcase and produced a pair of aspirin and a bottle of sparkling water. Mead took both and nodded to the man. "David may have no memories of his crimes, but, at heart, he is still a killer with all of the same desires he's always had. Add to that the fact that his father, the person he trusted most in this world, has kept him locked up for three years for no obvious reason ..." Mead could only shrug helplessly as he twisted the top off of his water, popped the aspirin, and chased them down. He then looked at his Rolex. "He has now been loose for as many as fifteen hours. I'm afraid," he said, again closing his eyes against the increasingly glaring lights of the interrogation room, "that it is not a question of *if* or even of *when* he might kill again, Detective. The question is only whether he has done so already."

CHAPTER TWENTY-TWO

The city was hot. Waves of heat rippled off of the white and grey concrete, causing the landscape behind it to shimmer as David took in his surroundings. He had forgotten what summers were like in Texas. He had been educated at private boarding schools all across the country, including one semester at a prestigious school on the Big Island of Hawaii, but always he had returned home in the summers. It had been necessary to gain his education at so many schools because he continually encountered problems with members of the faculty at the various schools he attended. He did well with most of the men, but the women were another matter. Inevitably, there would be … incidents. He was always whisked away and the matters swept under the rug, usually after a sizable donation to the school by his father. Eventually though, he had to be brought home for good. So, for the last three years, he had seen nothing but the four walls of his room and the face of the man who had put him there.

At the thought of his prison and his father, revulsion crawled up David's spine. He both hated and loved his father deeply. He was hardly the only son to find himself in such a place, he knew, but he was fairly certain that his own situation was unique. He knew that his father felt justified in locking him away as he had done. It had been for what his father truly believed to be the greater good, but he was also certain that he could never be what his father wanted him to be. No matter how long he stayed in that God-forsaken room, David knew that he would never be able to make the changes his father wanted him to make. He had simply been born the way he was, and he cursed his father for not being able to accept him. Not that it mattered anymore. He was free now to be what he wanted, to be who he wanted. One day soon, he would find his father and make him understand that.

It had taken David months to figure out how to open the lock from the inside, and months longer to find the courage to leave. Now that he was free, he knew he had made the right choice. Here, he could do anything he desired without having to worry about whether his father approved. The trouble was only in deciding where to go first.

He hadn't been to a movie theater in years. Or to a shopping mall. Or even a grocery store. In fact, he realized, he hadn't been anywhere. Now that he could go anyplace, it was difficult to decide where to begin. Up until this point, he had merely wandered with the sole goal of getting as far from his home as possible. Where would he go first? It needed to be crowded, within walking distance or close to public transportation, and, above all, cheap. His video game consoles had brought him less than he would have liked from a local pawn store, so conserving cash was important for the time being. He cycled through the options in his mind, considering and ultimately rejecting each based on the criteria he had chosen. He was becoming increasingly frustrated at his situation until fate intervened in the form of a city bus lumbering by that advertised the perfect solution across its side.

David smiled to himself as he pulled his cap lower to shield his eyes from the bright sun and ran to the nearby stop to catch the bus before it could pull away. This day was getting better and better.

CHAPTER TWENTY-THREE

"Wait. Say that again slowly so I'm sure I caught it all."

Stephanie was sitting on her sofa, resisting the urge to fall back on the cushions and drift away for a few more hours. "I'm serious. He walked right in of his own free will, admitted everything," Stephanie repeated. "Of course, that's only because his kid is on the loose again. Don't go thinking he had some sudden change of heart. He's no humanitarian," she cautioned. "And I don't buy his bullshit apology or excuses about you getting the memories either."

Robert could only sit and slowly absorb the information. Stephanie had rushed home to share the news with him as soon as the meeting had concluded, but it was taking a while to digest it all. On the one hand, Mead had agreed to reveal everything he had done to Robert, fully exonerating him from any criminal activity. He even offered to have the memories of the killings removed to whatever degree was possible. On the other, David Mead was loose in the city and likely to begin killing again soon. It was hard to take any pleasure from his own good news knowing the kind of predator who was on the hunt again.

"I don't doubt that one bit," he said. "Still, at least he tipped you off that his son got out. He could have kept it hidden."

"Agreed. It gives us a chance, but it's still going to be harder than finding a democrat at an N.R.A. rally."

Robert conceded her point with a nod and walked toward the coffee pot with his empty mug in his hand. Determined to find a silver lining, he tried again. "Okay, but at the very least you're going to get a really bad guy off the streets. Maybe not the killer you wanted, but the dad is nearly as bad in his own way."

Stephanie winced as sour bile rose to the back of her throat. She had not wanted to tell Robert the bad news, but she had known it was unavoidable. "Actually, that picture is still kind of coming into focus if you know what I mean."

Robert's forehead wrinkled. "How the hell could anyone possibly know what that means?"

"Fine," she said. "Dr. Mead is at home." Robert's eyes went wide. Stephanie rushed to add, "He's wearing an ankle monitor and there's a patrol car parked outside of his house for the time being, but, yeah, he's sort of free at the moment."

Robert had to clear his head. Surely he was dreaming.

Stephanie knew Robert had a million questions, but she had anticipated most of them because she had already asked her captain and the D.A. the same ones. "The problem," she explained, "is that his tech is newer than our laws. Something isn't illegal automatically, no matter how wrong it might be. Laws have to get passed, and there are none regarding memories. What he did to you was inexcusable. You can probably sue his pants off and never work another day in your life, but it wasn't illegal."

"Okay," Robert stammered, "but how about aiding and abetting? Or maybe imprisoning his own son?"

Stephanie massaged the back of her neck with her hand. "Yeah, those are trickier. Let me work backward. Imprisoning your own child is called grounding. Parents do it all the time. There isn't a time limit that makes it a crime. It has more to do with how the kid is treated. And, by Mead's account, his son consented to the confinement and lived like a prince while locked up. Since no one is around to say differently ..." Stephanie bit her lip and waited for Robert's reaction, which, as usual, was annoyingly mild.

"But from what you said, his wife would have had to know something, wouldn't she?"

"It's irrelevant. Mead swears he told the rest of the family that the son had gone on some excursion across Europe and just hadn't come home. Says he had the kid write letters occasionally pretending to be on some soul searching journey or something. I don't know if they believed it, but I guess they were just happy he wasn't around causing trouble."

Robert nodded. "The old ostrich approach." He returned to the living room and dropped himself back into the recliner where he had occupied the last several hours. He had made it only as far as the chair that morning, too exhausted even to remove his shoes, before he slipped away into some badly needed rest. He had been pleasantly surprised to find his sleep free of any dreams.

"If it's true, yes. Even if it isn't, we'll never be able to prove otherwise unless we find David. We're stuck on that front for now," Stephanie lamented.

Robert tried his best to put on a hopeful face. "Okay, but surely you still have him for covering up the murders, don't you? That's the one that counts, right?"

"I wish it were that simple. Mead claims, at least in his written confession, that he always considered his son's admissions to be dark fantasy that he was afraid would come true if he didn't intervene. Everything else he told us in person was strictly off the record, and since we can't link him to the actual bodies, there's no way to disprove his claim. When you add in the fact that he is now coming forward to aid in his son's capture, the legal waters get really murky. We could still charge him, and we might, but we have to get a jury to both believe he did it and not to be overly sympathetic toward a father desperate to help his son. The D.A. feels that might be a tough sell."

Robert wanted badly to be outraged, but he knew there was no use, so he grasped one final straw. "But I do still get to have my memories switched back, right?"

"Definitely," Stephanie agreed after a nearly imperceptible pause.

Robert caught the pause and thought he might have a mild heart attack any moment. "Wait. Why did you hesitate like that?"

"Sorry. I didn't mean to throw cold water on the good news parade." Robert scowled at her poor humor. "It's just that you and your memories are still our best hope of finding David, so—"

"You mean like the way I wrote those Bible verses that I didn't understand?" he cut in.

Stephanie's eyes sparkled and she sat upright at the mention of the verses. "Exactly. I told Mead about those, by the way, but I think he thought I was making it up. I don't know why, but those verses are important, maybe more than we knew."

Robert's stomach turned in great waves that threatened to empty themselves onto the floor of Stephanie's apartment. This experience had been enough of a roller coaster ride already. Now, apparently even the inventor of the damned technology didn't seem to understand all of the ramifications of the process.

"Stephanie, this connection I have, these memories, he didn't happen to mention how long they would last, did he? Or how deeply they go?"

Stephanie was puzzled. They had always assumed the transfer was permanent. "No. Why?"

"I'm not sure. Something's been different the last few days though. I can still remember things, but the vibes I was getting, the bad feelings, they seem to be getting a little better. I even slept straight through last night. I just wondered if the effect of the transfer wears off at some point."

Stephanie struggled to keep the concern that suddenly flooded her as far from her voice as possible. "I don't know, but if you're feeling better, that has to be good, right?" She knew the answer already. Burns had been quite clear that Robert was better off with the burden of his guilt keeping him in check.

"I guess. I still want the memories gone though. I hate knowing I have a connection to this psychopath, especially one that bastard doesn't even think should exist."

"A very temporary one," Stephanie insisted. "The instant we find this guy, we can remove everything that's happened since the moment you walked in the station."

Stephanie knew that Robert must take her up on the offer. It had been the agreement all along and the only way to bring him peace. Still, if he did that, if he lost *all* of his memories … Stephanie preferred not to think about it.

Robert considered her words carefully. On the surface, the decision she offered him should have been an easy one. Things were often not as simple as they seemed though. "What if I don't want to lose everything?" he asked.

Up until that point, by unspoken agreement, the pair had kept a playful banter of relatively harmless flirtation. Robert had now knocked on a door that she had assumed they would both leave closed until this case got resolved. She formed her words cautiously. "I would say that anything is an option once this case is closed."

Despite his efforts to still play it somewhat cool, Robert's face lit up like a Christmas tree.

"I meant with your memories, hotshot," she amended, smiling and rolling her eyes at him. "Come on. Where's that bad ass military investigator? I could really use his help on this one."

"Fine, but when this is over, you and I are having dinner together. And we aren't going to discuss this case or our jobs or anything remotely related to anything like that. Deal?"

"Deal," Stephanie agreed. "But if you take murder and mayhem off the table, what does that leave for normal people to talk about?"

He shrugged. "I don't know. Do you like baseball?"

"Not really. You?"

"It isn't my favorite. There. We have that in common. Let's talk about our mutual lack of interest in baseball like regular people on a date."

Stephanie held out her hand for Robert to shake. "I can't imagine anything I'd rather talk about. For now, I am assuming that you have selflessly volunteered to help the H.P.D. find an amnesiac killer, so let's get started."

"Actually," he said, easing farther back into the recliner opposite Stephanie's sofa, "I was going to say that I wanted to go home and never so much as read about this case again, but now you've made it awkward. Thanks a lot."

"My pleasure. Seriously though, where would you go first if you were David? You've been locked up for years for reasons you don't understand, you've got a mysterious urge to kill young women, and you have little or no money. Oh, and you are also absolutely bat-shit crazy."

Robert had been wondering the same thing. "I don't suppose there is any chance that he runs to the authorities and reports that he's been locked up against his will all those years?"

Stephanie grabbed one of the many throw pillows that adorned her sofa and hugged it tightly to her chest, tapping her fingers against it. "If he were going to, he'd have done it already."

Robert reached both arms high in the air in a gesture of surrender. "Then I hate to disappoint you so early, but I have no idea. Where does a psychopath go after he gets his get-out-of-jail-free card?"

Stephanie stood and indicated the door with a jerk of her head. "I have no idea either, but I'm pretty sure it isn't here. Let's head to the station. I want to talk to Bullet and see if he's come up with anything."

Robert rose with her and followed her to the door. "Think he's got coffee?" he asked.

Stephanie held open the door and allowed Robert to go through first so she could find her keys. "It's a good thing we're going to see a shrink. You might actually have a real problem."

"Given the last week of my life," Robert offered on his way out of the door, "if a coffee addiction is really ever my biggest issue, please let me know. Besides," he added once he had moved what he judged was a safe distance away, "the way you drive, I'll probably need something much stronger by the time we get there."

CHAPTER TWENTY-FOUR

The Houston Zoo was crowded, especially given the day's heat. The combined odors of a thousand visitors sweating their ways through the park and those of the many large animals doing their best to outdo the patrons were nearly overwhelming to most people. David overheard several families complaining about it as they sought shade any place they could find it, but David didn't mind. In fact, he loved it. The room in which he had lived for the past few years had been so sterile. The sour, sticky air here was a welcome change. Besides, ever since he had seen *her*, he had hardly registered anything else.

So far, he had kept his distance, using the time to build his courage. David had never been especially good at talking to women. Perhaps, he thought, it was part of what separated him from his father when it came to girls. His father could attract them so easily when he wanted to. For David, it had never been like that. Women were creatures to be admired certainly, the way he was doing now with the young, short haired, blonde beauty he had been eying for the last several minutes, but they were in no way easy to approach. And they were even harder to actually communicate with. He had never once given up trying to talk to them, but no matter how charming or witty or complimentary he tried to be, they always ended up ignoring him.

Sometimes, they were even rude about it. It made him very angry just thinking of those times. He looked down at his hands and saw that he was gripping the railing of the lemur enclosure so tightly that his knuckles had turned bone white. He blew his breath out slowly and forced himself to relax. *Patience*, he thought to himself. *Talk to her. See where it takes you. You never know. I mean, what's the worst that could happen?*

CHAPTER TWENTY-FIVE

"What do you think, Doc?" Stephanie asked Dr. Burns as she and Robert sat huddled together on the doctor's small office sofa.

Burns noticed the two had grown increasingly familiar and comfortable in each other's presence and the physical space they had been careful to maintain had practically disintegrated. Though he could engage in some fairly obvious conjecture, he was unsure exactly what their new closeness signaled, so he opted for keeping his observation private for the time being.

"I think, my dear, at the risk of stating what is already plain, that you have a difficult and unenviable task ahead of you. That goes for you, as well, Mr. Grayson."

Robert only smiled weakly. Stephanie had a somewhat stronger reaction. "No shit there, Doc. Thank God we came straight here."

"Stephanie, if I had something more helpful to offer you, I would, but think what you are asking me. You want me to help you predict what a man who has no knowledge of his own past actions might do next. As far as he knows, there is no behavior pattern in place for him to follow. It's as if he was born anew just yesterday."

Stephanie tried to interrupt but was silenced by a simple gesture from Dr. Burns. Robert thought for a moment he ought to try to learn the move, then discarded the idea as pointless.

"As I was saying, he has no pattern of which he is aware that he can repeat, but that doesn't mean one doesn't exist." As he finished speaking, he eyed Robert sadly.

Robert acknowledged the doctor's message with an exasperated nod. "Very subtle. Stephanie and I have already been down that road. I've agreed to help with anything I can think of, but I haven't had any new memories in a few days, just the old stuff rehashing itself. Maybe that's why I haven't had as much trouble sleeping lately. I don't know what else I can add to the party that's going to help establish a pattern."

At Robert's announcement of his new sleep habits, Dr. Burns' head had whipped over to him like a slingshot.

"What?" Robert asked.

"It's … nothing," Dr. Burns answered. "Look, Mr. Grayson, I don't know specifically what you have to offer either, but what Stephanie needs *is* still in your head somewhere."

Robert knocked on the side of his skull and cocked his head as if listening for an echo before looking back at Dr. Burns. "Any number of my teachers and nearly all of my ex-girlfriends have assured me there is virtually nothing in here, but if you can find anything, it's yours. How's that sound?"

Stephanie cut in before Robert's unstable temper could flare. "May I suggest that we simply go back to the beginning and compare the various victims again? The last time you looked over the profiles, you still thought you might be the killer. Maybe now you'll be able to see things from a fresh perspective. It certainly can't hurt, and we might find a pattern we didn't see before."

Robert stood up. "Fine, but, for the record, I don't think it will do any good."

"Why's that?" Dr. Burns asked.

"It sounds like this David kid was pretty screwed up to start with. Then his old man got in there and did even more damage with his machines. Won't forming a pattern from all of that be like trying to take puzzle pieces from different boxes and fitting them together into one big picture?"

"Possibly," Dr. Burns and Stephanie answered at the same instant and in the same tone of voice.

Clearly, Robert thought, one of them had rubbed off too much on the other. "My hand on a stack of Bibles, you two, that's the creepiest thing that's happened to me all week, and believe me, that is saying something." He rose and headed for the door, still shaking his head. "I'm going to grab some coffee before we get started."

The department, at Robert's request, had added a new coffee maker, the Bonavita 8-cup model with the thermal carafe. It didn't make quite as much brew at one time as other top models, but what it lacked in size, it more than made up for in quality in Robert's estimation.

Stephanie went to follow him but paused when Dr. Burns made no move to follow. "Aren't you coming, Bullet?"

He waved them off as he stared unseeing into the distance. Stephanie had seen this look enough times to know that it meant he was thinking seriously about something. There was no need to talk to him when he was like this, so she shooed Robert out the door and went to follow him.

"Stephanie," Dr. Burns at last called out from behind her.

"Yeah, Doc?" She turned to find him looking at her with an odd mix of curiosity and concern.

"I'd like a word with you privately before you leave."

Stephanie had never seen him quite like this, but she sensed that now was not the time to question him. "Sure thing," she answered before closing the door and stepping back out to find Robert waiting.

"What was that about?" he asked as they walked the halls of the H.P.D.

"Not sure. He gets like this sometimes," she lied. "It just means he's thinking something over."

"Let's hope it's related to this case. I don't think our other plan is going to amount to much."

"Maybe not, but it's better than doing nothing, so I'll get the files ready while you get your caffeine fix, and we can meet at my desk in five."

Stephanie didn't wait for an answer. Instead, she peeled away and left Robert to fend for himself in the lounge, which he was happy to do if it meant coffee sooner rather than later and Stephanie's uninspired plan later rather than now. Much of the investigative work done on any case involved boring grunt work, and Robert had done more than his share. In this case though, he felt that other people, any other people, were better qualified than himself to do what needed to be done. As far as he was concerned, his sole contribution to the department so far had been a decent coffee maker, and that had only happened because Stephanie had pretty much insisted on it on his behalf. Filling his cup and heading back out the door and down the hall, Robert could only hope that Stephanie could see something in these killings he could not.

"You ready?" she asked needlessly as he approached her desk and saw the files laid out before her.

He took a healthy sip from his mug and shrugged. "Guess so. Where should we start this time?"

Stephanie indicated the first three files. "We think these are his first victims. The time between killings is far enough apart to determine the order. These folders," she said, pointing to another stack, "we're less sure about. We have a vague idea of the time of death, but that's it. They're definitely after these three, but we can put them in only a rough order."

Robert grimaced. "See what I mean about the difficulty of establishing a pattern? If we get the order wrong, and the order is mostly guesswork at this point, we'll probably throw off the pattern too."

Stephanie started to suggest they take an early break, but Robert quickly waved her off. "It's okay. I don't mind helping with this. I'm just not sure that's what I'm doing. Mead was very careful to remove any information related to time frames, and nothing stands out about any of these women to suggest an order of any kind. And even if we can figure out the order, we have no idea whether that will even tell us anything useful."

Stephanie sensed he needed a gentle shove to keep him going. "Yet everything I know tells me that there is a pattern of some kind. Killing on this level is never random. He picks his victims for a reason. His father said in his file he considers women impure and evil and all that macho bullshit that some guys spout, but he isn't just killing every woman he sees. What made these women special to him? That's where our pattern is. The order is just to help us see them the way he did. So think. What do they have in common?"

"Age?" Robert offered. "They're all the right age to have children if they wanted."

"And, therefore, to be sexually active if they chose," Stephanie agreed. "That's likely a very important element to him, but that doesn't narrow down our list too much. What else?"

"Well, they were all at least fairly attractive."

"Again, true, but that isn't enough. There are a lot of pretty, sexually active women in Houston, Robert. He didn't target them all. Why not?"

Robert felt like he was in high school algebra again and having about as much success. "Opportunity?" Robert asked lamely.

Stephanie frowned. "Doubtful. If that were the case, he would have snatched as many as possible, way more than what he did. What else?"

Robert thought of them all again, all of the faces he had memorized so well from seeing them in his sleep. What was their connection? They were different races, different occupations, different marital statuses, and different walks of life. There was no evidence that any of them knew one another or their killer, and there was no evidence that any of them had been abducted from a single place. Robert grew increasingly angry as he went around and around with it all. A snapping sound brought his focus back to the present. He looked down to see a pencil he did not remember picking up now in two pieces in his hand. He placed the broken halves on the corner of the desk and hoped Stephanie might not notice, even though he knew very little got past her.

"I give up," he said. "I can't think of anything they have in common with each other. I told you this wouldn't work."

Stephanie tried not to look at the yellow, No. 2 elephant in the room as it clearly bothered Robert more than it should have. "Hey, don't get down on me now. We already know he targets pretty, young women. If we can narrow that list even a little more, we've made a huge step."

Robert eased his large frame into the little chair next to Stephanie's desk and stared blankly at the folders again without opening any of them. There was no need. He knew every detail of every one of them. There was one suspected prostitute, one definite one, five students, one drifter, four exotic dancers, one of whom was also a student, and, of all things, an Episcopal priest. Robert sighed heavily. When the victims ranged from priest to prostitutes and everything in between, what was he expected to find?

Wait, Robert thought. *Maybe not from priest to prostitute. Maybe the other way round.*

Stephanie saw the look on his face as the idea came to him. "What? You've got something. What is it?"

"I don't know yet. The first victim we know of, what was her occupation? Prostitute, right?"

Stephanie opened the file to be sure, but, like Robert, she knew the contents by heart.

"We think so. Alondra Escobar. Twenty-three. Undocumented from Venezuela."

"How was she found?"

"Let's see." She scanned down the page quickly and pointed to a spot. "Workers found her in a swampy field way out by Clear Lake. They were breaking ground on a private road that was being put in. If not for that road, it might have been years before she was found, if at all. There are still a fair number of gators in that area."

"Was she reported missing by anyone?"

"No. She was the perfect victim. No one who knew she was missing was ever going to go to the cops. Typical first victim for someone looking to get his feet wet, but after that, he only ever killed one other prostitute."

"That you know of."

Stephanie frowned. "You think there are other victims?"

Robert shook his head and leaned his huge frame across the desk. "No. I think there was a smart hooker."

CHAPTER TWENTY-SIX

Robert spent the better part of the next hour explaining his theory to Stephanie, who absorbed the information without judgment, nodding as the pieces came together. It wasn't as clear cut as Stephanie had hoped, but something was there. Where there had been only jumbled chaos, a pattern emerged.

"All along, you've been looking for one continuous pattern that fit all the girls, one thing that connected them. And the whole time you've come up empty, we've assumed it's because you just couldn't find the connection."

"Right," Stephanie agreed. "That's how it's always done. There's always a connection with serial killers. You think there isn't one?" She frowned. It was hard to explain to Robert, but serial killers simply weren't jihadists. They didn't change patterns to suit a new objective or to cover their tracks. They killed in predictable ways and for predictable reasons.

Robert shook his head. "No, there's a pattern, but it was hard to find because it wasn't just one. I think he had several patterns, like a progression of women he thought deserved his wrath. But as he acted out his plan, it wasn't solving whatever problem he thought he saw, so he progressed to different victims he thought were a better fit. One thing always stayed the same though. He always killed in threes."

"Like three women at once? Time of death on some of these girls rules that out."

It felt morbid, but Robert couldn't help smiling at his discovery. "Not three at a time—three of a kind. He started with prostitutes and then worked his way up."

"Um, no offense, Robert, but if that were true, we'd have three prostitutes among the victims." As she spoke the words, she realized what Robert must be thinking, and she shared his smile. His words resonated in her mind—*a smart hooker*. "We do, don't we?"

Robert grabbed one of the stacks of files and handed it to Stephanie. "I think so. I think one of our students was earning her tuition money the hard way."

Stephanie looked over the files quickly, trying to guess which one Robert had in mind. Nothing stood out. "Which one is she?"

Robert shrugged. "No idea. Not my area of expertise, but you'll find her if you dig hard enough. There are three. Some part of me or him or … well, one of us is sure of it anyway. I don't know how I'm sure, but I'm right about this."

Stephanie grimaced slightly. Going on hunches was a part of police work, but this was something else. On the other hand, this kind of insight was exactly why she'd asked him stay on and help.

Robert sensed her hesitation. "You're going to need to trust me on this one. It's like with the Bible verses. I don't know how I know, but I am sure of what I know."

"Okay, but even if you're right, none of the other killings comes in threes. There are thirteen victims, first of all. Second, that would leave four students, four exotic dancers, one priest, and one drifter. No groups of three."

Robert shook his head. "I think we're just classifying them

wrong. Look at one of the dancers, Heather Gillespie. She was also a student, and she was the only dancer who wasn't reported missing after a shift at work. He chose her as a student, not as a dancer. He didn't know."

"Fine. Three prostitutes and three dancers, but if you count her as a student, you're back to five students and a priest. You think he counted the priest as a student somehow?"

"I doubt it. He's pretty careful about the women he chooses, and he wouldn't break this pattern of threes."

Stephanie was growing impatient. "What then?"

Robert rubbed the back of his head, trying to coax an idea out of it. "What were the girls studying?"

Stephanie again found and opened the correct folders and began reading. "Pre-dentistry, business, divinity, English, and world religions. You think maybe there's a connection between the priest and the divinity and world religions majors?"

Robert tugged at an ear as he thought. "Got to be. Maybe he wasn't breaking the pattern with those two. Maybe he was just being proactive. If you check, I bet you anything they were about to graduate. Think about it. He didn't see them as students. He saw them as religious authority figures in the making and one who was already there. And my guess is that he killed them last."

Stephanie scanned the files to confirm times of death. Sure enough, these were the most recent killings. "How'd you know?"

"I think it's his pecking order. He started with the women he saw as the most obvious problem, like prostitutes and strippers, but after a while, he moved on to women who were doing damage to society in other ways."

Stephanie saw it then. "He started with women who were using their bodies to get by."

"And moved on to ones who were using their minds, like students," he agreed. "Finally, he went after women who dared to become priests or other religious figures. I think he really believes he's doing God's work." Robert began flipping through the files, searching them for clues that might confirm his suspicions.

Stephanie leaned back in her chair and watched him work. He'd have made an A+ detective if things had worked out differently for him. Maybe it wasn't too late. A lot of guys left the service and joined the force. He'd even make a good partner, a thought she'd never had about anyone before. Though she couldn't say why, the realization that her desire to partner with him might be driven by more than his excellent detective work bothered her more than it should have. She shook the thought off and concentrated again on the case.

"There's still a problem, you know," she pointed out.

"The drifter," he agreed. "That one's an anomaly, but there are a million explanations for that. His father wouldn't have necessarily found out about the killings just as he completed a cycle of three, for example."

"Maybe," Stephanie grudgingly acknowledged. She didn't like loose ends like victims who didn't fit an established pattern, but there was nothing to be done about it at the moment. "Okay, so for the moment, we forget about the drifter. The important thing is, we have a pattern. You're pretty sure he's going to start with a prostitute again?"

"Or he already has. It would make sense. Like you said, a lot of them are the perfect victims. No one reports them missing, and their circle of friends doesn't exactly run to the police."

Stephanie thought it over. She wasn't quite as convinced as Robert that the pattern would repeat itself, but it was at least something. "Okay, it's a place to start, and you're the one who understands him best. I'll put the word out, and you and I can take a drive to some of the most likely areas, maybe talk to a few of the girls."

Robert and Stephanie rose in tandem to begin their new search, but before either could get away from Stephanie's desk, an officer approached and acknowledged them before handing Stephanie a folded note and taking his leave.

Robert watched closely as Stephanie quickly unfolded and scanned the small slip of paper. Her brows furrowed as she read the report.

"What is it?" Robert asked.

"It's from Captain Bates. Some guy was at the zoo harassing women. He's already gone, but he tried to get a young woman to leave with him. Got pretty angry when she said no." She collected her keys and a notepad from her desk and gestured for him to do likewise with his cup. "I'm going to find out what Bullet wants, and then you and I are heading to the zoo."

"You really think it could be him?"

"There's only one way to find out."

CHAPTER TWENTY-SEVEN

Stephanie knocked only once before pushing open the doctor's door and squeezing in her head. Dr. Burns waved her in and gestured to one of his chairs. Something about his demeanor told Stephanie that this was a more serious conversation than she had been hoping for.

"You look worried."

A quick grunt escaped his lips before he could turn up one corner of his mouth. "That's because I am. I am extremely worried, actually. About Robert, and, therefore, about you."

Stephanie had assumed as much. "Because he said he's doing better?"

"Exactly. You remember that I told you he possessed the killer's emotions as well as his own, or at least that he could remember how the killer felt?"

Stephanie didn't try to disguise when she let her eyes roll back. She tried to remember how many times she'd given the same look to her father. Of course, she realized, on most of those occasions, he'd usually been right.

"Fine. Then what do you think it means that he no longer

has his own feelings of shame and guilt over those deaths? And has he mentioned whether he retained the positive emotions the killer had?"

Stephanie had tried not to consider this possibility since Robert had as much as told her this was the case back at her apartment. She knew what it implied. As much as she wanted to believe the opposite, the connection between Robert and the killer was somehow strengthening. It made sense now that Robert had been certain about the victims the second time they had reviewed them after having felt nothing the first time.

"You needn't bother answering, you know. I can see that you share my concern."

"Of course I'm concerned!" she snapped. "And you didn't have to call me in here like some child who's in trouble at school. You could have said these things in front of him."

Dr. Burns leaned forward across his desk and held Stephanie's gaze as only he could do. "Do you feel better now?"

She said nothing.

"Pouting does not become you, my dear. And, as a matter of fact, I could not have this discussion in front of him because I don't want him to know I am aware of the change. Robert is a very intelligent man, but he's also very guarded. I want him relaxed enough to share whatever he wishes without worrying about what it reveals about him. I know you trust him, and I don't ask lightly, but please do not reveal to him the details of our conversation. At least not for now."

He sat back in his chair and let Stephanie think over his request. She knew it was for Robert's own good, and she trusted Dr. Burns completely, but she didn't like the idea of, for lack of a better word, investigating Robert while he was helping her catch a murderer.

"The guilt might be unpleasant, but it really is the only way I can help him for now. That, and for you to report to me whatever he tells you."

Stephanie slowly nodded her consent and thanked Dr. Burns for his concern and his candor. As she walked out to join Robert at her car, however, it was not Dr. Burns' words that she remembered; it was Stephen Hennerman's—*"It turns out that people need a certain amount of shame in their lives to keep them on the straight and narrow. We found that removing that burden often changed people's personalities—and not for the better."*

CHAPTER TWENTY-EIGHT

"I told the other officers everything already, but I'll be glad to tell you again if you think it will help."

Though she had known David, or whoever he turned out to be, would be gone, Stephanie had still driven quickly, even by her standards. As expected, by the time they had reached the zoo, the suspect had indeed long since fled, leaving behind only a badly rattled, but cooperative, intended victim.

"Thank you. It really would," Stephanie assured her while producing her phone. The young woman was upset but there were no signs of any obvious trauma. Her information was likely to be about as accurate as eye-witnesses ever were. Of course, if she knew just what David would probably have done to her if he had succeeded in grabbing her, she might well be having a different reaction. "Just start from the beginning and tell us everything you can remember, no matter how trivial it might seem. I'm going to record everything so I can review it later if that's okay, Miss …?"

"Emily Hinds," she answered, swallowing against the dryness in her throat despite the half-empty bottle of water she held. "I was just standing here watching the people go past the enclosures.

I'm an art student at U of H, photography mainly. I was scouting the zoo for a possible shoot for an upcoming project. Anyway, I was standing by myself when this guy approached me and said hi, but, like, not in a normal way." Emily paused to raise the bottle to her lips. She'd made it halfway when she lowered it and began speaking again as if she needed to repeat what had happened before it could slip away. "Right away, my radar went off. He was strange. You could just tell he wasn't wired right somehow."

"How do you mean?" Stephanie asked.

Emily rubbed her arms as if trying to ward off a chill. Stephanie glanced at her phone. It was 96 degrees, and the humidity made certain that you felt every degree of it and then some.

"I'm not sure. Like, at first, I just thought maybe I was overreacting or something. He was strange, but he was trying to be friendly, at least I think. I didn't know if he was hitting on me or if he was just special in some way, you know?"

"You thought maybe he was mentally handicapped?" Stephanie clarified. "Why?"

"Well, he was all smiles and everything when he approached me, but you could see how nervous he was. Then, right away he starts rambling about the weirdest stuff. He kept talking about his father and about how I'd never meet him. He got really pissed then, too. The weirdest part was when he told me that I needed to go with him somewhere. He didn't even ask me to leave with him. He just told me that it was time to go and that I'd be safe with him forever. Then he started talking about his dad again. He was all over the place. I tried to tell him nicely that I didn't want to go with him, but …"

"But he didn't take the hint?" Stephanie guessed.

Emily was chewing one corner of her lower lip. She had been more scared than she was letting on, Stephanie guessed. "Worse. He understood perfectly, and he flipped out. Thank God he started screaming at me. A crowd formed pretty quickly then. He tried to pull me away with him, but I managed to get my arm free. By then, there were tons of people, so he ran off, and somebody went and got security. A few minutes later, there were cops here asking the same questions you are. That was it."

Stephanie followed up with more questions until she had enough information to be reasonably certain that the man who had accosted Emily was David Mead. Only then did she produce a photo for the witness. The hair was different she said, but she was pretty certain it was the same man. Stephanie would check the zoo security footage they were emailing her in order to verify it later, but she had more than enough to know it was him.

"What does this do for my he's-going-to-start-with-a-hooker theory?" Robert asked on the way back to Stephanie's car. Police were continuing the search for David in the unlikely event that he had stuck around the zoo, but Stephanie had more pressing business.

"Nothing. Only a tiny percentage of sexual assaults are ever reported, and those are the successful ones. Who knows how many failed attempts go unreported? Besides, as far as we know, he tried to pick up some random girl but was unsuccessful the last time too. Or maybe that's who the drifter was—the warm up act. Until we know for sure or have a better plan, we stay with yours."

Stephanie unlocked the car door, and they slid into their respective seats. Robert gave his seatbelt two extra tugs to make sure it was functioning properly before Stephanie turned over the engine. She shot him a sideways glance and turned the key. "Why does everyone always do that when they ride with me? I'm a good driver. Did you know I've never had one wreck?"

Robert muttered something about all of the other cars in Houston being alerted to her presence by now and then spent the next several minutes rubbing the sore spot on his left arm.

"Where do we search first? Even if he does go after a hooker, there's no telling when or where he'll do that. And what about a place to stay? Won't he need that? Or maybe he's looking to get out of town now? We've still got way more questions than answers," he complained.

"And we have way more answers today than we had yesterday, so no whining. As far as him leaving town, I doubt it. If he didn't hit the road the instant he broke out of his father's jail, I don't think he'll leave at all. Plus, as Bullet could probably tell you, I doubt he's aware he's done anything wrong beyond offend some confused girl. Once he escaped the zoo, he had no reason to keep running."

"And what about the rest?"

"Well, you're right about the place to stay. He has no friends, and I assume he has only a little money. He'll sleep on the streets, or he'll have to find a cheap hotel. Either way, his field of play is going to get a lot smaller a whole lot quicker than he realizes. We're going to get him, Robert. Soon, I swear. And if we can't, you aren't going to have to keep those memories, okay?"

"I'm sure you're right," Robert murmured. He noticed she had been wound tight ever since she had left Dr. Burns' office. He had wanted to ask what they had discussed, or, more precisely, who, but he was pretty sure he knew the answer. No need to make things awkward for her by pressing. "Where are we going anyway? Shouldn't we have stayed behind and interviewed other witnesses or whatever?"

Stephanie's head shook hard enough to send strands of her brown hair dancing back and forth. "There's no reason. We already know who we're looking for. Unless you think he yelled his destination out to one of the patrons back there, we can't gain anything by looking where he's already been. We need to change directions."

Robert feigned surprise. "I honestly didn't know we had a direction we could change from. What did you have in mind now?"

Stephanie revved the engine on her Ford Mustang and threw the car into drive, pressing them both back into their seats. The tires squealed slightly and gravel rained down on the asphalt from the rear tires as the car shot forward. "When you're at a crossroads in life, you sometimes have to make tough choices. The way I see it, we either need to find religion or a prostitute. Which one do you want to try first?"

Robert placed his hand protectively over his sore arm and stared straight ahead. "Easy choice. The way you drive, I'm always ready to find religion."

CHAPTER TWENTY-NINE

"I thought we were going to see a priest," Robert complained a short time later from his usual spot next to Stephanie's desk.

"We are," she said, indicating the department's laptop Robert had been assigned. "Robert, meet Father Google. He knows everything, and he doesn't give me a hard time for missing the last few hundred masses."

Robert groaned. "Seriously, why don't we just offload this to a real priest and move on to something better, like looking for David." Since Stephanie had told Robert they were going to go back to the drawing board on the Bible verses, he had been less than enthusiastic. In truth, a part of her would rather have been searching for him as well, but her instinct told her to keep Robert off of the street and away from David if she could. She also had no idea where to begin searching unless she was willing to cruise every seedy part of town for the right lady of the evening at the same time that David happened to. She'd have better luck waiting on him to walk in the station the way his father had.

"We are looking for him. These verses are the only loose end we have," Stephanie had insisted. "And the department doesn't really keep any Biblical scholars on the payroll, so keep looking. If we find something, we'll call a priest."

Robert sat back and appraised Stephanie as she worked. He looked over her profile, the way her jawline sloped down to her long, graceful neck. She was beautiful from any angle, but Robert had never noticed this one before because of Stephanie's habit of always looking him in the eye—something she was carefully avoiding doing at the moment.

"You don't want me to go out," he said through gritted teeth.

Stephanie tried to look puzzled. "What are you talking about? We were just out."

He tilted his chair back on two legs and grinned, though he found the situation far from funny. "Yeah, but you didn't expect to actually find David. We got close, and it scared you. You're afraid of how I'll react if I see him." He waited for Stephanie to look up from her computer, a gesture she had no intention of giving him the satisfaction of. "Say it," he added.

Stephanie growled and looked up. "Fine. I'm afraid of what might happen when you see him, but I'm willing to risk it if it means saving more women. Not to mention you. And anyway, the greater Houston area is over 10,000 square miles. How much difference do you think adding one more car to the manhunt is really going to make? The uniforms can look for him just as well as we can." She jerked her head back down to her computer and began pecking one at a time at the keys there. Each tap was much louder than she intended, but she wasn't about to adjust anything for Robert's sake.

He sighed. He hated it, but she was right. He was far more comfortable engaging the enemy in the field, especially now that the enemy had a face, but there was no need to run off and play cops and robbers when the real police were already doing all they could. He looked down again at the quotations he had by now memorized. "These are all about death, just like I told you after I wrote them," Robert offered as an oblation." But that's all I know."

Stephanie was silent for a moment longer. Dr. Burns was right about her, she decided. Petulance didn't become her. "That's what I get when I read them too, but there are probably lots of verses about death in the Bible. He specifically chose these three. There has to be a reason. Plus, they showed up in your brain when nothing else did, so they're worth at least looking at again."

The argument settled, they commenced exhausting every search engine tool they could think of. Hours and, in Robert's case, mugs of coffee, slowly were consumed before he came across something that caught his eye. "Check this out," he told Stephanie. "You remember reading about that guy Manasseh from that Isaiah verse?"

Stephanie slid her chair over next to his and peered at his computer screen. "I think so. Some ancient king, right?" she asked as she read.

He nodded. "That's the one. Get this. In Hebrew, his name means, 'causing to forget'. Any chance that's a coincidence given what his father was trying to do to him? And according to this, he had quite the checkered past, just like our boy. First, he was co-king of Judah along with his father for ten years before taking over when his dad died. I never heard of having two kings at the same time. Second, it says here he was imprisoned for some reason by some other high king."

Stephanie recalled reading some background about Manasseh, but nothing about an imprisonment. "Does it say what for?"

"Nope. There are theories, but no one knows for sure. What it does say though is that after his imprisonment, he changed his ways and embraced God. He was restored to his throne, and he had the longest reign of any king of Judah."

Stephanie scanned all of the information as Robert read it. "Okay, so what does any of that mean, and is it relevant to our case?"

"I'm not sure exactly, but there are some coincidences here, don't you think? The imprisonment thing for one. David was locked up, and he doesn't know why. Maybe he felt a connection there, maybe something so strong that it got passed on to me when it wasn't supposed to. Second, once he got out, he repented and everything was great for him. Maybe that's what David wants, or at least what he knows his father wants."

Stephanie could see where Robert was going. It was obvious now, she thought. The only reason she had missed it the first time she searched was because she hadn't known David was a prisoner.

"I don't know what it proves by itself," Stephanie said. "But the connection *is* too strong to be a coincidence. Still, I doubt Manasseh killed a bunch of prostitutes, did he?"

Robert gave a half-shrug. "Maybe. I mean, if he was on the outs with God and then came back in the fold to be king again, it's not hard to believe he sacrificed something pretty special. Not hookers, but definitely something big. This isn't your run-of-the-mill kill the fatted calf kind of thing, I'm guessing."

"And you think these prostitutes might be David's sacrifice for his deliverance?" Something in the way Stephanie asked the question told Robert she didn't agree. What had he missed?

"But that doesn't make sense, does it?" He looked at Stephanie and could see in her eyes what he had just reasoned for himself. "The timeline is off. Why would David relate to Manasseh if he only got locked up *after* he made all of his sacrifices? If Manasseh did it at all, he did it after he was set free." Robert ran his hands through his hair and tapped the heels of both feet against the polished concrete floor.

"It fits perfectly otherwise. I don't get it. How can everything else fit together except this one piece?" Robert reached over and picked up a printed sheet from the desk and read, "Those for death to death. And I'm telling you, Stephanie, I can *feel* it somehow—

this relationship between David and his father is seriously screwed up. Respect is right at the heart of it, too. It's critical somehow."

Stephanie thought it over. They'd need to find an explanation for the disparity in the timeline for the Manasseh thing to be an exact fit. Otherwise, though, it all made perfect sense. Why then, she wondered, did she keep asking herself about the damned timeline?

"So David was doing this all for his father, and his father was doing everything he could to stop him," she said. "Shit, I didn't think this case could get sadder."

Robert sighed. "In a strange way, the saddest part may be that David is never going to get to explain all this to his dad. I don't think it counts for much in his mind unless he gets to present it all to him like some kind of trophy." Robert shook his head while he traced circles with his index finger around the rim of his coffee mug.

Stephanie immediately sat up in her chair and gaped at Robert. *How the hell did I miss it?*

"What?" he asked. "Are you okay?"

Stephanie rattled off something that sounded vaguely like, "I'm fine," and continued to think for a moment longer. She needed to be certain before she said it out loud.

"I think you're right about him wanting to see his father."

"And the fact that I'm right about something has thrown you for this much of a loop?"

Stephanie leaned forward and grabbed Robert's wrist. She stared straight into his eyes, which were only inches from her own. "You're not getting what I'm saying. He's going to see his dad at some point. If we can't get to him before, we can at least pick him up when he's done and goes to report his good deeds. Like you said, the trophy doesn't count unless he can show it off to the old man."

Robert leaned back a bit and scratched his head. "I'm probably missing something, but if he only goes to Dad once he's killed a bunch of women again, won't that be a tad bit late for our purposes?"

Stephanie scowled and pushed her chair back to its original spot where a dark cloud had seemingly formed in order to rain on her pending parade. "Better than not at all," she growled. "But I get your point. What if," she offered, her bright mood returning as quickly as it had gone, "we can force his hand a bit? After all, he's got no money and no place to stay." She was reaching. She could only hope it didn't show.

"How? It's not like you can convince him that he's killed a bunch of women when he hasn't." Robert slammed the brakes on his train of thought. "Except that he *has* killed a bunch of women, hasn't he? He just doesn't remember it. You think you can convince him of what he's done in the past and make it seem new?"

Stephanie threw herself against her own seatback. "Probably not, but Mead might be able to. If we get him to go to the media, David's bound to see it at some point. With no money, no friends, and just a little luck, maybe he'll head straight home."

"The place he just escaped?" Robert asked.

Stephanie waved off the idea. "You said it yourself, he has to go home at some point or none of this counts. I'm just gambling we can move the clock ahead before any more damage gets done."

"Well, it's better than sitting here waiting for him to kill again. Think you can convince Mead to do it? The way you described it before, he's sitting pretty from a legal standpoint. Doesn't sound like you have a lot of leverage."

Stephanie smiled. "Leverage comes in all kinds of forms."

Robert was no fan of Mead. Neither though did he want Stephanie feeling pressured to do this on his behalf. Ultimately though, this was her case. Anyway, he decided, one of the things you have to love about Stephanie Monroe, nobody makes her do anything she doesn't want to. He looked at his watch. It was late, but maybe that was better. "Want head over there now?"

She thought it over before deciding against it. "I'd like to, but we're both exhausted. I want to be in top form when I question that son of a bitch, and I could use some time to form my game plan for this interview. Come on," she said, rising. "You can crash on my sofa again."

Robert hesitated for just a second before rising. "That sounds great, but you know I can go back to my place now. You can just put one of your uniformed buddies with me. If you don't want me at your place, I mean."

Stephanie detected just a hint of scarlet rising in his cheeks. It was incredibly, awkwardly cute.

"No," she lied before she had time to think about why she did so. "I doubt I could get an officer on such short notice. You can stay with me one more night. As long as you promise to be a good boy, what's the worst that could happen?"

CHAPTER THIRTY

It took his eyes several moments to adjust to the ink-black space. His ears picked up the familiar sound of the clock ticking the seconds away from down the hall but otherwise detected only silence. Everything was as it should be. He had been in the apartment enough times when she wasn't home to know his way in the dark, though he did pause by her bed when he entered the room, not to gain his bearings but to savor the moment. This was, after all, the only time he had ever killed a girl in the dark.

Ideally, he'd have the lights on so he could see her face as she transitioned out. Equally, he'd prefer her to see his, to see the appreciation he held for her. But he was no fool, and there were times when aesthetic considerations must be traded for caution. She was beautiful and intelligent and all the things he always looked for in one of his girls, but she was also very dangerous. She could just as easily send him from this world as he could send her, so the lights would stay off. When she woke, it would be to the exquisite agony of his hands crushing her throat. That was his favorite part, of course, that intimate moment that can only be achieved between two people when one is squeezing the life from the other, his hands wrapped firmly and lovingly around her throat. He reached for her as he smiled to himself.

"Robert! Wake up!"

Robert's eyes snapped open as a brilliant, overhead light flashed on and equal parts panic and confusion flooded him. His heart was a machine gun inside his chest. His eyes adjusted to the light and took in his surroundings. Somehow, he was standing in Stephanie's bedroom. She was looking up at him from her bed, obviously frightened and as confused as he was. He took a long step back and looked down at his outstretched hands. He had been dreaming about something ...

"Robert, what the hell are you doing in here?"

He put up his hands apologetically and shook his head. "I ... I don't know. I'm not even sure how I got in here. I'm so sorry."

Stephanie eyed him carefully. He was more frightened than she was. That much was obvious, but of what? She had been sleeping soundly when she had heard a strange noise in her room and had reached for her clock to check the time. When she did, she had just made out the silhouette of someone in her room. Immediately, she had flipped on the light and retrieved her personal weapon from its hiding place behind her headboard. When she saw it was Robert, she had stashed the gun under her covers and begun shouting to him to wake up.

"I think I was sleep walking," he mumbled.

Stephanie could see that he wasn't sure he believed what he said any more than she was supposed to believe it. Her sister, Caroline, was a sleep walker, and she had never looked the way Robert had just then. It was hard to explain, but Caroline had always seemed herself, just out of touch with reality. Admittedly, she had seen him for only a few seconds, but Robert's body language was all wrong. He had held himself differently, and the look on his face was almost gleeful. Robert was a lot of things, but giddy wasn't one of them.

"Sleep walking? Is that something you do? You've never mentioned it."

"I don't know for sure. Not that I know of, except for the night I wrote out the Bible verses at my apartment." He remembered suddenly what he had been dreaming about when the lights had come on, and, more importantly, who he had been dreaming about. He took another step toward the door. "Stephanie, I'm so sorry, but I was having one of my dreams, and I think I was acting it out or something. I'm so sorry," he repeated. His face and palms were clammier than he could ever remember them being, even during heavy action on the front lines, and his heart was still hammering in his chest.

"Robert, it's okay. Nothing bad happened. It was just a close call. You'd probably have woken up on your own anyway." Stephanie was not at all sure that would have been the case, but Robert was obviously in bad shape over the episode and needed reassuring. "Look, it's nearly morning anyway. Why don't I put on some coffee, and you and I can get an early start on the day? What do you say?" She was appealing to far more than his love of coffee, and he knew it. One look at Robert, and she knew that this case needed more than ever to get resolved quickly. Leaving him with those memories simply wasn't an option much longer.

Robert nodded. He was, at least, thankful he would not have to return to sleep anytime soon. "Thanks, and, again, I'm so—"

"Sorry. I know. It's okay, really. Now, go rinse your face off while I make some coffee. You look like hell."

CHAPTER THIRTY-ONE

The morning was a strange one as both Stephanie and Robert attempted to ignore what had happened and prepare for the day. The pall of what he had nearly done hung over the apartment, clinging to everything and making even normal conversation difficult, but with enough coffee and awkward jokes, they were able to restore at least some semblance of normalcy and move on as scheduled. Robert had assumed that the correct course of action would be to run up the chain of command and notify Stephanie's boss about the next step in what seemed to him an increasingly unorthodox plan, but Stephanie had no such intentions.

"Better to ask for forgiveness than permission," she told him on the way to Mead's house. "Especially when I'm not planning on taking no for an answer. Not after last night," she added.

Robert thought it over and decided that he was inclined, at least in this case, to agree. Lawrence Mead was almost as responsible for the deaths of those girls as David Mead was. Whatever means Stephanie intended to employ to get him to talk would probably pale in comparison to some of the things he'd done back in Iraq. Still, he was a bit apprehensive about the coming interview. He wasn't at all sure how he would react to meeting the architect of this private hell he had found himself in.

Stephanie could see the worry in the way Robert held himself, and she knew it was more than just his usual nervousness at being in the passenger seat of her car. "I wish I could tell you that you could sit this one out if you wanted to, plausible deniability and all, but I think I'm going to need you for this to work. You going to be okay?"

Robert clutched the sides of his seat cushions and tried not to look at the road. "Hey, in for a penny and all that, but I do hope you realize that I'm not sure how well I'm going to handle seeing him."

Stephanie had considered little else over the last hour. It was risky. Anything could happen when the two met, and no one would be more aware of that than Mead.

"If it matters," she offered, "I wouldn't bring you along if I didn't think you could handle it. Still, if it's too much to ask, I'll find another way."

"I'll be fine," he insisted with a confidence that was hard to come by, especially with Stephanie driving. "But, if I do manage to avoid killing him, you can pay for dinner when we finally do get around to our date."

Stephanie swerved quickly to avoid traffic that was moving only slightly faster than the legal limit and saluted the drivers with a pointed gesture as she passed them. Robert's feeble attempt to see if she was still interested in keeping their date was not lost on her, but any promises about the future needed to wait until after the coming confrontation. Her safest bet was to answer his question with a question.

"Haven't I bought you dinner every night for like the last two weeks?"

"Yeah, that was actually the county, and I've ridden in this seat for all that time without ever pulling a citizen's arrest on you for your driving. Plus, I nearly let everyone think I was a homicidal rapist. So there's that on my side of the ledger."

Stephanie took a gamble. "And nearly killing me in my sleep?" She refused to look at him now for fear of losing her battle to keep a straight face.

Robert turned away sheepishly to stare out the front windshield. "So we'll go Dutch, then?"

Twenty minutes later, they pulled alongside one of the marked patrol cars that took turns outside of Mead's residence. Mead had an ankle monitor, but the D.A. felt a little extra precaution was more than worthwhile due to the host of technophiles and computer geeks to which Mead had ready access. The patrol was more than happy to take a coffee break and had asked no questions when told not to rush it. Robert smiled. Apparently, the code of silence that existed between soldiers applied to cops as well.

Mead's home, Robert noted as they approached the door, was a lesser mansion but a mansion nonetheless. In true southern style, there were white columns and an expansive front porch with a pair of simple white rocking chairs off to one side of the door. They appeared comfortable, welcoming, and, most of all, purely ornate. Robert suspected that Mead did not welcome guests to stop by and rock away an evening on the front porch while he tended to his homicidal offspring in the basement.

Stephanie ignored the bell and rapped sharply on the door with the butt of her police baton. She then removed her badge from her belt and flashed it impatiently at a small camera lens hidden just above the doorframe. Robert begrudged that Stephanie was either very good or he was out of practice as he had not noticed the device. Then again, very few of the buildings he had entered in the Middle East had had electricity, much less home security. Unless you counted the improvised explosive devices that often greeted him and his men on their raids. Either way, it was a good catch on her part.

After a brief wait that felt longer for the heat, the door opened unceremoniously to reveal a haggard looking Dr. Lawrence Mead. Gone was the refined man with his regal bearing and his team of high-priced sycophant lawyers from only thirty-six hours ago. In his place was a tired man, a beaten man, whose clothes, a simple blue and white tracksuit that rose up at the ankle to reveal his blinking monitor, hung loosely on his sagging frame. Judging by the faint and all too familiar smell, Robert thought they might have seen more than one day's use. Mead offered no welcome or other comment. He simply moved out of the way and dragged himself to the parlor. His guests would follow him or not. It was clear he did not care which.

"Dr. Mead?" Stephanie asked, following him to the small chamber just off the entry. "Are you okay, sir?"

Mead ignored the question until he had taken a seat in a recliner that seemed to have molded itself to his shape from frequent use and then looked at Stephanie through glassy eyes. He stared at her openly, but if he saw Robert at all, he gave no indication.

He finally spoke. "My dear Detective, why ever would you ask that? Everything is going swimmingly. I am under house arrest, my wife and daughter have left town, and most of the contents of my bank accounts seem to have followed them. Oh, and my company is soon to be in absolute ruins. Don't forget that part."

Stephanie refused to pity him, and if Robert did so, it was only enough to consider putting him out of his misery. "I hope they're okay, Doctor, but you can cut the crap. Anyone crafty enough to hide an entire room in his house from his wife surely has a few bank accounts stashed around that she knows nothing about. And if you're going to spend your time worrying about your family members, there's a different one I'd focus my energies on."

Mead inclined his head almost imperceptibly and then waved them to a love seat opposite his own chair. "Indeed. Forgive my manners. Have a seat, both of you. You've clearly come here for some purpose beyond taking stock of my well-being. Let's hear it, and then you can do me the courtesy of removing yourselves."

They obliged him without protest or thanks. The loveseat they shared was something out a Victorian era novel, both small and rigid. She would be forced to look ever so slightly up at Mead when they spoke. It was the kind of furniture a man who wanted to make his guests ill-at-ease might have. But Stephanie was planning on busting his balls hard enough already without quibbling over seating arrangements. "Dr. Mead, I'm here for your help. As you know, you've caused a problem, a big one, and I think you can do something to help fix it."

"It's nice of you to ask, Detective—" Mead began before Stephanie cut him off. Her voice was cold steel.

"But, you see, I'm not asking, Doctor. The thing is, we found your son yesterday. At least for a minute." Stephanie waited for a response she knew was unlikely to come. Mead was speechless and appeared largely impassive, but Stephanie knew it was mostly shock that held his tongue. She could see the vein in his temple suddenly throb as he took in the news. "I see you appreciate the gravity of this. We were close to having him. Very close. It was at the zoo, by the way. Tried to grab a young woman there and take her away somewhere. We both know what would have happened if he had succeeded. The bodies," Stephanie indicated an imaginary pile with her hand and raised it higher and higher, "would have started piling up already."

Mead refused to make eye contact, settling instead for a barely discernable shaking of his head.

"It's begun again, hasn't it, Doctor? And we both know how it ends. When he's had his fill, he's going to come home to you.

You can say whatever you want in that so-called confession of yours, but you always knew the killings were real." She leaned forward and stared hard at Mead. "You helped hide the bodies, a fact I can pursue or not pursue. It all depends on how the next few minutes go."

Mead knew better than to respond, and Stephanie hadn't really expected him too.

"This time, Doctor, we need him to come home *before* he kills, if he hasn't already. We need you to help us call him in. For his own good, we need you to take advantage of your son one last time. Shouldn't be too hard for a man like you."

Impossibly, Mead sank farther back into his chair, pressed down there by some invisible weight. Invisible, but plain to them all nonetheless. It was the burden of his sins, past and present, Stephanie thought. Mead sighed and gave her a sad, cryptic smile. "Detective, you are certain of so much, and yet you know so little."

Stephanie appraised him coolly. "Are you saying he won't come if you call him?"

He reached up and began massaging his temples slowly. "It doesn't matter. I'm not going to do it. I couldn't even if I wanted to. I have no idea where he is, except probably not at the zoo," he said, smiling sarcastically, "and I can promise you he will not come home until he feels his work is done."

"Agreed," Stephanie said. "Which is why you are going to help me convince him that it is."

He sat up. Against his will, Mead's curiosity had been piqued. "How would you go about that?"

Stephanie shook her head. "Nuh uh. Not me."

Mead pointed a quaking finger at himself. "Seriously? Why don't I just arrest him too while I'm at it? You do know that I'm the one who pointed you to him in the first place, right? What have you two accomplished while I've been doing my civic duty?"

Stephanie felt Robert's weight shifting up off of the sofa in Mead's direction. She placed a steadying hand on his thigh. His muscles were taught as iron, but his face showed none of the rage he felt. Years of practice interviewing the worst kinds of bad guys, Stephanie reasoned, had taught him to keep his cool. It had been enough though for Mead to see it, and he was as relieved that Stephanie had intervened as he had been scared when Robert had moved.

"Thank you for keeping him on a leash. For a moment there …" Mead started, but he never finished.

As she had calmed Robert, Stephanie had withdrawn the collapsible baton she had used on the door earlier and extended it to its full length. She made a show of testing its heft in her hand and then swung it sharply in a small arc that stopped only when the tip of the rod met the inside of Mead's left knee and found it could move no farther. She appeared to Robert to have used hardly any force at all. Except for snapping her wrist, she had barely moved. The effect of the blow, however, looked as if it couldn't have been greater if she had swung a Louisville Slugger with both hands and a running start.

Mead's head immediately snapped back as his face formed an awful grimace, and although no sound emerged, his mouth formed a distorted oval. He went white with agony, and his hands reached down and clasped the injury in a futile attempt to stem the pain. He looked as if he might be sick at any moment, and Robert couldn't blame him. The crack of steel on bone had made his own stomach lurch despite the fact that he took some private pleasure in Mead's pain.

Ignoring his silent screams, Stephanie leaned farther into Mead and spoke softly. "Listen to me, Dr. Mead. The pain you are experiencing is absolutely nothing compared to what over a dozen women experienced at the hands of a monster you created, a monster you tried to shelter from the justice system and from people who could have tried to help him with real medicine and real science. Do you hear me? It's *nothing* right now, but it will become something very real as soon as I let Robert here—you do remember Mr. Grayson, the man you tried to frame for your son's murders? Good. Where was I? Oh, yes—the pain you are experiencing is nothing compared to what Mr. Grayson would like to do to you. And I plan on letting him do every one of those things unless you become very cooperative in the next couple of seconds. Do you understand?"

Mead had not yet found his voice, but his expression spoke volumes as he glared at Stephanie through pain-soaked eyes. Stephanie understood the unspoken message and raised her baton meaningfully. Mead's eyes widened and he quickly relented, nodding furiously at her before she could strike again.

Stephanie smiled and collapsed the weapon, returning it to its holster on the back of her belt. "That's much better. Now, what's going to happen is that you are going to convince your son of the truth about what he did. You're going to record it, and I'm going to help you get that message out to the world. We're going to broadcast it so widely there will be no way David could miss it. Then he's going to come to you the way he always does. Understand?"

"You … you want me to go on record as saying that I helped my son cover up murders?" Mead groaned. "You know I can't do that. I'd go to prison for the rest of my life."

Stephanie nodded emphatically. "As well you should, Doctor. I still very much hope that happens to you, but that is secondary to my desire to find your son. For the time being, we'll agree that you don't have to admit anything you did specifically. You'll just say what happened, not that you did it."

Despite his agony, Mead was clearly struggling to decide.

Stephanie understood his trepidation, but she had neither the time nor the inclination to indulge him.

"Doctor, as you may know, it takes twenty pounds of force to break a human knee cap, a little more when the force is applied laterally as it was in your case. I hit you with about half that much. Half," she repeated. "Care to try for the full twenty on the other knee? I won't quite break it, but you won't really be able to tell the difference. And don't forget that Mr. Grayson still gets his turn as well. In his condition, I don't think he's capable of showing the kind of restraint that I have today."

Mead looked over at Robert, who glared menacingly at him, and addressed him for the first time through gritted teeth. "I'm sorry for what happened to you, Mr. Grayson. For what I did, I should say. But I've been in your head. I know your mind nearly as well as you do. Are you seriously trying to tell me that you're the bad cop?"

Robert stood slowly and approached Mead, towering silently over him. There were many things he'd have liked to have told the doctor, but none of them could have had the effect that his hulking presence was having. Mead made the point moot by cowering back into his chair and casting his gaze away from Robert's own and down to the floor.

"No, Dr. Mead," Stephanie answered softly for him. "I'm still the bad cop, at least where you're concerned. And I'm not even pissed off yet. Mr. Grayson here is the trained killer whom you tried to have put to death by lethal injection, courtesy of the state of Texas and my office. He's the man who, if he decided to kill you right now, has the built-in insanity defense that you created when you scrambled his brain. He's the man whom no self-respecting Texas juror could ever find guilty, no matter what he did to you. And, as for me, I take your security tapes with me when I go, and I was never here. So, which of us are you more comfortable pissing off right now?"

Mead had no choice, and he knew it. He nodded reluctantly through the pain.

"Excellent," Stephanie said, her voice syrupy sweet and her face beaming. "Let's get started then."

CHAPTER THIRTY-TWO

Stephanie's plan, such as it was, went off without any major difficulties or further instances of police brutality. Mead recorded what Stephanie wanted him to, although he did insist on using his own wording on the basis that if the message didn't sound authentic, David wouldn't respond. Stephanie had found it difficult to argue with his logic and had yielded to his one demand after hearing his version of the message. When he finished the recording, Robert and Stephanie listened to it several times.

"David, I know you're lost, you're scared, and you're traveling alone right now. We both know that for some people that can be very dangerous. It's easy to be confused about who your friends are, who you should trust. But you can trust me, David. I know you have work you think you need to accomplish before you can truly come home, but you don't need to worry about any of that. Because of you, it's all taken care of. You've done what you needed to do. If you come in now, I can explain everything. We can start all over again. Let's just go back to the beginning, and I can make it right this time. I promise you, son, a new beginning."

It was a little cryptic in places, but then, it wasn't as if he could just say, "Stop killing girls and come home." Mead assured Stephanie that David would understand the message the way it was and respond to it. If not, he would record another one.

Now, all that remained before she could air the message was to have the district attorney and her captain approve it. Gaining the tape without permission was one thing. Letting it see the light of day was quite another. Though there had been more than one raised eyebrow when Stephanie glossed over exactly how she had gone about acquiring Mead's further cooperation, she had eventually gotten the blessing she sought along with a reminder to keep her distance from Mead.

The technical experts, or lab geeks, depending upon whom one asked, immediately went to work posting the video to whatever magical places videos went to become viral. News outlets ran with it on the promise they each would receive exclusive access to the son mentioned in the recording. Stephanie assured them it would be their lead story for a week, a promise they were incapable of ignoring. All the stations teased the video at least three times every hour. It was their lead story with a follow up between weather and sports. By 10:00 p.m. that same night, it was hard to imagine there was a soul within a hundred miles of Houston who hadn't seen the father's plea to his desperate son.

"How long?" Robert asked without elaboration after the nightly news wrapped and Stephanie clicked off the television. Without any discussion of the previous night's events, Robert had accompanied her home to her apartment. He was unsure whether he would remain for the entire evening, and it seemed that the later it got, Stephanie was equally unwilling to broach the topic.

"A day," she shrugged. "Two at the most. I'm on stakeout there starting tomorrow morning. I'm hoping he doesn't show before then."

"So this stakeout," Robert began, but was cut short as Stephanie's phone began an erratic dance across the top of the coffee table. She grabbed it before it could shimmy its way off the edge.

"Don't worry. You don't have to come," she told him as she thumbed the phone alive and answered it.

Robert wanted to tell her that he had not meant that, but he immediately saw that it would have been pointless. Stephanie's attention had turned totally to her phone call. Whatever news she was receiving, it was clearly important. And bad.

"Hold on, Bullet. He's right here. I'm going to put you on speaker."

Stephanie punched a button and laid the phone flat on the coffee table from where she had picked it up a moment before. "Go ahead, Doc."

A tinny voice responded back, speaking faster than Robert could remember him ever doing. "Hello, Robert. Well, as I was just telling Stephanie, I'm afraid I have rather bad news. Your plan to get David to come in out of the cold to his father was well intentioned, but I think there's a problem."

"What?" Robert interjected. "You don't think it'll work?"

"Oh, I'm almost positive that it will work, or at least that David is going to come home at some point. The problem is what he intends to do when he gets there."

"You're killing us here, Doc," Stephanie urged him. "Out with it."

"Well, I went back and looked at those Bible verses again. Something about one of them didn't sit well with me. I just couldn't say which one or why at the time. Today, it finally came to me. It was Isaiah."

"The one about the Manasseh guy? We're way ahead of you, Doc. It was how Robert figured out that he'd go back home again, to make atonement."

"I'm sorry to disagree with you, Robert, but I don't think David wants to atone for anything at all. In fact, I believe it's quite the opposite. He wants to take over for his father. He wants to be the king."

They had the same thought, but it was Robert who spoke first. "And you can't have two kings at the same time."

CHAPTER THIRTY-THREE

Benjamin spent the next several minutes explaining his findings to Robert and Stephanie, who sat huddled around Stephanie's phone, absorbing details and questioning Dr. Burns here and there. He had explained patiently what little he felt would make sense to them, but mostly he reminded them that he was an expert in human behavior and they would simply have to trust him. Basically, David believed the Bible condoned killing. He also believed in a destiny predetermined by God. The first two verses made those findings obvious. It was also this sense of divine destiny that made Bullet so sure that David wanted to eliminate his father.

"It does make more sense than our original theory," Stephanie conceded after Bullet had hung up.

"Probably," Robert agreed. "Your friend is a hell of a lot smarter than I am. I'm just not sure what to believe anymore. Every guess we've made so far has been based on hunches. Even now, he can't really know what David is going to do. Not for sure."

Stephanie nodded. "He would agree. But then that would apply to your theory too, so it just comes down to playing the percentages."

Robert chewed his bottom lip pensively as he thought over Dr. Burns' explanation again. It was an old habit from childhood that he thought he had left far behind him. David, it seemed, was not the only one doomed to repeat the past. Perhaps, he thought, that only reinforced the doctor's idea. *Maybe we all spend our adult lives repeating our childhoods, running from them, or trying to fix the damage done by the ghosts we thought we had left behind,* Robert thought. Certainly, both he and Stephanie fell into one or more of those categories. Dr. Burns had been kind, in Robert's opinion, not to mention that fact as a way to reinforce his position. Then again, unlike Robert's own theories, Dr. Burns had had plenty of research and facts to do all the supporting he needed.

"Manasseh had not been the sole monarch of his country at first. For a decade, he had shared rule of Judah with his father," Dr. Burns had begun. "Once his father died, Manasseh quickly set about correcting what he perceived to be many of his father's mistakes, mostly by restoring all of the pagan idols and traditions of his ancestors that his own father had taken down in favor of Christianity."

All of this, of course, had been information that Robert and Stephanie had already uncovered. It was also where they had stopped digging.

Dr. Burns, ever the scholar, had considered the surface barely scratched. "You assumed that the killings had a religious significance attached to them," he had pointed out. "I don't believe they did. Most religious killings have a good deal of ceremony about them. They follow some patterns established somewhere. Beheading for infidels of Islam, or stoning for Islamic women who are impure. Christians were big fans of burning at the stake for witches and heretics. Aztecs cut the hearts out of their victims while they were still beating. These types of killings are always consistent with regards to some methodology. Not to mention the mythology that goes along with it."

"We get it, Doc. But David did have a pattern. He strangled his victims," Stephanie had said.

"No," Dr. Burns had countered. "Not at first. He had to find that method after trying many others. He stuck with it because it felt good and because it was so intimate. Speaking of which, the things he did with those women's bodies afterward certainly weren't in keeping with any religious text."

The entire trio shivered at the image of David and his victims' remains. A silent pause seemed appropriate, but time was short so Robert spoke. "Even if you're right though, what about the Bible verses? Are you saying they don't matter? They *felt* important."

"I think they're incredibly important, actually. I think David, like so many others before him, found religion after his incarceration. When Dr. Mead imprisoned him, he needed an explanation, especially since David couldn't recall anything about the killings. I think that's when he latched onto his father's religion and identified himself with Manasseh. And it would make sense that Dr. Mead would choose to lecture his son about Manasseh, after all. He is considered by many to be the most wicked figure in the entire Bible. Worse than Saul or Judas even, but according to Christians, even he was eventually forgiven for his sins when he repented. He would have been the perfect Biblical model for Dr. Mead, and if it worked as I believe it did, it would have been enough to give anyone hope."

"Sounds like it worked too well," Stephanie had observed.

"Indeed. David began to see himself as Manasseh in more than a symbolic sense, so now that he's repented, it's time for him to go home and assume his rightful throne and usher his family into a new era of peace and prosperity. The trouble is that I doubt his father will go along with the plan seeing as how he needs to be dead in order for it to work."

"Which David won't perceive as a violation of his spiritual awakening since it's all part of God's plan," Stephanie had added.

"Wait," Robert had then interjected. "Are you saying that David isn't a threat to women anymore? What about that girl at the zoo?"

Dr. Burns was quick to reassure him, though. "Whether David thinks he is or not, he is still very much a threat to anyone he encounters. He is, after all, a sociopath. His conscious efforts may be directed at his father, but all of his old impulses to kill are still there. He'll just need to justify certain killings now, like he'll do with his father; whereas before, he killed simply out of habit or desire."

"So why didn't he return right away and do the deed? Why even sneak out in the first place? He could have just gone upstairs and killed dear old Dad in his sleep," Robert had wondered aloud.

"A million reasons. Who knows? He needed a sign from God first? He was just so happy to get out that he temporarily forgot the plan? He was afraid? What I can tell you with reasonable certainty is that now that Dr. Mead has invited him back, he will return. Soon."

"Okay," Robert conceded as he and Stephanie sat and went over Dr. Burns' new ideas. "But I still think Burns is off somewhere. Something about it doesn't feel right."

Stephanie knitted her brows. "I trust your instincts on this, but I trust Burns too. Tough call. What does your memory mojo tell you?"

Robert shook his head and gave a small shrug that meant he had nothing to offer. "Okay, assuming all of this new information is correct, what's your play? We just wait on David to show up and arrest him when he does? We were going to do that anyway."

"Got a better plan?"

Robert didn't need to think it over. "Not really. Burns might be off somewhere, but at least he's giving us something to work with, and it isn't like it changes anything for us."

Stephanie stood and took his coffee mug, the contents of which had long since gone cold, a rarity for Robert. "Then we'd better put on a pot for you and get out the thermos because it does change one thing. Our stakeout just became guard duty, and it starts now."

CHAPTER THIRTY-FOUR

The house had lain dark and quiet when they had arrived. The sun had brought with it no discernible changes. Apart from the ankle monitor that revealed his location, it would have been impossible to know Mead was even at home. Would David know? They supposed it didn't matter. Mead could be in Acapulco for all they cared, as long as David came looking for him *here*.

Robert urged parking up close so that they could easily see the front door. Stephanie had insisted that they take a more cautious approach and park down the street.

"David doesn't know what your car looks like, and he's never seen either of us. There's no need to be subtle."

"You don't know that. He could have stayed behind at the zoo and seen both us and the car."

"Unlikely," Robert grumbled.

"Agreed, but not impossible. Just be a good little addict and drink your coffee, will you?"

Robert declined the suggestion, adding, "I'm not tired. Or thirsty."

"Yes, but you can't talk and drink at the same time."

Robert had no choice but to agree, and it wasn't like they were surrendering any tactical advantage. They could see any approach to the front door from where they were, although the angle was a bit odd and partially obstructed by large azaleas that grew in the corners of the front beds. The other unmarked car at the opposite end of the street shared a similar view but from the opposite angle. Between the two cars, the front was more than covered. In any event, they both agreed that David was far more likely to come in through the back door, the entrance they would have preferred to watch had the layout of the street allowed it, but with a short, narrow alley as the only way in or out of the rear of the property, there was no place to hide and watch. It was one or the other, so they had settled for unmarked cars at the ends of the block where they now sat. They settled for being able to see the entrance to the alley, if not the door itself.

"Fine," he muttered. "But I wouldn't be so uneasy if you would have talked him into letting one of your guys inside."

"I tried, believe me. He was being totally unreasonable about it. Didn't want to surrender his privacy. Or so he said."

"Could it be that he didn't want to surrender his other knee to one of your guys?" Robert mumbled over his coffee cup.

Stephanie fired a warning shot over his bow in the form of her darkest scowl, the one that said, "Choose your next words carefully."

Robert pretended to be temporarily transfixed by the contents of his mug. When he risked looking her way again, Stephanie was steadily switching her focus between the front door to the alley and back again. It was like watching a spectator of an invisible and interminable ping pong game. Only this was even less exciting, especially as late night gave way to overnight, then to early morning, and, finally, to mid-morning. Robert could stand it no more. "You sure David got the message?"

Stephanie shrugged. "Of course not, but I don't know how he

could have missed it. If he's near a computer, television, newspaper, or radio, he's aware of it. Besides, if Bullet is right, it might not matter."

"So you busted that guy up for no reason, huh?" He had wanted to broach the topic with her since she had practiced her backhand on Mead's knee, but the timing hadn't felt right before.

"Got a problem with how I handled my interview? Strange since you said you did some pretty back-alley stuff yourself with your suspects back in the day."

Robert nodded. "True, I did, but the rules were different for me. Enemy combatant label gives you a lot of leeway. You don't have that protection. And just because I did it doesn't mean you should."

Stephanie snorted. "Great. Aren't you going to ask me what I would do if all my friends jumped off of a cliff, Dad?"

"I'm not trying to bust your ... whatevers. I just want to make sure that whatever lines you might choose to cross are for you and not for me. I don't want you getting in trouble on my behalf, and, worse, I don't want you resenting me for anything you felt forced to do. That's all."

Both had maintained the façade of looking for David to avoid making eye contact during their discussion. When Robert finished, Stephanie risked looking his way and caught him doing the same. "That's really decent of you, but don't worry about me, okay? I make my own choices, and I'll be fine. Once all of this is over, anyway," she added. "Speaking of which, how are you doing? You holding up okay since the other night? Neither of us have had much rest. That can't help."

The shrug Robert offered was noncommittal. "I try not to think about it too much. I want to. I want to face it and beat it down so it knows to stay away, but I can't do that yet. As far as the lack of sleep goes, I haven't minded that too much. Sleeping in little bursts keeps the dreams from coming on as badly. My only worry now is how long I can keep this up."

Stephanie had no reply. She had the same worry. Bullet had said anything was possible, but if Robert was coping with his emotions by burying them, she was afraid that gravesite was already full. Robert might be right to worry about what might come crawling out and when.

He knew well enough what her silence probably meant, so he changed the topic. "I still think Bullet is off, about the verses or David's desire to kill his father or something. I just don't know what it is yet."

"Still no guesses?" Stephanie asked though she knew it was pointless.

"For one, I don't get the sense that David is in any hurry to get here. This place has too many negative memories associated with it. It's like I can feel them crawling up my spine sometimes."

Stephanie's brow knotted as she juggled her hands back and forth as if she were balancing some invisible scales. "I believe you, but we've been through this. We aren't leaving, so unless you want to see if you can get us an invitation in there, you might as well get comfortable. Breakfast will be here soon. Try to focus on—hey! Where are you going?"

Robert had abruptly popped the handle on Stephanie's Mustang and swung the door wide open to allow his large frame to slide from the car. Stephanie did likewise on her side and jumped out to follow him.

Robert didn't look back when she called his name again. "I'm doing what you said. I'm going to get permission to go in. And you need to stay here until I have it. You aren't even really supposed to be here." Robert stared her down with his most matter-of-fact look, hands jammed in his jeans pockets, waiting on her to return to the car as if there were no other possible outcomes. "The longer you drag this out, the greater the odds are we'll be seen, but I can wait as long as you want, 'cause I don't think he's coming."

Finally, Stephanie gave up and made a show of throwing her hands in the air. "Have it your way. I'll be in the car."

Robert immediately turned and resumed his trip up the street and to the front door with its large columns and still empty rocking chairs. He had no particular plan for gaining entry, no logical argument or persuasive speeches. He was just going to ask to come in and hope for the best. Maybe it would be easier than Stephanie made it out to be. She could be a bit rough around the edges for some people. Okay, she could be like sandpaper and broken glass to some people, but it was worse with Mead. Robert knew and appreciated that her aggression was somewhat on his behalf, but it wouldn't serve their cause to let her anywhere near him right now. Her way had gotten them the video they'd needed. His job now was to get them in the door. Time and place for everything, he reasoned.

Robert rang the bell and waited. It was a loud and deep chime that he felt as much as he heard. Robert stuck his hands back in his pockets. There would be no need to ring twice. He suddenly remembered the camera above the door and looked up at it. Awkwardly, he withdrew one of his hands and waved at the little lens. Was Mead even looking at him right now? There was no way to tell, so he stood and stared and waited. And waited.

After two or three minutes and no sign of Mead or anyone else, he decided to ring the bell again after all. The result was the same. He turned and looked at Stephanie's car. The glare off the windshield made it impossible to see her, but he knew she was there, shaking her head at him and possibly grinning. There was no way he was walking back to that car empty handed to face her, but he couldn't wait on the porch forever either. If he couldn't go back or stand still, the only option was forward.

Hesitantly, he reached for the ornate brass knob and turned it, fully expecting it to resist. Instead, it turned easily in his hand. There was a deadbolt above it though, so when Robert pushed gently on the door, he still expected it to remain closed. He was zero for two. When the heavy door gave way before his hand and he was greeted by the site of the familiar entryway, he called out loudly for Mead. He knew though that there would be no answer. Everything about this situation felt wrong to him. A man who was security conscious enough to have cameras mounted didn't just leave his front door unlocked, especially when a homicidal maniac was expected to pay him a visit.

He hesitated only a moment before entering. Stephanie would need probable cause to enter a private residence. He, however, was just an acquaintance stopping by. If he found anything that concerned him, he could return to Stephanie with all the probable cause she needed. It was a good plan, except that he was unarmed and out of practice for these kinds of situations. It couldn't be helped though. He'd crossed the threshold, and he wasn't going to stop now.

He moved on cat's feet through the house, torn between calling out and maintaining the element of surprise. After several silent seconds, he opted for the loud way. If Mead, or anyone else, was here, he or she could easily be watching him from the cameras that Mead had everywhere. He would have to trade surprise for confident bravado. Bravado, he reminded himself, didn't make one bulletproof, so he cautiously resumed his search of the bottom floor of the home, simultaneously calling aloud for Mead and ducking around corners as he did so. He felt foolish. If whoever was here hadn't answered that doorbell, they weren't likely to answer his calls, but it was all he had, so he continued nervously.

It took nearly five minutes to complete his sweep of the downstairs, and he knew the top floor would take just as long. He also knew Stephanie would not keep waiting with no word from him, so he decided that an empty bottom floor and no answer to the bell or his calls would have to constitute reasonable cause on this occasion. He retraced his steps to the front door and was about to make the walk back down the street when he realized it was unnecessary. He simply leaned his torso out the door and waved her down, signaling her to join him. Robert smiled. There could be no argument about what to do next if he didn't give her the chance until *after* she was inside.

Stephanie exited the car, shrugged her shoulders, and raised her hands to signal, *"What?"* Robert ignored the gesture and waved again for her to join him. No need to let the bravado go just yet. He might still need it to save his life when she arrived. When she had done so, instead of finding Robert gloating that he had gotten them in, he was giving her his best apologetic look.

"What's wrong? He change his mind about letting us in?"

Robert shook his head. "No, not exactly. Here, come in."

Bewildered, Stephanie stepped across the threshold and craned her head around as Robert had done, trying to locate Mead. "Where is he?"

Robert gestured to the open door. "When I got here, the door was unlocked. Nobody answered, so I let myself in. Didn't think the door would open, but it did. I've been all over the place. I think something is wrong."

Stephanie agreed, a fact for which Robert was immensely grateful. "Why the hell would his door be unlocked? I told him to keep it locked tight. I was really specific about that."

"I can't think of anything that makes sense. He still has the bracelet, right? I mean, you'd know if he had left?"

Stephanie ignored his question and looked up the stairs and then back through the hallway that led to what she assumed was the kitchen. "You been back there yet?"

"Yeah. All over the first floor. That still leaves the upstairs and his little dungeon in the basement. Want to split up?"

Stephanie considered it briefly before discarding the notion. "No, but I'm on point. Clear?"

Robert answered with a simple nod. Carefully, with as much quickness as caution would allow, they made their way up the stairs and through every room, every corner, of the top floor of the home before repeating the process on the first floor with no sign of Mead. When they approached the entrance to the basement, a narrow door off the white and black tiled kitchen, they looked at one another. Whatever awaited them almost certainly was not good. Mead must surely have heard them and would have responded if he were willing. Or able.

Moving with more urgency now, Stephanie pushed the thin door inward and flipped on the light switch. Bright light flooded the stairwell and what could be seen of the large room at the foot of the stairs. After calling out yet again with the same result as on the other floors, Stephanie unfastened the catch on the holster at her hip and adjusted the weapon within, making sure the humidity would not cause it to stick if she needed to draw it quickly. Robert saw the move and was momentarily envious. He had made many of these entries during his military career but never without a weapon. Or Kevlar body armor. And ten other guys who were similarly outfitted.

"Ready?" she asked, bringing him out of his nostalgia.

"If you are. You're the only one with a gun."

"Yeah," she said, jutting her chin to indicate the room at the end of the stairs. "Let's hope so."

CHAPTER THIRTY-FIVE

Figuring that whoever was there would already be well aware of their presences, Stephanie and Robert opted for going in fast, hoping to take whomever they found by whatever surprise they could still manage. The plan was tactically sound but, in the end, wholly unnecessary, the basement being almost as empty as the rest of the house. The object of their search, Mead, was certainly nowhere to be found, but they made two other discoveries that were nearly as helpful if infinitely more frustrating.

The first was Mead's ankle monitor. Still functioning perfectly by the look of it, it lay on a workbench with various small tools, its tiny green light flashing in two-second intervals just as it was programmed to do. Presumably, the various little implements had been used to pry it off Mead's ankle without triggering the alarm, a nearly impossible task. And a very risky one. Had he failed in the attempt, a judge would have issued a new warrant for his arrest, and Mead would be in a lock up somewhere in Harris County right now, a destination at which he would still find himself sooner or later thanks to his disappearing act. Mead had little left apart from his temporary freedom and his many precious possessions.

Stephanie couldn't see him risking either of those lightly.

The second discovery was more interesting than the first but also more troubling. A door that was not a door, but a section of wall that had blended perfectly with its surroundings stood ajar at the end of the room closest to what had been David's luxury suite for the last three years. Stephanie was tempted to close the door in order to see how she had missed the damn thing. She knew if she did so though, it would become invisible again with no obvious means of opening it from the inside. Mead was proving infuriatingly clever.

"What do you think?" Robert asked her after giving her an appropriate amount of time to absorb the details.

Stephanie wasn't sure at first, but she had a hunch. "Like, did he run, or was he taken? Ran. The son of a bitch definitely ran."

Robert had the same feeling, though perhaps for different reasons than Stephanie's. "Why do you say that?"

Stephanie withdrew her phone and began punching in numbers. "Simple. I assume that only he and David knew about this door here. If David had come for him, would he have left with him willingly? Even at gunpoint? He knew there were cops out front everywhere. Couldn't have been too hard to signal one somehow, and there are no obvious signs of a struggle down here or anywhere else in the house."

"I agree, and I'll do you one better. You figure either member of our father-son picnic is capable of getting that monitor off by himself? That's a pretty specific skill from what I understand. You don't just look it up on YouTube. That means a third person loaned a helping hand, and they probably did it on a webcam or something because we know no one came in."

Stephanie saw where he was going. "And why not trigger the monitor's alarm if he's being abducted? Would have looked like an accident even if David were aware it had happened, which I doubt he would have been. Nothing happens when you remove them. They're that way on purpose so the perps think they've gotten away with something. All the cavalry Poppa Mead would have needed would have been here in under a minute. Anyone skilled enough to get the bracelet off would have known that."

Stephanie put the phone back in her pocket and informed Robert that they would soon have company. Apparently, calling in for backup had now been replaced by texting it in.

"Want to see where this door goes while we wait?"

Robert nodded. "I'm guessing it's the garage, but let's check."

They followed the short passage that Stephanie lit by using her cell phone's flashlight. In almost no time, they emerged through another hidden door into a three car garage that conspicuously held only one car, a blue BMW 7 series. Stephanie tipped an imaginary cap at Robert who gave a small shrug in reply.

"Where else could it have gone?" he asked. "It's not like the tunnel could have gone on forever, and if you need an escape tunnel at all, you generally need it to be a pretty short trip."

"Especially if you're smuggling out your first born in the middle of the night, which is why I assume Mead had it built. Probably figured that if worse ever came to worst and he had to get the kid somewhere, he couldn't exactly walk him up into the living room and out the front door. I should have seen this coming," she spat.

Robert continued to look around the garage, peering around corners and behind boxes as if Mead might come popping up out of one of them. He knew this was bad for Stephanie professionally, but he was also angry that Mead had outwitted the police again. It was bad enough that he might escape the judicial system through his cleverly worded confession. Now he might not even have to face the prospect of seeing his son again.

"What happens now?" he asked.

"We put out an alert with his picture, and we hope we get lucky."

Robert had once marveled at the way the legal system was forced to deal with its prey. In Robert's world, there had always been an enemy, someone to take the fight to when you needed it. Stephanie's world was filled with a lot of guesswork and waiting around. He didn't know how she handled it, and he made no attempt to hide his frustration.

"Take it easy," she urged as Robert began to pace around the concrete floor. "We also do what we've done all along. We deal with what we know, and we take the next logical step."

Robert continued to pace slowly in circles, squeezing his eyes tightly and trying to decide what Stephanie thought they knew. He could think of only one thing. Dr. Burns had been right. Mead ran because he knew his son would come and because he didn't want to be here when that happened. He's afraid, Robert decided, but why? He and Stephanie had decided against sharing Dr. Burns' theory with Mead. Mead was, as far as he knew, in no danger. And taking off the monitor was a clear violation of his agreement with the D.A., one that was sure to land him back in court and probably even behind bars. What would motivate him to do it?

"Earth to Robert?"

He had stopped pacing and had been staring at one spot on the floor while he thought. His old drill instructor had called it his thousand-yard stare. "Sorry. I was just wondering what would make Mead scared enough to risk jail by running. By definition, it has to be something at least as bad as prison, and I don't think he'd do too well in prison, you know?"

"I had the same thought. David is the obvious answer, right?"

Robert shrugged his shoulders. "Maybe, but if that's true, why? He didn't know what we know about his son. Did he? I mean, about David wanting to kill him?"

It was Stephanie's turn to be noncommittal. "Not to be disagreeable, but we don't really know what he knew. He's been smart about things so far. It's not a stretch to say that there are things he hasn't shared with us. Maybe David threatened to kill him every day while he was locked up here. Maybe Mead figured out the Bible thing the way we did. Who knows? However he figured it out, I'd bet my next paycheck that Mead knew he was in trouble if he stayed."

"I don't like this at all," Robert said, shaking his head. "We missed something." He knew police work and soldiering weren't exactly aligned, but neither were they that different. Searching for terrorists had made him very good at reading people and situations. He had gotten to the point that very little surprised him in the field, and he was sure Stephanie would have said the same. Neither of them had seen this escape act coming, which meant something was out of focus somewhere. He gave up agonizing over it long enough to focus on solving the current mystery—the location of Dr. Lawrence Mead. "Okay, at least we know for sure now that Bullet was right, don't we? I hate to admit it, but Mead confirmed that for us when he ran. That's the why and the who. And we know how and at least approximately when, of course. Got a guess as to where?"

"No clue, but it doesn't matter. Wherever he goes, we'll eventually find him. It's not nearly as easy as you think to disappear completely these days. Besides, as long as David doesn't know he's missing, we don't absolutely have to have him. We'll just grab junior at the front door when he shows up to get Dad."

Robert gave a half-hearted smile. "You make it sound so simple."

Stephanie flashed back a smile of her own, but Robert suspected that it was more out of kindness toward him than out of any real enthusiasm she might have felt. "Hey, cheer up. Something about this case eventually has to go our way, right?"

CHAPTER THIRTY-SIX

Mead had not turned on a radio or a television since liberating himself from that awful and irritating device the police had installed on his ankle. But, even without radio or television, he knew the only two pieces of information he cared about at the moment—he was now a wanted man, and his son was still at large. Removing the monitor had been a costly move. His lawyers had assured him it would take them considerable legal wrangling to keep him out of jail if he moved forward with his plan, but what was a father to do? His only care at the moment was that he find his son before the police did.

David would not return to the house. No amount of begging or trickery could accomplish that, but it made no difference. Mead was as confident as ever in his plan to be reunited with his child, to help him *before* the police could arrest him. Maybe his years of work and planning hadn't ever been able to change David the way he would have liked them to, but it had given him an understanding of his son. If he couldn't use that understanding to control him, he could at least use it to influence him. And to predict where he might go next if he could be influenced in just the right way.

The problem had been the means—until that detective had come along and given him the perfect opportunity. As difficult as she was making things, she was still instrumental to Mead's plans. It pained him to admit it, but he was glad she had come along.

How long before David will get the message and make his move? Mead wondered. There was no way of knowing for sure, but he suspected it would all come together fairly quickly from here forward. David would respond. That was certain. The police would probably figure out that David wasn't coming back to the house, even if they didn't understand that Mead was complicit in that. He thought of that detective and chuckled drily to himself. Okay, he acknowledged, she would definitely figure it out. The only remaining question was how long it would take them to figure out where he had sent David. Did he have enough time to try just once more to cure his son? Even if the police found him and things worked out for the worst, he owed it to his son to try one last time. If he couldn't, or if he failed … Mead closed his eyes and shuddered against the thought.

But it had to work this time, for he would not free his son if he could not be repaired. That would be unthinkable. Too much damage done already for that ever to happen. *No*, he vowed, *even if I'm left with only one other choice, no member of my family will ever see the inside of a prison again.*

CHAPTER THIRTY-SEVEN

While Mead's escape from the ankle monitor, no doubt through help from one of his many technophile lab rats, could not be blamed directly on Stephanie, the fact that he felt the need to run could be blamed on her, something Stephanie's boss and the D.A. seemed intent on reminding her of repeatedly. It had been Stephanie's idea to use him as bait, hadn't it? Plus, the D.A. was certain that the only reason he had agreed to help her at all was because of her less than hospitable nature. Thus, it fell to her to apprehend him while not forgetting her primary duty, the capture of his son.

"Think of it as a two-for-one special," her captain told her. "The son is your priority, but if you find them both, you get to keep your detective's shield. And on the off-chance that you should find either of them, try not beating them to death on the way to the station!" she had yelled as Stephanie sulked out of their meeting. She had ground her back teeth together against the urge to say something unprofessional, but she had made it out of the meeting without speaking and, thus, with her job. She didn't like being chastised for something that was clearly not her fault, but she had been around long enough to know that things worked a certain way. The people at the top would pretend to be pissed at her in the hope that their own bosses would direct their pretended anger the same direction. The only person whose opinion really mattered, the only real boss, was the public. If the killer was apprehended before anyone else died, all would be forgiven. If not, then the anger would become real. A scapegoat would be needed.

Fortunately, she was confident that Junior would still be easy enough to catch. No reason he wouldn't be walking up to his own front door any minute now. Senior was going to be a bit more problematic, she acknowledged, but not much. His passport had been revoked, his picture was up in every train station and bus stop for one hundred miles, and every means of communication he possessed was either cut off or tapped. Cockroaches might be hard to catch when they're operating in the dark, but when you shine a bright light on them they always scurry for the safety of the familiar.

"Come on, sleepy head," she said, rousing Robert from Dr. Burns' sofa. "It's time for us to get back on watch."

Robert groaned audibly. It had been fewer than four hours since they had gotten back to the station, and he was less than eager to return to sentry duty.

"Unless you'd rather I took you home first and let you miss seeing this guy get my lucky bracelets put on him," Stephanie offered, jangling her handcuffs above him.

Robert didn't open his eyes or even attempt to adjust his large frame before speaking. "You're very chipper for someone who didn't bring any coffee with her."

"Hey, a girl can't give away everything on the first date. Come on. Move your ass. We'll get your stupid coffee on the way out."

Nothing.

"I even made a fresh pot for the road."

Robert opened one eye and peered at her. "How fresh?"

"I don't think David is going to wait for us to have this fascinating discussion about coffee, Robert. Let's go."

"How fresh?" he repeated.

"I had to mug a Columbian guy for the beans. Are you coming or what?"

He sat bolt upright and rubbed the sleep from his face with both hands. Once he was sufficiently awake to be sure he could dodge a blow, he responded. "What? And miss your driving? It's the only excitement I get anymore."

"Keep up the jokes about my driving, funny man, and it really will be the only excitement you'll get. At least from me."

Robert placed his hand over his heart and winced. "Ouch. Okay, but for the record, I'm doubting this will be as fast or easy as you make it sound."

"It will be. I promise."

Two days later, after spending sixteen hours of each of those days parked outside of Mead's house with no sign of David, Stephanie was grudgingly forced to reevaluate her promise. "I don't understand," she repeated for what Robert was sure was at least the twentieth time. "He should have shown up by now."

"Agreed, but I'm not sure that saying it again is going to help. You're starting to sound like me."

"Annoying, isn't it?" Stephanie responded without turning away from watching the house. After investing so much time in the stakeout, she was reluctant even to blink for fear that David would slip in when her eyes flickered shut.

Robert had no desire to wander into a trap from which he

could not easily walk out, so he let her comment go. Besides, he reasoned, she was right. It *was* annoying to be on the other end of these conversations. As long as they were exchanging roles for a time though, he figured he might as well press his luck and try to move things along in the search. Otherwise, he might die in Stephanie's car, and, while he had accepted that risk, he had assumed it would be while it was in motion.

"You can usually tell when someone is lying. You told me that, right?"

"I did," she answered, still without looking away.

"And you know I can pretty much do the same."

"Do you want to know if I think Mead was telling the truth about his message working? You know I do. And we know that his running confirms that he believed it."

So far, this was going about as well as he had figured. "I know that. What I'm saying, for what I'm sure you're going to tell me is the hundredth time, is that we're missing something obvious. If he wasn't lying, but David still hasn't shown up yet, what does that leave?"

Stephanie turned to look at him finally, rubbing the tension out of her neck as she did so. "You playing the knowns and unknowns game with me now, Grayson?"

Robert gave a half-shrug of his shoulders and let them drop wearily back down. Every little movement was beginning to make him sore after so long in the same seat. "It appears so, so play along, please. If we know Mead was telling the truth, what could explain the unknown of why there's no David?"

Stephanie had thought about it, of course, but the answers were no more help than the questions were. "Either Mead was wrong, which we think is unlikely since Bullet also confirms that David would show up, or ... or I don't know." She slapped both hands against her steering wheel. "David wants to come, but he can't? Like maybe he's injured somewhere or something?"

"Maybe," Robert agreed. "But there's nothing we can do about that if that's true, so let's move on. What is the only other option?"

Stephanie sighed wearily. "I'm working on too little sleep for your Socratic seminar, Professor. Can't you just tell me?"

"Fine. Benjamin might be right about David, but what if it's Papa we're wrong about?"

"What?" she puzzled, her brows knitted so tightly that Robert was afraid they might permanently merge. "You just said that we know we're right about him because he ran."

"But correlation doesn't equal causation. What if he's not afraid at all, even if he should be? What if he's been in communication with Junior somehow, and they've run off and met somewhere else? Is that possible?"

Stephanie sat and thought it over. *Impossible. And yet, it would explain everything. No Lawrence Mead and no David Mead is awfully suspicious. Still…* "No," Stephanie finally said with certainty. "We found out how he made the call to his lab to get help with the monitor. We even think we know which technician did it. It's that specific of a tracking system. No other calls or emails were detected coming in or out. He's smart. I'll give him that. He can make communication hard for us to find for a little while maybe, but we've got more bugs planted in that house than a crooked termite inspector. He couldn't hide anything from us for this long. No way."

"Yeah, but what if he didn't have to? Hide it, I mean. The jihadists I used to track were able to use our communication networks against us all the time. It wasn't even that complicated for them, and they were using mostly stone age technology."

Stephanie cocked her head. "What are you saying? He tapped into our surveillance and used it to get a message out? That would be tough with what he had in the house. Probably impossible."

"No," Robert answered, beginning to bounce around in his seat a little. "I don't think he had to. I think maybe we delivered the message for him."

CHAPTER THIRTY-EIGHT

Stephanie hated to admit it, but Mead had outsmarted her again. First with the rigged confession, and now with her own idea of a message. Unfortunately for Robert, her anger was doing nothing to improve her driving. If it was possible, she seemed even more aggressive than usual behind the wheel. The only benefit of this channeled rage was that she and Robert arrived at the station quickly and were already listening to Mead's recorded message less than twenty minutes after Robert first suggested it. On the third time through, Stephanie heard it.

"Damn," she whispered, pausing the playback on her computer.

Robert knew he had missed something. He asked her to play it back again, but nothing jumped out at him. Finally, he admitted defeat.

"Listen," she urged. "It's right there in the beginning. He said they both know how dangerous it is for some people to travel alone. He's not speaking hypothetically or metaphorically. He's referring to something specific, something they both remember."

"Like what?"

Stephanie shrugged. "Who knows? It could be anything, but

it's important whatever it is." Stephanie played the recording again several more times. Each time, they tried to absorb little details, nuances of speech or anything that would give something away. "Hear anything?" she asked.

"I don't know. I mean, if they met somewhere else, wouldn't he need to give a location?"

"Seems reasonable, but I didn't hear one. Did you?"

"I'm not sure. Maybe at the end? Play it again." Stephanie pressed the button and listened as Robert closed his eyes and did the same. She was prepared to admit defeat once again, but as she was about to speak, Robert's eyes shot open. "There! He says they need to go back to the beginning. We thought he meant the beginning of their relationship, like he wanted to start over, but the beginning of their relationship would literally mean the hospital where David was born, right? I think we'd have heard if they were there. The beginning of their new relationship in which David was locked up was at the house. That's out too, naturally."

"The beginning of what then? David's first kill?"

"I don't think so," Robert said. "David killed alone. *Their* beginning would be someplace where they shared an experience of some kind, something that would be important to David. It would have to be a place he would remember and that he could get back to pretty easily."

They sat in silence, listening to the clock on the wall tick the seconds away as they thought. Stephanie agreed with Robert's guess, but without more information about their shared backgrounds, it was impossible to guess what beginning he was talking about. It could be nearly anything. It was driving them both crazy, but it was Robert who finally slammed his palm into the table in frustration.

"There's got to be something we're missing again, something in David's past that would stand out. I would give anything to be able to look in his mind right now the way I'm supposed to be able to do. Just a hint from him. Something!"

Stephanie looked on, sharing his frustration but too tired to share his outburst. And it would hardly be a good idea to encourage Robert to get angry anyway. He had been even more on edge the closer they'd gotten to finding Mead, or at least to finding his son. "It probably wouldn't do you any good. That kid's mind has been wiped. It's practically a clean slate."

Suddenly, Stephanie's jaw went slack, her eyes shot to the size of saucers, and she repeatedly mumbled something under her breath. Robert had to twice ask her to repeat herself.

"It can't be," she mumbled only slightly more clearly. Robert couldn't tell if it was for his benefit as she had given no other outward signs of having heard him. Instead, she began rifling through the stacks of files and papers on her desk, casually tossing aside those she did not want until she came across her prize. She tore the rubber band from the file and began frantically searching through it for something. Robert wanted to ask her what she was doing but thought better of it. Whatever she was after, he knew better than to step between her and it.

"Son of a bitch, here it is," she said, running her finger across a particular line and reading it again to herself before handing the file to Robert and sinking back into her office chair. Robert took the file from her, careful not to lose the page she had been reading. He quickly scanned the paper and found it was a transcript from her interview with Stephen Hennerman, the head of sales for Happy Memories. Robert perused the paper until his patience left him entirely. Whatever Stephanie had seen, he was blind to it. "I give up. What did you read?"

Stephanie shook her head in disbelief. "It's the beginning that Mead talked about. Look at the name of the company before they became Happy Memories, Inc."

Robert read until he found the right paragraph. "Clean Slate?

This was before they started doing memory transplants, right? They were just doing removals then."

"Correct. Did you notice where they were doing them?"

It didn't take Robert long this time to find the information he needed. "In Hennerman's apartment," he read aloud. "You really think that's the beginning he meant? The beginning of the company?"

Stephanie nodded. "It makes sense. We know David was patient zero for the company—the *beginning*."

Robert wasn't convinced. "That's a pretty good theory, but there's a problem. David wouldn't remember it. It isn't much of a message if David can't decode it."

"Who knows what he remembers? Maybe Mead told him about it later as part of his therapy or something. Maybe he caused him to think he was there for some other purpose. There are a million maybes here, but it's the only beginning I've found so far. How about you? Got any better ideas?"

Robert gave a small humph. "Virtually never."

"Okay then. It's probably a long shot, but what do you say to one last road trip?"

Robert didn't budge. "Stephanie, I appreciate the offer, and I do want to come if you're serious, but I've seen the way you've been looking at me lately. You're even more worried about me than normal. I get it," he threw in before Stephanie could object, "we both know I'm a little unhinged. Be honest. You don't really need me anymore. Not for this anyway. My job was to help you figure out what David's next moves might be, nothing more. All that remains now is for you to find out if you're right about Hennerman. If so, you get your bad guys. If not, I think we both know I'm just dead weight at this point. I'll go see Burns and get some more of his magic pills while you go do your thing."

Stephanie slipped both hands onto her hips and stared at

Robert. "What a piece of work. You seriously think I'm going to let you bail out on me now? Do you have any idea where this investigation would be without you? I wouldn't even be able to see square one from where I'd be sitting. And by the way," she added, her voice picking up in pitch and volume as she pointed at him with an angry finger, "your *job* is to help me catch a killer, and I haven't done that yet." She continued to stare at Robert for a moment through wide eyes while she focused on slowing her breathing. She calmed herself until her voice softened. "I'm counting on having you with me when I see Hennerman again. With you there, I think I can make him crack without resorting to more ... direct methods. So, to use your words, all that remains is to finish this, and we're going to do that together. Unless you want to quit. I'm not your damn boss." She crossed her arms and scowled.

Robert rose, stretched his tired back, and, to Stephanie's complete surprise, moved quickly to her and pressed his lips to hers briefly and softly, backing away again before she could react. "Sorry," he whispered, "but I've waited as long as I could to do that." He cleared his throat a little louder than was needed and spoke as calmly as if nothing had happened. "So, we stay together and bring this thing full circle, back to Hennerman?"

Stephanie could taste him on her lips. Coffee, of course. The kiss hadn't been the lingering, romantic kind, and it had been totally unexpected, but it had also been warm and comforting and somehow familiar. She could get used to those, she decided. She smiled and nodded. "Back to the beginning."

CHAPTER THIRTY-NINE

"We need to make a stop by my place," Robert said after they had left the station. Something about the way he said it made Stephanie think this wasn't just a casual stop.

"It's pretty much on the way," she observed, "You need to pick up something?"

"Yeah." He nodded, offering no other explanation and inviting no further discussion of the topic.

They reached Stephanie's car and popped open both doors wide to let the imaginary breeze blow some of the brutally hot air out. Stephanie leaned across the roof of the car and gave Robert her best non-menacing stare. "You know you can't bring a weapon, right?"

He copied her posture. The difference was that his longer arms and torso meant he could lean practically all the way across the car. He smiled at her, appreciating that she knew him well enough to make the objection without feeling the need to make a long preamble. "I never said I wanted a weapon."

"No," she answered, pulling her arms back and lowering herself into the still-roasting car to fire up the engine and the A/C. "But you'd be crazy not to. I'd want one if it were me."

Robert dropped heavily into his seat and drew the belt tightly across his chest in one smooth motion. "I *do* want one too," he said. "But I don't know if that's the best idea in my condition. Anyway, we're going after one bad guy and one fugitive Radio Shack employee with delusions of grandeur, neither of whom carries a gun as far as we know. I think one gun is enough for the two of us."

Stephanie nodded. He was right, of course, but her pistol at her hip was still reassuring. "Mind my asking what for then?"

Robert examined his feet. He'd need new tennis shoes soon. His were getting worn down in the heels. "Just a superstition. Something I carried with me on all my missions. Always made it back alive. I figure it can't hurt to bring it out of retirement one last time, especially with the luck we've had."

Forty-five minutes later, they found themselves standing in front of Stephen Hennerman's apartment door. They had confirmed with the tired and overweight guard who passed for security that he was in for the evening before coming up, but the guard was unsure whether he was alone.

"Anybody who has the code can get in anytime," he had complained. "And that don't even count all the people who might sneak in through the back entrance or the employee garage. They say we're security here, but the only bad guys we could keep out are the ones who'd be dumb enough to try to check in here at the desk on their way in. It's a damn shame is what it is."

Stephanie was apprehensive about entering a room without backup, especially one that might contain two fugitives, one of whom was a mass murderer with a taste for women, but she had little choice. She had no warrant and no case she could present to a judge to get one. Their only hope of gaining entry was through invitation, something she wasn't going to get with a SWAT team in tow. But as Robert had said, these weren't exactly elite commandoes they were after.

"You want me to knock?" Robert offered.

Stephanie ignored him and rapped solidly on the door, the sharp sound somewhat muffled by the rich carpet that lined the hallway. Neither said anything as they waited, and Robert passed the quiet seconds by shifting his weight back and forth from foot to foot. Stephanie saw his nervous energy but opted to say nothing. Stephanie's own career, at least in the near term, hung on the outcome of this case, but Robert, she knew, had much more at stake. She silently renewed her vow to see this through for him as quickly as she could. He had earned the rest that would come when this was over. Of course, all of that hinged on Hennerman eventually opening his damned door.

As Stephanie raised her hand to knock again, the apartment door eased open halfway to reveal almost total darkness. With all of the lights off inside, it was difficult to see Hennerman as he retreated.

"Come in, Detective. You too, Mr. Grayson. I've been expecting you."

Both Robert and Stephanie's senses were immediately on high alert. The darkness, something about the sound of the voice inviting them in, all of it had an eerie quality that raised the hairs on the back of their necks.

"Mr. Hennerman, are you okay, sir?" Stephanie asked. Neither she nor Robert had moved an inch. At least the apartment was now open to them, but neither was entertaining the notion of entering while it was engulfed in blackness.

Robert longed for the days of being able to throw a nice M84 stun grenade ahead of him to level the playing field. Without one, he sure as hell wasn't going in that door unless the lights came on.

"Is the darkness a problem? Here, allow me." With that, he

flipped on a switch and the entryway was immediately flooded in brilliant light. Robert realized too late that Hennerman had improvised his own flash grenade. Although the effect would have been far worse had they entered the total darkness of the apartment first as they had been intended to, they were still temporarily blinded. They had, in fact, had time to notice two things before they were robbed of their sight. The first was that the man inviting them in was not Hennerman as they had expected. It was Dr. Lawrence Mead. The second was the gun he was pointing at them as casually as if he were holding a rolled up newspaper.

"Well," he said cheerfully as they blinked heavily. "Don't just stand there staring. You're letting all the cool air out."

Stephanie held her hand up against the harsh light. "We wouldn't want to intrude," she offered. She kept her voice devoid of any of the surprise she felt for no reason other than to rob Mead of the satisfaction. "That would just be rude of us."

Mead's smiled vanished, and he raised the semi-automatic pistol for effect. "Not to sound too cliché, but I'm afraid I really must insist."

Minutes later, still at gunpoint and stripped of Stephanie's weapons and both of their phones, the pair was seated in Hennerman's living room, and they were not alone. The apartment's owner sat limply, tied to a straight-backed kitchen chair that had been moved into the room. Stephanie wasn't sure how long he had been there, but he was obviously exhausted. He resembled a worn out rag that had been cast onto the chair more than the man who owned it. He recognized them, of course, but could offer only an apologetic shake of his head.

"Why are you doing this?" Stephanie asked, turning her attention back to Mead. "We came here to help, to honor our part of the deal to find your son. You don't have to be afraid of him."

Mead sneered and gave a dismissive laugh. "Of David? Once

again, Detective, you understand so very little. No, while I wish I could say I was afraid of him; sadly, he is not his father's son. Though the Lord knows I've tried everything in my power to change him, there is just too much of his mother in him, I think." He sighed. "As always, leave it to a woman to ruin a man."

Robert sat silently and tried to make sense of what was happening. Mead had obviously played them from the beginning, but to what end? How did this help bring David in?

"What the hell is going on, Dr. Mead? Where is David?" Stephanie demanded.

"Hmm? Oh, don't worry, Detective Monroe. He'll be back shortly. Just running a quick errand for me. I needed some time to talk to Stephen here privately, but I suppose we can expand our little *tête-à-tête* to include you both. It's not as if it will matter in the long run." The grin he gave them this time was somewhere between terrifying madness and genuine pleasure.

Stephanie needed to keep him talking. In her experience, rule number one when your shit is plastered to the giant fan of life is to delay the inevitable as long as possible. Your own situation isn't likely to get worse in the meantime, and you never know what sort of miracle might come along if you give it enough time. To that end, she asked, "Why won't it matter, Doctor?"

Mead sauntered over to the end table where he had laid Stephanie's things and eyed them carefully, pretending a great deal of interest in each item. He ignored Stephanie's question as he gently ran his hand over the top of each of her belongings until he came to rest on the only item that had really interested him all along, the baton. He lifted the rod carefully and tested its weight and balance in his hand before snapping it open to its full length and pointing it wickedly at Stephanie. "Because, my dear lady, as you have already surmised, both of you will be dead. But first, let's see about that knee of yours." Mead walked to stand over Stephanie, raised the weapon back as far as he was able, and then paused there for effect. "Twenty pounds of force was it, Detective? I've not had the kind of practice you obviously have, but let's see how near I can come."

CHAPTER FORTY

For Stephanie, the worst of it was over much more quickly than she had anticipated, but whatever she gained in expediency, she traded many times over for in pain.

Mead had simply walked up to her after his threat, his arm still drawn back as far as it would go across his chest, and delivered a vicious backhand with the tip of the baton coming down across the outside of her right knee. Had she been standing, she would have collapsed immediately. Seated, at least the knee had not been locked in place when the blow was delivered, but that did nothing to keep the cap from shattering. Stephanie's reaction was similar to what Mead's had been in that she offered no sound, but where his reaction had been the involuntary result of the pain, hers was by choice. Every nerve in her body lit up simultaneously with electric bolts of white hot, searing light, but no matter how much it hurt, she was determined to not give Mead what he wanted— her cry of agony to signal his victory. True, the pain she felt was unreal, but she had endured worse in silence. She had survived that ordeal when she knew she could not. She would survive this too. Somehow.

Robert immediately leapt to his feet, but Mead motioned him back down with the gun.

"I can see you're upset, Mr. Grayson. There's no need. It's only fair, after all. Besides, if it helps, I don't intend to let her suffer for long. Or you either, for that matter."

"Those destined for death to death, huh?" Robert growled.

Mead nodded. "And those for the sword to the sword, though we'll have to improvise on that end," he answered, gesturing to the gun as if to apologize. "It's good you understand."

Every inch of Robert's body shook. He had been this angry only one other time in his life. He had let that son-of-a-bitch off a lot easier than what he was going to do to Mead if he got the chance. Calling upon every reserve of strength he possessed, Robert turned his focus inward and concentrated on his shaking hands as he tried to calm himself. Images of that young officer he had nearly beaten to death came to his mind, but instead of his face, it was Mead to whom he delivered blow after punishing blow. That man should have died but was allowed to live because Robert's own men had intervened. *There's no one here to save you, pal,* Robert thought.

He looked down at Stephanie, who was doing her best to let nothing show. She had gone almost completely white, and her face had instantly been covered in a fine sheet of sweat. He had seen the same thing in men who had been shot in the gut. They had nearly always lived, and they had nearly always wished they hadn't, at least in those initial moments. Thinking back on those men reminded Robert that things for Stephanie would get worse before they got better. Right now, the adrenaline was flowing and masking some of the pain. That would not last much longer. Mead would be lucky in comparison. He would suffer only as long as it took Robert to squeeze the life from his crushed and broken neck.

Robert glared up at Mead, a wicked scowl now stretched across his face. "I meant you."

"I understand. The urge to kill can be a powerful thing. Undeniable really, once you've heard its call. Once you've answered." He smiled suddenly. "But who am I telling? I've seen your memories, Mr. Grayson. I know you. You're no innocent when it comes to answering the siren's song."

"You're insane," Stephanie moaned as she blinked back her tears. Her words were heavy in her mouth, and each syllable was laced with traces of the agony she tried to hold in. "What happened to you? You can't kill us. You'll be caught, and you'll be executed."

Robert and Mead both turned to her in surprise. With the severity of her injury, Robert couldn't believe she was able to form a coherent sentence. He had known she was tough, but still. Mead seemed equally impressed as he took a seat across from the pair and next to Hennerman, who had yet to make a sound, but who was now crying silently in his chair, his head hung low against his shaking chest. Mead's dark eyes appraised them for some time before he answered.

"By whom?" he finally asked. "The police? I doubt that very much. I've had no difficulty staying ahead of you and your people so far. I imagine it will be the same for as long as I wish."

Stephanie glared back at him. She formed her words carefully, letting each one slowly form a path through the labyrinth of pain. "Staying ahead of us? We found you here easily enough, didn't we? We saw through your little message to David and tracked you here because of it. And we were barely trying. Others will do the same. Count on it."

"Oh, I am, Detective. Believe me, I am. And please don't try to make yourself look smarter than you are. That message that you so cleverly cracked? It wasn't for David. He would have eventually worked out where to find me, though I'll grant you that you did move the timetable forward ever so slightly. But that is insignificant really since the message was actually for you." He leered down at her so he could see whether she understood just how pathetic she had been all along. "Here is where a less kind man might point out that it took you days to figure out a message that you forced me to record." He made a show of shaking his head and sighing. "Sad, really, what passes for modern detective work."

Stephanie was having trouble concentrating. *Could he be telling the truth?* She didn't want to believe it. *What was his game? Why would he do all of this? And why involve the police if he truly is so far ahead of us as he says?* Nothing made sense. She looked over at Robert.

Robert saw Stephanie's quizzical expression through the pain in her eyes. He shrugged his shoulders helplessly. He didn't know if Mead was lying, but, save for the fact that he knew it bothered Stephanie, he was unconcerned. His thoughts were more basic. He cared only about how he was going to distract Mead long enough to kill him without putting Stephanie at risk. He knew he needed to be patient, but for how much longer?

Mead saw the exchange and frowned the way one does when a small child has endured some minor scrape or bump, a frown meant at once to show sympathy and yet to diminish the significance of the event. "Oh, forgive my insults, Detective. I was having a bit of fun, but I can see that you remain a professional until the end. You're still trying to work things out for yourself. Kudos for that. Well, since we have to wait on David to return, I may as well satisfy your curiosity. Would you like that?"

"There's nothing about you worth discovering, you crazy bastard. Just shoot us and get it over with."

Robert tried desperately to catch her eye from where he sat. Was she insane? He thought she had been buying them time, and here she was begging him to rush things along. Perhaps the pain was even worse than he imagined.

"Oh, I would like that very much, but it is not to be. David needs to be the one to complete this task, his last one for me. Besides," he reached out and stroked the sides of her neck lovingly with his free hand, "if I were going to kill you, I'd much prefer to do it the right way, the way I always do. I'd use my hands."

CHAPTER FORTY-ONE

Stephanie's mouth was agape. She had certainly reached the obvious conclusion that he was stark raving mad, but Mead had just freely admitted to being the killer they had been seeking. How was that possible? Were he and his son working together? "You? What about your son? You ... taught him to do what you do?"

Mead's shoulders dropped and he shook his head. "One cannot be taught to do what I do. At least not directly. I have tried to pass on the knowledge to him in other ways, but it never worked. My son was not blessed the way I have been, but that doesn't mean that he cannot play his role so that my work, God's work, can continue."

"What other ways?" Stephanie asked, suddenly realizing what Mead meant. "You transferred your memories to him in order to make him a killer?"

Mead's wicked smile returned. "Not just a killer—an instrument of God, Detective. There is a difference."

Robert heard the pride in Mead's voice and could not resist speaking up. "Maybe there is, but you wouldn't know anything about that. You're not an instrument of God. You're a monster, and you've made your son into some kind of monster too, only not the kind you wanted, apparently. Congratulations. You've passed the sins of the father onto the son."

"Ah, I was wondering when you would rejoin our little conversation. Let me assure you that you don't know the first thing about what you're saying, Mr. Grayson. Not the sins of the father—the legacy. My father gave it to me, and I tried to give it to David. He rejected it." Mead looked down at the gun he was holding as if it were a framed picture of his son instead. His voice was melancholy, even nostalgic. He seemed suddenly to remember where he was, and his head jerked back up to look at Robert. "You were, in some ways, an adequate replacement, but on the whole you would never have worked."

"Wait. What legacy could your father have given you?" Stephanie asked before Robert could respond. "Didn't I read that it was just you and your mother growing up?"

Mead nodded. "Yes. Marcus Winston. Convicted in 1974 of killing four women. I was thirteen then," he reminisced. "He was put to death two years later. My mother dropped his name from ours to avoid the stigma and relocated us from Lubbock to Houston. In a city the size of Houston, even back then, we could disappear and start over. She thought that with a few miles and a name change, I could be free of his influence and free from learning any more about the supposedly horrible man who was my father." He rolled his eyes as he spoke. "*Obviously*, she was wrong."

"Obviously," Robert and Stephanie retorted in unison.

"What you think of me matters very little. No man is ever a prophet in his own town, but for whatever it's worth, I agreed with people like you for many years. So much so that finding out what drove my father became my obsession. I worked hard in school, took every class they offered in psychology, biology, chemistry, and genetics. I *needed* to understand. Try as I might, though, science offered no explanations." Mead's eyes took on a glassy look as he thought back to those days. He seemed temporarily transported back to his youth, and Robert saw in his distraction the opportunity he had been waiting on. Stephanie saw it too, but it didn't feel right. It was too easy. Mead might only be baiting them.

"What did you need to understand?" she blurted, bringing Mead back to the present, if, in fact, he had ever left. "Why your father killed?"

"Yes," he nodded again. "But more than that. I wanted to know why I desired the same thing. Killing, after all, is wrong. Or so we are deceived into believing."

Stephanie was not overly given to pity, especially to men who had bound and attacked her, but she could not help but acknowledge some small bit of it for the young boy who grew to become this deranged man. She felt it even more deeply for David, who had apparently resisted the urges to which his father had eventually given in, only to become part of his twisted game anyway.

"Right out of college, I threw myself into the area of genetic memory and encoding. I wanted to know if there was some irresistible, invisible cord pulling me toward my destiny. That's how it always felt to me. It was like gravity. It was always there, biding its time and waiting for me to stumble so it could do its work."

Mead stood and began to pace around the room. The more he spoke, the more agitated he became. Stephanie would have given anything for Dr. Burns to have been there. He would have known what to say.

"Eventually, of course, I came to realize that I could not just ignore it and wait for it to go away. That was getting me nowhere, so I finally gave in. It was difficult at first, naturally. The guilt was unimaginable," he closed his eyes and set his jaw as he recalled that first time. "But then, so was the ecstasy." His eyes opened, and a smile flashed across his twisted face. "Over time, I lost the guilt, but the joy always remains. Isn't that so, Robert?"

In that instant, everything made sense to Robert. His sudden and inexplicable ability supposedly to cope with the murders he thought he had committed. He was reliving the same emotions that Mead had experienced himself. With each murder recalled, the guilt had faded until it was nothing more than a dull ache. Robert had falsely hoped it was simply the knowledge that he wasn't guilty of the crimes. He'd known all along it was something more.

"You said the way I reacted was special. I picked up something more than just your memories, didn't I? The Bible verses, the sleep walking, all of it was you. Some part of you imprinted on me somehow." Robert's stomach rolled at the realization he had been trying to deny. "Given time …" He was unable to finish the thought.

Mead smiled happily. "Yes, Mr. Grayson. That's what made you so special and so very hard to find. You were such an excellent match in some ways that you not only absorbed the memories, but you also took something extra, something unexpected in a subject to whom I wasn't closely related, but it made sense in a way. With that many memories, there were bound to be changes to the brain. Subtle ones, perhaps, but changes nonetheless. What happened to you is what I had always hoped would happen to David. But," Mead continued, though now considerably crestfallen, "you also were processing so many issues of your own that the guilt took hold much more strongly than it should have. It was my fault, perhaps. Too many memories at once. Too much to process for most people, especially someone like you. You're far more soft-hearted than you realize. It's a pity. I could have fixed that in time."

Two minutes alone with me in a room right now might change that opinion somewhat, Robert thought through gritted teeth. He remembered to keep his breathing even and his pulse steady, to give away none of the rage he felt that might make Mead aware of the danger he faced.

Mead paused to sigh heavily. When he spoke again, his eyes were wider than before and his pace quickened somewhat. "I was luckier than most, you see. I realized who I was destined to become. It was hard wired into me. It's who my father was, it's who I am, and it's who David should have been. He has no choice!" His nostrils flared and flecks of spittle flew from his lips as he raged.

Robert shook his head, still in shock at the realization that he could become like this monster should he live long enough. What might he have done that night in Stephanie's bedroom had he not woken up? An icy hand ran its way up and down his spine. A part of him felt it and wanted to give up. Just charge Mead now and take the bullet he would surely receive. *There are fates worse than death. No*, he decided. *Regardless of what he might deserve, if I die, Stephanie would be alone with this lunatic. Whatever happens to me*, he promised himself, *she lives*. His bout of self-pity evaporated as the sound of Stephanie's voice brought him around.

"I understand your anger, Doctor. You want David to follow in your footsteps because if he doesn't, then that makes him stronger than you. You know the science. Hell, you're an expert in it. You share the same DNA, the same genetics. If he can say no when you couldn't, then it's about more than just science. You are who you are because that's who you chose to be and because you're weaker than David is. And you're definitely weaker than Robert. David didn't become like you, and Robert would never have either." She turned slowly to look at Robert. Her eyes told him she wasn't sure she was right, but that it wasn't his fault, that she didn't blame him. He tried to return the look, but she could see that he didn't believe, that he couldn't, so she turned back to Mead and glared at him once more. "All of your research was just an attempt at finding an excuse for the sorry-assed human being you became. When David did what you never could, you couldn't stand it, so you decided to change him."

"Shut up," he growled.

Stephanie threw her head back a little and laughed. "It makes so much sense. I figured that you had no picture of your son because you were ashamed of having a killer in the family, but that wasn't it at all. You were ashamed of yourself for your weakness. Of course, I can't really blame you for that. Seeing David's picture was a reminder of your failings, so you hid it from yourself. You can't stand that he's stronger than you, and you hate him for it." She laughed again. "Man, I thought you were crazy when I figured you were just a serial killer with daddy issues."

Mead stepped closer to her and raised a hand threateningly. "You are playing a most dangerous game, Detective Monroe. I know what you're trying to do. But I'm still smarter than you, and I have a plan."

"Oh, and what's that? After you kill us, you might be able to convince the police that David did it, but for how long? They'll eventually catch him, and when they do, he'll talk. I promise. They'll run a few tests, and confirm your presence here and the fact that you fired a gun. It'll be enough for a jury. The last thing you're going to feel is a needle in your veins."

Mead shook his gun at her as if he were wagging his finger. "Now, now, Detective. That's no way to talk. Besides, I doubt very much David will ever tell the police anything. You see, along with both of you, he'll soon be dead as a result of the shootout you're going to have with him. I will come out of hiding when I hear the tragic news of my son's death. I'll be devastated of course, but not surprised. I'll ask the D.A. to keep the news of your abusive behavior toward me a secret. I mean, I was forced to run out of fear of you and of my son, but I don't want the entire department tainted by your behavior, especially so soon after your death in the line of duty." He gave her his familiar grin. "The police will have the killer they've sought, and I will be free to rebuild my company's image and start over. I rather think the market will eat up the story of the grieving father who threw himself into his work in order to help himself recover."

Robert hung his head at the news. Mead had not been bluffing. He truly had been expecting them all along. "That's why you gave me the memories, isn't it?" he asked, his brows twisted together in anger. "You knew I might turn myself in, and you knew the police would eventually find out about David and suspect him if I did. Either I'd replace him, or I'd help you frame him. Either way, you'd be free of him." Robert couldn't stop shaking his head. "You couldn't get him to kill for you, so you're going to get him to die for you instead? You're a first-class piece of shit, Mead, and it's only fair to tell you that I'm going to kill you for it, for what you did to him, to me, and to all of those girls. You should thank me for that, by the way. At least you won't have to live with your son's death on your conscience for very long."

Mead shook his head and laughed to himself as if he were the sole recipient of some private joke. "Oh, Mr. Grayson, you have a fine mind, and I admire your drive, no matter how misplaced. I truly do." As he spoke, Mead casually drew Stephanie's Taser from where he had been hiding it behind his back and pointed it at Robert, looking at it as if he were unsure what the device might do. He continued to point it as he walked over to where Stephen Hennerman sat bound to his chair. "Everything you said is exactly correct, right up until the part where you're going to kill me. That would throw a rather large wrinkle in my plans, you see. Oh, and, of course, you were right about one other thing. I wouldn't want to live with my son's death on my conscience. That would be unbearable for anyone. But," he said, gesturing to Hennerman, "thanks to my technology and my friend here, I won't have to. Not for long anyway."

He was right. Stephanie and Robert both knew it. He'd be able to wipe away the pain of what he'd done as soon as he did it. He'd go on with the rest of his life as if none of this had happened. No wonder he was always smiling.

"But back to your original point, I don't doubt one bit your resolve to kill me. Takes one to know one and all, eh?" he teased good-naturedly. "Best thing would be just to kill you now, but forensic science being what it is," he said, rolling his eyes, "it might look strange on your autopsy if you were shot after you were already dead. Still," he said, hem-hawing, "I can't have you running around, so I'll have to settle for the next best measure right now. Good night, Mr. Grayson. Try to have pleasant dreams for a change. After all, they're going to be your last."

With that, Mead waved goodbye playfully at Robert and jammed the weapon into the solid flesh of his shoulder. He pulled the trigger on the electric device, smiling cheerfully as 1,200 volts of searing and debilitating pain pulsed through Robert nineteen times each second, dropping him to the floor almost instantly. Mead followed him down, unsure how long he should hold the trigger. He didn't wish to do any permanent harm, at least not yet, so he resolved to hold it no longer than until he bored of seeing Robert's body seize and convulse. Unfortunately for Robert, Mead did not bore easily.

CHAPTER FORTY-TWO

When Robert's convulsions and the sharp, guttural moans he had made had mostly subsided, Mead turned his attention back to Stephanie. Her face was inscrutable. Mead had expected her to react to Robert's pain, but she was as silent as when he had shattered her knee. He was uncertain whether her restraint was more a product of strength or of coldness, but it amounted to the same thing. He thought it sad that he could not take his time and kill her the way he would have liked, but the needs of the moment outweighed his personal desires. And there would certainly be time for other women later. For now, he needed to make short work of binding her hands and feet. Even unarmed and on one leg, she could be a problem if she chose to be.

Sour bile tried to force its way up from Stephanie's stomach and into her throat as Mead touched her while he worked, but she managed, with great effort, to choke it down. Retching in front of him would somehow have been worse than crying out. Still, even with every particle of her brain that was not devoted to blocking out the pain focused on controlling her revulsion, it was difficult to hold it in check because, as much as she hated even to think it, his plan was brilliant. Hennerman was going to erase Mead's memory of murdering his own son. The police, thanks largely to her own work, already thought David was the killer. Once they found his dead body and those of a police officer and a war hero, they were going to be only too happy to close the case as quickly as possible. And should anyone even think to implicate David's father in his own son's death, which there was no apparent reason to do, he would pass any interview they ever administered. Add to that the fact that Robert now lay crumpled in a heap in God knows what condition on the floor of a strange apartment just waiting to die, and her impending illness threatening to erupt at any moment.

Mead finished securing her bindings and moved around in front of her, his face only inches from her own. "Detective, you don't look at all well, and, for once, you're quiet. Whatever is troubling you? Could it be that you've finally realized that everything I've told you is the truth? It's good, really," he assured her, nodding confidently. "No one should die without accepting the truth. I've always felt that way."

"You're a monster," she seethed. "And you don't deserve to philosophize or even to speak to me about what you believe. You think you're a what? An instrument of God, you said? You're not. You're a pitiful, little man who's going to burn in hell one day, and sooner rather than later if I have anything to say about it. You too, Hennerman," she said, craning her neck around Mead to get a closer look at his other prisoner. "Why are you even doing this? Why would you help him?"

Hennerman could only shake his head. Other than when they had walked in, he had not been able to make eye contact with her, and he still would not, even as he began to speak. "I don't want to. I have no choice. I have a family!" As he spoke, he briefly came to life, twisting against the ropes that held him in place and looking up at his boss, his eyes begging for mercy they knew could not be found.

"Tisk, tisk, Stephen. Don't make this solely about them. You're always handsomely rewarded for your help in these matters. You will be this time too. You'll see. Now, buck up. We're almost done. In the meantime, I need to attend to David's arrival, so I'll just leave you two to chat." Mead then glanced down at Robert's unconscious form and apparently decided that he was satisfied and left them quickly before Stephanie could ask what he had meant, but it made no difference.

Stephanie knew what she needed to, that Hennerman had erased memories for him before, presumably to cover up killings. It seemed to her that since the day this case had fallen in her lap, every dark corner she had turned had held another equally dark surprise. She fumed but resisted the urge to think that things couldn't get any more twisted only for fear that some cosmic force would insist on correcting her.

Frustrated at her lack of an accessible target for her anger, Hennerman's nearly silent sobs brought her fury back to bear on him. "You've helped him before." It wasn't a question, so Hennerman didn't bother replying. "He said you get paid for helping him. How much could he possibly be paying you that you would help him murder innocent women over and over?"

Silence.

"How much?" she demanded. She was loud, but she didn't care if Mead heard them. What difference could it make?

"It doesn't matter," Hennerman muttered. "That isn't why I do it. At least, not anymore."

He had said he had a family. Mead might be using them as leverage. Not that his excuses mattered, but Stephanie softened slightly at the thought of his children being pawns in Mead's cruel game. "What did he say would happen if you didn't help?"

He closed his eyes and shook his head. "That doesn't matter anymore either. Nothing does."

Stephanie tried her best to sound sympathetic. "Then it won't matter if you tell me. What did he say?"

Hennerman opened his eyes and looked at her. She was holding it together better than he ever had. She was the one facing certain death, but she looked as if she were only stuck waiting in traffic. Annoyed, maybe, but totally in control. Perhaps because of her calm demeanor or perhaps because he had never had the chance to talk to one of Mead's victims, his own victims, he decided he owed her the truth. And she was right. What difference did it make now? "I have two children, Detective Monroe, a boy and a girl. I used to have three until Lawrence killed my oldest daughter. I would like to keep the other two. They're my only concern now. I'm sorry, but I can't lose either of them. I can't go through it again."

Stephanie was incredulous. How could Hennerman work for the man who had killed his own daughter? Maybe he didn't think he could risk turning him in, but why hadn't he at least grabbed his children and run? How could he see him every day knowing what he had done? It made no sense.

"I can see you're wrestling with all of the same questions that have haunted me every day for the last three years. Don't bother. It never makes sense. Only gets worse the more you think about it, actually," he said, staring at a blank space on the wall over Stephanie's shoulder.

"Don't start thinking this is some shared bonding experience for us, asshole. My friend and I are going to be dead soon, along with Mead's son. And your own daughter is already dead, so don't pretend to hand me some Zen bullshit about how you're coping with it by not coping with it, okay?"

Stephanie looked down again at Robert, who lay sleeping peacefully on the floor. In a way, she envied him. He'd get to go in peace while she sat and thought about what was coming. *No*, she realized, *he would have wanted to die on his feet or with his boots on or however the saying goes.* Instead, he would die flat on his back in a Houston high rise while she did the same, except on her ass or however Mead was going to arrange it. It suddenly came to her that it was not her looming death she feared. It was the helplessness that went along with it. She resolved in that instant to do something about that, even if it was only some small gesture.

Hennerman interrupted her musings. "You're right. I don't deserve your forgiveness, and I'm not asking for it. Anyway, I wouldn't expect you to understand."

Stephanie glanced at Hennerman now and saw a man who was utterly broken. She expected only anger, but as she sat waiting on her death she was consumed with an intense curiosity. What had happened? How could a man's life spiral so utterly out of control? She could not resist unraveling this one last mystery. "So explain it to me. If I can't offer you forgiveness, maybe I can do understanding."

Hennerman had nothing left to lose. He nodded. "I can try."

CHAPTER FORTY-THREE

"My daughter's name was Tracy," Hennerman began. "She was our first. We loved her, but my wife and I knew from the time she was in elementary school that things would be tough with her. And on her."

As Hennerman recalled his daughter, Stephanie could hear the change in his voice. His words stripped away the thin veneer that time had laid over his feelings, and he had to pause and gulp hard before continuing. Stephanie doubted he had ever spoken of the things he was about to say.

"She didn't fit in with things the way other kids did, and she didn't want to be made to. Give her a rule, and the first thing she would do was try to find a loophole. It's not that she was bad; she just enjoyed the challenge. When that didn't work, though," he admitted, "she just broke it outright. It got to be like a game for her, and the more we pressed, the more she wanted to play. Eventually, she grew tired of the game and left. She never stayed gone though, you know? She would come back home from time to time and act like she'd never even been gone. She never said where she went when she left either, but she always looked okay.

Didn't seem strung out on drugs or starving or anything. We still worried, of course, but we tried to tell ourselves that it was normal behavior for some kids. She just needed to find herself, work things out her own way maybe. But then we'd wake up one morning and she'd be gone again."

At some point in his story, he had begun crying.

"I think we always knew that there would be a day when she wouldn't come back, but we still hoped. We couldn't help it. She was lost, but she was still our little girl."

Stephanie nodded as she listened. She had heard similar stories many times since becoming a homicide detective. They never got easier to hear, and if she was the one hearing them, it meant they wouldn't have happy endings. This one, she already knew, was no different.

"I had only been with Mead a few months when she finally disappeared for the last time. Strangely, as bad as things were at home, they couldn't have been better at work. I was making a fortune, far more than I'd ever imagined. I was getting paid to sell a miracle product that people couldn't buy fast enough, and I was great at it. Mead loved me for it, of course. I tried to tell him once that a trained monkey could sell what he had made, but he kept calling me his golden boy and piling on the stock options and bonuses."

Stephanie smiled the way people do when they know something isn't funny but know they have to do something. "I smell a set up."

He nodded absently. "That's because you're smarter than I was, I guess. Or maybe I didn't want to see what should have been obvious, like with my daughter." He paused again to collect himself, breathing long and deep before speaking again. "He came to me one day. Said he had a memory he needed removed, something bad. He told me I was the only one he could trust. I knew what he meant though. Somewhere along the way, I had sold him my soul, and he knew I wouldn't risk giving up my meal ticket. He was right. It made no difference to me what he'd done, and I told him so."

Stephanie's smile was replaced with revulsion at the realization of the memory Mead needed removed. "You helped him cover up your daughter's murder for some stock options? And now this? You really did sell your soul."

Hennerman shrugged in agreement. "I'd trade places with you if it would save you, but it wouldn't. And for whatever little it's worth, I didn't know it was my own daughter's murder I was covering up."

"You knew it was somebody's," Stephanie spat at him.

He looked to Stephanie as if he wanted to cry again, but that well had apparently run dry, so he simply nodded feebly and continued. "Yeah, I knew it was somebody's. Anyway, I found out who he had killed as soon as I wiped the memory. There's a monitor that lets you see what the subject is wiping out. We didn't often use it, but I was curious. I guess I wanted to see what the blood money I was taking had bought." He winced at the memory. "I made him watch it after, and he admitted that, while he couldn't remember killing her, he did remember the rest of his plan and why he had chosen her. He said he knew I would agree to help him when he came to me as long as there was enough cash involved. He was right, I guess. The bastard is always right."

Stephanie could never remember being so conflicted about anyone. Hennerman was at once victim and criminal. She was unsure which mantle he had taken on in greater proportion. More importantly, she wondered, did he know? "So what happened next?" she asked quietly.

He laughed bitterly. "Nothing. Life went on. I mean, I was now an accomplice after the fact to her murder. I was going to turn him in, of course, but I would have been in jail along with him, my kids would have had no way to pay for school, and my wife at the time, God bless her, had zero marketable job skills. No matter what I did, I couldn't take back what he'd done. Or what I'd done. Not to mention that the technology was so new then that I wasn't even sure he'd ever be convicted. In case you hadn't noticed, he's disgustingly brilliant."

"So you just took his money?" Stephanie's nose crinkled at the thought of it.

"I think that staying near him was a form of self-inflicted punishment, though at first I just told myself that being poor wouldn't make my situation any better. I thought I could work even harder than before for just a short time and then cash out, get away from that monster. My family and I would live out our days on some tropical island somewhere, and all of this would be just a bad dream."

"But you're still here. What happened to the dream?"

Hennerman indicated her with his chin. "The same thing that happened to you. Mead is even smarter than I realized. He knew I would try to run, but he didn't want to lose me in case he had other murders to erase. One day, he called me in his office and showed me a bunch of pictures of my wife and kids at school and at the store and at the park. He had some private investigator or somebody following them. His message was clear. He had the resources to get to them anytime he wanted. After that, I had no choice. I worked even harder trying to forget what I'd done. My wife eventually got tired of me never coming home. I didn't blame her, but I was just trying to protect them all by staying away. At least when she left," he said, sighing audibly and smiling, "she took the kids. I was grateful for that. The farther they are from me, the safer they are from him."

Stephanie let out a low whistle. "You know that's probably not true, and they shouldn't need that kind of protection anyway. For a few lousy shekels, you opened the door to hell. Don't complain now that you've met the devil."

Hennerman shrugged once again. That simple gesture seemed all he was capable of anymore. "No complaints. It's like you said. My life is hell, and that's where I'm headed in the next life too, if it exists. Figured I had to get used to it at some point."

"And in the meantime?"

"He'd bring me in every so often and have me remove some memories for him. I quit looking at the monitor, but I always knew what they were. He was storing memories to give his son, but he always kept plenty for himself. Said he didn't want to lose sight of who he was, sick bastard." Hennerman took a moment to regain his composure, which had slipped away somewhat as he had confessed to more and more crimes. "Now, I live with the guilt but also with the knowledge that my kids are as safe as they can be. It's all I have left."

Stephanie looked down again at Robert, who had not moved since Mead had put him down. His breathing was even and reasonably deep. Perhaps he'd get to sleep through it all. She was as happy for him as the circumstances would allow. When she looked up at Hennerman again, it was with an entirely different set of emotions. "Wrong, shithead. You also have time, something we don't. You could be using it to try to make things right instead of being a selfish prick."

A noise over Stephanie's shoulder drew her attention, making her crane her neck. As she had expected, it was Mead entering the room. At the same time though, she heard the unmistakable sound of a key turning in a lock and the apartment door swinging in.

Mead gave a resigned sigh and a sad smile before looking at Stephanie. "Well, Detective, I for one am terrible at goodbyes. What do you say we not drag this out?"

CHAPTER FORTY-FOUR

"Dad?" a voice called from the entryway. It sounded as if it belonged to a child. "Is someone here?"

Mead's face immediately took on the mask of a happy demeanor. Stephanie knew he was faking it given that he was planning on killing his son in the next few minutes, but it certainly seemed convincing.

"Yes, son, we have company. Please do come in and say hello."

David walked gingerly into the main room carrying a brown paper grocery bag overflowing with various items. He saw the two people bound to chairs and the third laying dead or unconscious on the floor and stopped short. He looked quickly to his father, his eyes question marks and his mouth open. "What's going on, Dad?" he stammered.

Every image Stephanie had held of the boy-turned-serial-killer vanished like a grain of sand in a windstorm. He was small, shy, and obviously terrified of his father. He was about as threatening as a kitten, and twice as nervous.

Mead waved his hand impatiently, beckoning his son over. "Here, David. Oh, put those down on the table. Good. Come here. I've someone I want you to meet. This is the lady I've been telling you about."

David looked nervously down at her and back to his father. "The police woman? Wh … why is she tied up like that? And who's that?" he asked, indicating Robert.

Mead looked mildly chagrinned, as if he had been caught using the wrong fork at a seven-course dinner. "How rude of me. I nearly forgot our other guest. David, this is Robert. He is a friend of the detective. You'll have to forgive him for not getting up."

He clearly had no intention of answering his son's other question nor of offering an explanation as to why Robert was unconscious. Stephanie could see that David wanted to ask again, but he hesitated. Then she understood. This was a test of wills. David understood that he was both not supposed to ask and yet that his father very much wanted him to muster the courage to do so precisely because it was forbidden. Some version of this scene had doubtless been played out many times over the years. It would have only one outcome.

Desperate for something else to discuss, David pointed at the grocery bag he had deposited on the dining room table. "I got all of the stuff you wanted."

Mead nodded seriously. "Of course you did because you're a good son, an obedient son. Now, there's something I need to tell you." He indicated that David should have a seat on one of the dining room chairs. He complied dutifully, easing gingerly onto the nearest one. "I've invited our guests here tonight for a very special reason. Do you have any idea what that might be?"

David shook his head fervently, but the way he avoided his father's eyes told Stephanie that he was well aware.

Mead spoke sternly, keeping his voice perfectly even. "David, you and I both know that isn't true. We've talked about this moment before. We both know it's time to do what needs to be done for you. You'll never be complete until you do it. Trust me. I'm your father, and I know what's best for you."

David wouldn't look up or respond. Stephanie thought he was rocking back and forth in his seat a little, but it was hard to be sure.

"David?" his father asked.

"Don't do it!" Stephanie blurted. David's head shot up involuntarily at the sound of her voice. "He's only using you! After you shoot me, he's planning on killing you and framing you for all of his murders, including this one. Please listen, David. I'm telling the truth. You need to believe to me."

Mead gave no response except to duck his head down to meet David's eyes, which had returned to staring at the carpet. He raised his eyebrows and cocked his head slightly in a questioning glance at his son. "See? What did I tell you? It's you and me against all of them. They want to break us apart any way they can. It's just like I told you." At this, he reached out and hugged his son awkwardly. David eventually returned the gesture and nodded before looking down at Stephanie. She could see some of the confusion in his face had gone, and in its place was thinly veiled contempt.

Stephanie knew two things in that moment—that she and Robert were going to die and that Mead had beaten her again. He had known she would reveal his plan to his son. It was the sole reason he had told her. He had used that knowledge to warn David what she might say in an attempt to poison their relationship. She had played her part unwittingly and beautifully, and David seemed to accept it all without question. She shook her head in disgust at herself. From behind David's back, Mead winked slyly at her.

"You see it now, don't you, son? They want nothing more than to destroy all men. Nothing would make the average woman happier than to tear apart a father and son, especially ones as close as you and I. Even your whore mother and sister abandoned us in the end. They cannot be trusted. Do you understand?"

David nodded slowly at first, then with greater conviction. Tears were pooling up in his eyes as he stood and looked down on Stephanie. "What do I do?" he asked.

"Come stand over here," his father answered, gesturing to the space next to himself. "I have something special for you." As he spoke, he walked over to the table where David had left the groceries and reached into a black canvas bag Stephanie hadn't noticed earlier. He must have brought it out with him when he had rejoined them earlier. He slowly withdrew his hand and produced a dull gray semi-automatic pistol that Stephanie immediately recognized, a .45 caliber 1911 Colt, one of the most popular handguns ever produced. There were probably a million of them in circulation right now, making it a hard slug to match to a particular killer unless the police recovered the actual murder weapon, which also made it incredibly popular among criminals.

Mead reached back into the bag and produced a long cylinder that he slowly screwed into the barrel of the gun, twisting it tight at the end to be sure the noise suppressor was snugly in place. A handgun like the one Mead was holding would normally fire at around 150 decibels or so. The suppressor would take that noise level down to around 110, something in the range of a jackhammer. Its true value, Stephanie knew, was that the gun would no longer sound like what people thought a gun should sound like. They would assume it was a neighbor's television or a car backfiring or something else. Something loud, to be sure, but certainly not a gun. The thought that the shot that would kill her would be slightly less loud than it was intended to be did little to comfort Stephanie.

Mead held out the gun and nodded at it, a clear sign that David was supposed to take it. Slowly, like a dog drawn to a master who was as likely to deliver a beating as a meal, David approached and extended his hand uncertainly to take the weapon. His fingers closed around the pistol's grip, lifting it up and away from Mead's grasp. David looked at his father for assurance that this was a requirement. Receiving a decisive nod, David turned to look down at Detective Monroe as she sat in her chair.

"Dad," he mumbled, "I'm not sure I can do this. I want to make you happy, but this isn't right."

"I understand, son. This is a serious thing you're doing, and these aren't ideal conditions, but we can't leave with her. It has to be here, and it has to be this way. What you're feeling in your gut is nothing more than your mind's way of warning you about those things. You're smart to listen, but now it's time to fight through that and listen to your father instead. Always trust me."

David had never taken his eyes off of Stephanie. Now, he raised the gun and pointed it down at her. It would be a center mass shot. Stephanie knew that she'd bleed out very quickly even if the shot didn't take her heart. And the trauma would put her in shock long before any pain could arrive. The knowledge did little to comfort her, but there were far worse ways to go.

David inhaled slowly and closed one eye to take a bead on his target. He let his breath out slowly as a drop of sweat traced its way down his forehead and into his brow. His hand shook uncontrollably. It was now or never. "Dad, I don't think I can do this!" he moaned, lowering the weapon and retreating back to his chair. He placed the gun on the table next to the paper bag and held his head in his hands, rocking back and forth evenly again.

Mead marched over to him and cuffed him roughly on the side of the head. "Boy, you pick up that gun and you finish this job. Now!"

David flinched at the blow, but he would not look up and he would not answer. He simply continued rocking and occasionally mumbling something to himself. Stephanie couldn't make out what it was. As she watched the argument in front of her gain strength, movement on her right side caught her eye. She glanced down at Robert, but he still seemed to be out cold. Perhaps it was an involuntary movement, or perhaps she had imagined it. She turned her attention back to the father and son who were still playing out the same scene with the same results as before. Mead would yell and hit while David rocked and moaned. Her heart ached for the young man who would be her killer. He had never had a chance at having a normal life.

Her attention was quickly pulled back down to Robert as she again saw movement from where he lay. As before, she was unable to tell if it were real or imagined. She thought he might be slightly more curled than he was before, his head and hands closer to his feet, but she couldn't be sure. She thought of trying to get his attention somehow, but to what end? Better for him if he slept through it all and woke up on the other side.

She looked back to see Mead now down on one knee, talking to David and imploring him to get up and finish the job. David had finally raised his head and was listening to his father's words, but his look was anything but determined. Conflict was etched into every line on his young face, lines that shouldn't be there this early but that had no doubt arrived ahead of schedule due to the stress of having Mead for a father and from being locked away for years.

Movement. Her head whipped around. This time she was sure of it. Robert had moved, and he was definitely curled up tighter than before. His hands practically touched his feet now, forming him into a rough U-shape. She watched him closer this time for any signs of movement. He was completely still, and his breathing was smooth and even. He had moved, but if he was awake, he was hiding it well. She looked back to see if either of the Meads had caught the shift, but their attentions were now solely focused on one another, and their voices were getting louder.

"I'm telling you, Dad, I can't! Please don't make me do this,"

David begged.

"You *can* do it, and you will. *Now!*"

David was silent again as he wrestled with his conscience and his desire to obey his father. His pleading eyes sought out Stephanie, who in turn watched him with a degree of ironic admiration as he resisted the inevitable outcome as long as he was able.

"Now," Mead repeated again, slowly this time and with great finality.

David rose, grabbed the pistol, and stepped almost toe to toe with his father, attempting to stare him down. "Fine," he growled. "This is what you want? To make me a killer? To make me like you?" He stepped away from his father and toward Stephanie. Like an executioner's ax, he raised the pistol slowly.

Tremors rolled through Stephanie's stomach, and her body fell limp. The rush of adrenaline through her veins was simply too much for her muscles to process. Dozens of vicious words and final, defiant glares fought to escape and assemble into one last, brave stand, but Stephanie could see the way the gun trembled, and tears formed for the young man. More than fear, more than rage or fury, she felt helplessness again, but not just her own—David's as well.

David saw the recognition on her face, and for just a moment, the gun lowered.

"It's okay," she told him. "I know you have no choice. Do what you have to. I'll forgive you." Stephanie smiled, not because she felt any happiness for herself, but because she knew how proud Dr. Burns would have been of her. Maybe this would be her last defiant act, the refusal to give in to the hate that had been with her for so long.

"You won't have to do that for me," David said, raising the pistol a final time.

Stephanie willed herself to keep her eyes open until the end.

She wasn't sure, but it appeared his aim was drifting away from her and in his father's direction when a voice spoke out from beside her.

"Damn right she won't."

Time slowed for Stephanie as David turned toward the sound, bringing the gun's barrel in Robert's direction, though well above him since Robert had not yet risen from the floor. Stephanie saw it in his eyes then—the uncertainty, the defiance. Perhaps he would have refused to shoot her after all.

She would never know for sure.

CHAPTER FORTY-FIVE

Robert had produced a small black semi-automatic pistol, presumably from a hidden ankle holster, and had pointed it squarely at David's chest. When David looked down, Robert didn't hesitate. A shot roared out deafeningly as the bullet that took David's life hit him squarely in the chest. He spun in a half circle and fell limply to the floor, the pistol he had dropped lying temptingly between him and his father.

"Don't move," Robert warned before Mead could even think about it. Mead nodded, and Robert stood slowly, keeping his gun trained on the other man the entire time. He risked a glance down at Stephanie. "You okay?" he asked.

Stephanie was still watching David and had not heard the question. No matter what you see in movies, a gunshot wound anyplace other than the head or heart almost never kills instantly. Instead, the bullet clears a path through the body where no path should be. Blood rushes into that space and leaks or pumps out from the place where the bullet entered the body. The victim dies of exsanguination—blood loss. It's a death that takes some time, and David was only part of the way through the process.

"Stephanie, are you okay?" he repeated.

She looked up at him and nodded. Apparently, he had opted for getting a gun of his own after all. He was a better liar than she had thought. "Yeah. Untie me, and I'll call an ambulance."

Robert ignored her and waved the pistol at Mead, directing him to stand at the other end of the living room. He then walked over to the spot where the gun lay on the thick rug. He picked it up, then placed his own weapon into the waistband of his jeans. He ejected and then reinserted the clip, making sure it was loaded and then checked that the safety was still off.

Stephanie wished he would hurry. She was glad he had the presence of mind to secure Mead and the weapon, but if an ambulance didn't get here soon, whatever chance David had of surviving was gone. Not to mention that she would like to be untied and have her own injury looked at. "Hurry and untie me, Robert. He's not going anywhere."

He walked to stand behind her and examine her bindings. They would have been fairly easy to break if he had intended to.

"Thank God you woke up when you did. And I hate to look a gift horse in the mouth, but were you ever planning on telling me that you ignored your own advice about the gun?"

Still, Robert said nothing.

Stephanie willed him to look into her eyes and then tried to hide the shock she felt at seeing the hard determination that could mean only one thing.

"Hurry," she tried. "We're going to lose him if you don't hurry, and we might very well need his testimony in court. This bastard is slipperier than an eel."

Mead looked on with curiosity. He had always known that a trial would happen for him as it had for his father. His goal was to do as much as he could before that day and, more importantly, to leave a legacy. He had failed at the second bit of that, but maybe he would live to fight another day. The kind of money he had could buy a lot of justice these days.

"We don't need any witnesses, Stephanie. There isn't going to be a trial. Not for him."

"What do you mean no trial? What are you thinking of doing?" She already knew the answer. Panic began to set in now worse than it had when her own life was at stake. "No, Robert! You *cannot* do this." It was the reverse of the argument that had taken place in that spot moments before.

"Why not? What would be the point of a trial? We know he's guilty, and we know he's smart. Smart and rich is a not a combination I want to see tested by our judicial system on a scumbag like him, so I'm just going to jump to the end we both know he deserves."

"Maybe he would get away with murder if we tried him, but I doubt it. We have Hennerman's testimony. That should be enough. Besides," she begged, "you don't have unlimited money and high powered attorneys. You wouldn't get away with murder when your trial happens."

Robert gave a thoughtful nod. "Yeah, I've thought about that. I'm willing to take my chances. And it isn't like I don't deserve to be locked up. I've killed too, and it's obvious that I will again if I'm left free. Mead made sure of that. You think he'll ever take these memories back?"

Mead gave a low throated laugh, prompting Stephanie to give him an icy glare.

"Shut up, you bastard, before I decide to encourage him. He is right, after all. You do deserve to die."

It was true, and she knew it. Everything Robert said about him was absolutely true, yet it went against everything she was sworn to uphold. She would have traded everything at that moment to be anything other than a cop. She knew that for the average citizen, this would be a no brainer. It wasn't much of a choice for her either, but she had to try one last time.

"What about me?" she asked gently.

Robert jutted his bottom lip out and shrugged. "You're going to watch me do this, and then you're going to take me in. You'll be a hero."

She shook her head. "I meant what about me with you? What about us?"

He looked at her this time with a tenderness she had not seen before. It broke her heart to see it now. "I'm sorry, Stephanie. I truly am. For whatever it's worth, I love you. I was really looking forward to this being over." He looked back at Mead and all of the tenderness that had been there flew away. "But it will never be over until he's dead." He walked over to the table where Stephanie's gear lay and where Mead had returned her Taser. "We used to get zapped with these from time to time. Sometimes it was part of our training. Other times, guys were just so bored that we would think of the dumbest stuff we could to entertain ourselves. We had no money, so we'd play poker and the loser got tased. You get used to these the more you're hit with them, and I was a bad poker player. I was awake for a while there on the ground, so I heard a lot. He was smart enough to beat Hennerman, he was smart enough to beat us more than once, and he's smart enough to get out of this. Or rich enough anyway. I won't take that chance. This ends here. Now."

"Stop, Robert. This isn't you! This is all because of what he did to your mind. Don't you see?"

Robert nodded. "Please remember you said that. I'm planning on that being the cornerstone of my defense."

"Fine, kill him if you want, but I won't take you in. That would make me your accomplice. You'd do that to me?"

Robert looked down at her and smiled. "You're not a good

poker player either, Steph. I'm going to turn myself in to you, and you're going to take me in. We both know that. If you don't, I'll just turn myself in at the station where they'll treat me like a common criminal, and you're too good a person to let me do that. You're going to bring me in yourself and see that I get every privilege your department can throw at me. That's who you are. You can't help it. And it's why I love you. Goodbye, Stephanie. I enjoyed almost getting to know you better."

With that, he turned, sighted the gun in on Mead's heart, and pulled the trigger. The gun erupted, and Mead stumbled back into the wall behind him and stayed suspended there for a split second before sliding down the wall to the ground to meet whatever fate awaited him. His eyes stayed open but unseeing, and his back left a long, bloody streak where the bullet had exited. His death was almost complete by the time he hit the ground.

Robert walked over to where David lay on the carpet. He had quit moving, but Robert checked twice for a pulse. Satisfied that there was none, he placed his weapon on the ground and approached Stephanie. He said nothing more as he walked behind her and loosened her binding. He then helped her to stand on her good knee before leaning down gently and placing a kiss on her cheek. "I'm ready."

"Hand me all of my gear," she whispered. "If you're going to make me do this, I'm going to do it right."

"Of course." He made sure she could stand and then walked over to the little table to collect her things for her. He brought the baton, the cuffs, the Taser, her radio, and her flashlight. Her gun was not among her belongings, so Mead must have carried that to the back. He offered to collect it, but she declined.

"Just turn around and let me cuff you, you selfish asshole."

He complied slowly. "I am sorry. Fatal flaw, I guess. I always have to do what I think is right. I don't know how that keeps getting me in so much trouble."

"Me neither," she muttered as she placed his wrists in the handcuffs. "Too tight?" she asked.

He craned his head back around as far as he could to her. "It's fine. Hey, Stephanie, you know this wasn't me choosing my conscience over you, right? That would have been easy. I just couldn't have him out there thinking about you. If he got loose, he would've come for you. I couldn't live with that," he repeated.

"I understand," she answered, her voice barely above a whisper.

"Now, I guess I'll have to live forever with all of the memories he gave me. Not to mention all of this," he said, indicating the bodies on the floor.

Stephanie made sure that Robert's cuffs were secure before drawing her Taser and placing it directly in the small of his back.

"No," she said. "You won't."

Before Robert could ask what she meant, she pulled the trigger, and the same volts that had shot through him before did so again with the same effect, collapsing him to the floor in a crumpled heap. She cried out her anger at him, zapping him again and again until she was sure this time he would stay down.

CHAPTER FORTY-SIX

"Oh, Stephanie, dear. What a tangled web you have woven here."

Stephanie and Dr. Burns were seated in his private office away from the police station. Because of her injury, Stephanie had been given several weeks off to recuperate. Her knee had not needed surgery, but it did require extensive physical rehabilitation. Since she had taken little of her leave time over the last few years, she had plenty built up now and was taking advantage of it.

After making Dr. Burns swear, unnecessarily, he reminded her, that he never tell anyone what she was about to reveal, Stephanie told him the story of that evening, including what she had done after she had knocked Robert out. Stephanie had freed Hennerman and then laid out her plan for him. In return for keeping her mouth shut about him deleting Mead's memories of his murders, she would require that he perform the service one last time—with Robert as the subject. He was to remove the memories that had been implanted by Mead as well as any memories associated with tonight.

Hennerman had agreed without hesitation. "One catch, though.

Do you remember what I told you that day in the station when you asked me about this process? I can't just remove those memories without taking everything around them. And if you want tonight included, I'll have to take everything between then and now. He's not going to remember any of it. Including you."

Stephanie had remembered, and she had known this would be the price for her plan. "Do it."

Together, they had hooked him to the equipment that Mead had placed in Hennerman's apartment. It had been a nearly impossible task to drag him with her bad knee, but they had gotten him there eventually. Hennerman had completed the erasure, and Stephanie loaded a very groggy Robert Grayson into the back of her car and deposited him at the hospital anonymously. Judging by the tiny wounds the Taser had left, doctors told him that he had suffered some kind of an attack that had left him with some short-term memory loss. It wasn't uncommon, they said, and the memories would probably return in time. In a day or so, he could head home and back to work.

Stephanie had phoned his boss at the factory and told him that under no circumstances would Robert ever mention working with the police, and that he would do well to follow the same protocol. It was top secret. She made vague threats of legal action if he should violate the order. His boss had said it would be no problem, asking only that she not send police to the job site in the future. Some of his guys got a little jumpy if too much blue showed up in one place. Stephanie assured him he would never see her again as long as he kept his word.

Her bases covered to the extent they could be, Stephanie had driven herself to a bad part of town and called in for back up. She had been assaulted by masked thugs. They had probably meant to rob her, but when they opened her purse and saw the shield, they had run for it. The bastards were lucky she hadn't shot them.

As for Hennerman, she had debated about whether to have him call in the murders, but there was no good explanation for why the killings had happened in his home. Instead, she had placed calls to a couple of characters whose moral compasses did not exactly point straight north. In exchange for calling a few old debts even and a couple of Hennerman's more valuable trinkets, the pair had gotten rid of the bodies. The rest, Stephanie had told Hennerman, was up to him. He had agreed, and the matter had been settled.

"Can it, Doc," she told Dr. Burns now. "I'm not saying what he did was right, or what I did for that matter, but can you think of a better solution?"

"That isn't for me to decide, and you know that. But bringing Robert in certainly would have followed the letter of the law. Isn't that what you do? Have you not now started a course down what might be a very slippery slope?"

She shook her head adamantly. "I don't think so. This was a once in a lifetime case, Doc. At least I hope so. Anyway, no one went to jail, and the cases remain open, but I feel confident that justice was done. Speaking from experience, that's what matters most."

Burns removed his glasses and placed them on his desk before looking back at Stephanie. "And what remains now for you, my dear? Did you deserve what happened to you, losing Robert the way you did? That was quite a sacrifice you made, whether you're willing to admit it or not."

She had asked herself the same question many times over the last few weeks without finding any answers. "I guess all that's left for me now is to …" She left her sentence unfinished and rose to give Dr. Burns a longer than normal hug and a peck on the cheek. "You're the best person I've ever known, Doc," she whispered to him. "As long as I don't lose you too, I'll be fine."

Before he could respond, Stephanie grabbed her crutches and hobbled out the door. Behind her, her best friend and mentor watched her walk away as he shed for her tears he knew she could not yet shed for herself.

EPILOGUE

Three months after Stephanie's narrow escape from death and a series of even narrower escapes from Dr. Burns' office, she returned to work. Her desk was as cluttered as ever, and there were too many heavily masticated No. 2 pencils lying about to even count. Her boss was once again pressuring her to take a new partner, and she was resisting as strenuously as ever.

Things had settled back into their usual, easy rhythm with only two changes. One, Dr. Lawrence Mead and his son had been declared missing persons and fugitives from justice. There had been no further progress on their cases, and since every possible lead had dried up, there would likely never be any. Happy Memories, Inc. was still afloat and being run by its former head of sales, Stephen Hennerman, but the market was less certain than before that its stock was a no-lose gamble. Time would tell if it was to survive. Two, Stephanie drank far more coffee than she used to. Dr. Burns had remarked on it once in passing to her, and she had given him a strange look and declared that he might want to see a shrink himself. She consumed exactly the same amount she always had, at least by her count.

Dr. Burns had been watching her closely for most of her life and knew that the loss of Robert had affected her deeply. Somewhere inside of her, he knew she knew that as well. He had tried to discuss it with her several more times after that first day. Each attempt was less successful than the last until she finally just told him to leave it alone unless he would like to pick up his own rehab sessions where hers were leaving off. He acquiesced, but he kept a closer eye on her than ever. The woman in this world who was most like a daughter to him was heartbroken, and as any father would do when his daughter's heart was in need of mending, he attempted awkwardly and painfully to repair it.

He twice tried to set her up on blind dates and was twice told to screw himself.

Finally, after exhausting all other ideas and against every bit of good judgment he possessed, he texted her after work one day and asked her to meet him at a bar a few miles from the station. He told her that he needed to speak with her and that it could not be done at work. As he had known she would, she accepted without question. At the same time, he sent another text asking for a similar meeting but with a bit more explanation.

Five minutes after the arranged time, Dr. Burns texted Stephanie again and told her that an emergency had come up and that he would be delayed or possibly even be unable to make it. He apologized profusely and told her he would make it up to her somehow. Stephanie decided to give him as long as it took her to finish her beer. As she was nearing the end of her drink, a large, handsome man of about thirty-five with brown hair and an equally brown beard that he kept very well trimmed approached her hesitantly.

"Excuse me, ma'am? I'm sorry to bother you, but I think I'm supposed to meet you here."

Speechless, Stephanie stared up into the man's familiar brown eyes.

His smile was toothy and utterly sincere. "I'm sorry. I know how it sounds, but this isn't some pick-up line. I got a text that said I needed to be here tonight and that it was important." He held out his phone so she could see the screen. "The same number just texted me and told me to come over to you and introduce myself." He grinned even more crookedly and shook his head. "Normally, I'd never do anything like this, but, I don't know. It's been a weird few months for me, and I figured I had nothing to lose. I suppose none of this makes sense?"

Stephanie had worked tirelessly the last few months building walls designed to keep out the memories of this man, yet, there he stood in front of her, as honest and disarming as ever. She could feel those walls as they crumbled around her, and she wanted nothing more than to leap from her chair and throw her arms around him. But she knew she could not. They had both made choices, difficult ones, to do things they knew they would regret for reasons that felt … maybe not right, but necessary. The only way to honor those choices now was to wave him off, finish her beer, and leave. As hard as it would be for her, she took some solace in knowing that for Robert, it would be just a simple case of getting shot down by a stranger in a bar. He'd get over it quickly. She, on the other hand …

His smile was unaffected by her obvious reluctance. "I can see you're searching for a polite way to let me down easy. That's nice of you, but don't worry about it. I knew it was crazy when I came over to introduce myself. Speaking of which, I'm Robert. It was nice almost getting to know you."

Robert's words slammed into Stephanie with all the force of a runaway locomotive. He had said the same thing that night in Hennerman's apartment, and she found herself back there, reliving every moment of that evening just as she had done in her dreams each night since then. She finally breathed deeply, unaware she had been holding her breath. "Stephanie, and it's nice to meet you, too."

As that one sentence escaped her lips, Stephanie found her resolve disappearing with it and gestured for Robert to have a seat. She ordered beers from a passing waitress and smiled at Robert over the top of her empty bottle.

Confusion and relief vied for control of Robert. This woman had clearly been about to blow him off, and now she was looking at him as if they were long lost lovers. The turnaround might have been disconcerting under other circumstances, but there was something about her that made even this exchange somehow familiar and comfortable. Even now, they had been sitting together for nearly half a minute with neither having said a word, and Robert felt not even a trace of discomfort in their shared silence. Still, he supposed he should attempt to break the ice.

"So, Stephanie, since someone obviously wants us to get to know each other, what would you like to talk about?"

"Well, Robert, I don't know about you, but I have always hated baseball."

ABOUT THE AUTHOR

Scott is a married father of two who has spent the last nine years teaching high school English. When not busy with his family or correcting everyone's grammar, he enjoys reading, hiking the beautiful trails and beaches of Hawaii, lurking the internet as @_scottwrites, and finding ways to avoid going to the gym. This is his second novel.